Roberto's Return
A T. J. Jackson Mystery

by

Paul Ferrante

by Melange Books

Published by
Fire and Ice
A Young Adult Imprint of Melange Books, LLC
White Bear Lake, MN 55110
www.fireandiceya.com

Roberto's Return ~ Copyright © 2014 by Paul Ferrante

ISBN: 978-1-61235-861-1

Cover Art by Stephanie Flint

To my father, Natale Ferrante, who took me to my first Major League game - a man of few words, but a great storyteller.

Acknowledgements

Thanks to Jim Gates, Librarian at the Hall of Fame; Liam Delaney at the Hall for his information on the Clemente mannequin; Audrey Murray at Christ Episcopal Church in Cooperstown; Lisa Almeida for her assistance with the Spanish passages; Sarah Bell for her insights; Cooperstown Mayor Jeff Katz, Micah Lawrence and Karen Harman for their help on the book cover; artists Carol Young and Rob Monte for their work with the T.J. Jackson series; my publicist Carrie Ferrante and agent Maria Simoes; and my editor, Denise Meinstad, for her continued patience and guidance.

Prologue

December 31, 1972

Morty Barrett was in a foul mood. Here it was, New Year's Eve, and he was stuck in a second-rate airport on a third-rate island when he should be at the hotel bar of the San Juan Conquistador, or maybe poolside, knocking back one of those fancy multicolored rum drinks with an umbrella stuck in it. But no, he couldn't get out of this glorified hangar they called San Juan International because they'd misplaced his baggage, and every person with a name tag whom he'd spoken to was more inept than the one before. Not that they weren't friendly, but if just one more attendant shrugged their shoulders with a "so sorry, be patient, we look," he was going to scream.

Because Morty knew all about good service. He was the owner, general manager and head of entertainment at the Pocono Hideaway, a resort nestled into the Pennsylvania mountain range that lent the hotel its name. His wife Doris had tried to talk him out of buying it back in the mid-1960s, saying they were getting in over their heads, but he'd proven her wrong. The matching diamond necklace and earrings she was sporting at the moment were a testament to that. In fact, she'd come to be a valuable partner in running the place, whether it involved keeping tabs on the restaurant's waitstaff, calling out numbers on Wednesday afternoon bingo, or schmoozing with the mostly matronly women who'd schlepped their families to the Poconos from Pittsburgh or Philly instead of trekking to the distant Catskills scene.

The Pocono Hideaway could be all things to all people: a

1

honeymoon destination, complete with its signature heart-shaped bathtubs; or a wholesome family oasis where harried parents could dump off the kids at the well-staffed pool or lakefront, in addition to arts and crafts and such, and just *relax*.

But where Morty really shone was as the master of ceremonies for nightly adult activities as the Hideaway's restaurant turned into a top-flight nightclub, featuring singers, musicians and comedians from as far away as New York, some of whom had appeared on the Ed Sullivan show. Morty loved creating a steady patter with the audience, entertaining them with rapid-fire jokes that usually had them doubled over - especially after a couple drinks. There was no place on earth he'd rather be. In this dump he was just another overweight, balding tourist with a camera hanging from his neck. But at the Hideaway he was an *attraction.*

Maybe that was the source of his anger tonight. He and Doris had to close down the resort every winter for a few weeks of refurbishing and because, despite being in a mountain range, they were nowhere near a skiable slope, and that left the habitually antsy Morty with time on his hands. Most years the Barretts found themselves visiting Doris's parents in Boca Raton, but this season he'd let her talk him into a trip to Puerto Rico, mostly because he couldn't stand her folks to begin with. So he'd booked them into the swanky Conquistador on the recommendation of a longtime Hideaway patron. If he could only get there. It was coming up on 9:00 PM, the empty luggage carousel was going round and round, and to top it off, the kid was crying. Again.

"Doris, now what?" he moaned as his wife tried to soothe their wailing eight year-old.

"Morty, somebody stole his baseball glove," she hissed, hugging the child tightly.

"What! Where? On the plane? Cripes, we just got here!" he thundered. The boy looked up from his mother's embrace, his curly hair smashed flat where she'd held him to her breast. His eyes were red rimmed. "I... just put it down...for a...second," he said in halting gasps.

"But I told ya not to bring it in the first place!" cried the exasperated father. "I mean, who did you think you were gonna play ball with down here, anyway?"

Roberto's Return

At that, the child reburied himself in his mother's arms. "Have a heart, Morty," she admonished, her diamonds tinkling. "You know how much he loves that glove. He takes it everywhere."

She was right. The kid cherished his beat up glove. Why, he didn't know. Nathaneal was a disaster as a little leaguer, couldn't get out of his own way. He preferred to just sit in front of their Zenith color TV watching the Pirates, reshuffling his hundreds of Topps baseball cards into piles by position or team, and pounding his tattered glove to accentuate good catches or timely hits the Buccos were pulling off on their way to another solid season at Three Rivers Stadium.

Now Morty was stuck with a miserable kid for the next week. That is, if he could ever get out of this godforsaken airport.

"Why does the child cry?"

Morty turned to face a black man with close-cropped hair dressed in a Banlon shirt and slacks. He was every bit of Morty's six feet in height, but much unlike the tourist, he was sinewy muscle from head to toe. A small canvas carry bag was slung over his shoulder.

Embarrassed, Morty shrugged and explained, "We just got here, and somebody stole his baseball glove."

The black man frowned, then squatted down next to the boy and tapped him on the shoulder.

Hiccupping, Nathaneal wiped his nose and peered out from his mother's bear hug. His eyes opened wide, and Morty thought his son was about to have a seizure.

"You have lost your glove?" the man said in gently accented English.

The child opened his mouth to reply, but no words came forth.

"Say something, son," prodded Morty.

"Y-you're Roberto Clemente," the boy stammered.

"Yes, I am Clemente," the man answered quietly. "This glove, it is your favorite?"

"Yeah. I...wear it when I watch your team play on TV."

Roberto Clemente smiled broadly, his teeth a brilliant white. "You are a Pirates fan?" he asked, an eyebrow raised.

"Uh, yeah," said the boy, who was now just sniffling. "I like all you guys. Willie Stargell and Manny Sanguillen and Bill Mazeroski. I have all your bubblegum cards."

Clemente nodded seriously, his brow furrowed as if contemplating some great mystery. "Then I must ask a favor of you, *amigo*," he said earnestly. "You see that plane out there?" he said, pointing to an ancient DC-7 propeller cargo plane being loaded on the runway. "I am about to leave for Nicaragua. There was a terrible earthquake there, and I am personally bringing supplies to the victims who have been cheated out of the aid we have tried to send." He looked back out the plate glass window into the darkness where some palm trees swayed in the breeze. "I am going to make *sure* the supplies arrive this time. We are flying boxes and boxes of materials there tonight.

"But I did something silly, *amigo*. I packed my glove in this satchel because I thought I would maybe have time to play ball with some of the children there. Because of some mechanical problems my plane has been delayed, as you can see, and there will be no opportunity to visit the children. So, my young friend," he said, unzipping the bag and reaching in, "would you take care of this for me until I return?" He pulled from the carry bag a well-oiled, mahogany-colored Rawlings XFG-1 fielder's glove that glistened in the terminal's florescent lights and handed it to the astounded boy, who accepted it as one might the most fragile Ming Dynasty vase.

"Mr. Clemente?" said Morty, after clearing his throat, "you're serious here?"

"Yes, of course," the ballplayer replied. "I will return in a couple days, God willing. You will be staying in San Juan?"

"At the Conquistador," he answered, sticking out his hand. "Morty Barrett," he said, feeling Clemente's vise-like grip. "This is my wife, Doris."

"Pleased to meet you," she said, batting her false eyelashes.

Nathaneal just stared at the glove in his grasp.

Clemente grinned. "When I return, I will come to the Conquistador and bring the new glove for you. Then, you and I will have a catch, eh?"

"You mean it?" asked the boy.

"I tell you the truth, *amigo*," he replied, extending his hand.

Nathaneal Barrett shifted the glove to his left hand and shook with the great Clemente.

Roberto's Return

Morty, who had been peering out through the window himself, turned back to the ballplayer with a sense of alarm. "Hey, Mr. Clemente," he said with a pained look, "I'm no expert, but I was in the service during the war...Army Air Corps. And I gotta tell you, that plane doesn't look too kosher. In fact, it doesn't look like it'll even get off the ground. And you've got it loaded with supplies? Are you sure you want to do this?"

"I gave my word," he said firmly. "Don't worry, Mr. Barrett. God will take care of me." He looked down at Nathaneal. "So we have a date to play catch at the Conquistador?"

"You bet."

Clemente mussed the child's curly mop and threw the bag over his shoulder. "Happy New Year," he said in the deserted terminal. "I must get out to the runway. *Adios.*"

They were the last people to see Roberto Clemente alive.

Chapter One

"You want the top floor this time or the second?" asked Andrew Florio as he opened the back door to the panel truck.

"Makes no difference," said his brother Nick as he wrestled the steam carpet cleaner from the truck bed. "Geez, it's cold."

"What do you expect, Nicky? It's nighttime in the dead of winter in the freakin' mountains. It can't be above five degrees." He shivered involuntarily as he hefted a box of cleaners and rags.

"Well, the good thing is, we're getting paid extra 'cause it's New Year's Eve."

"Yeah, but not exactly the way I wanted to ring in 2012. There's a New Year's Eve bash down at The Dugout tonight that I wanted to hit. Gonna have lots of beer and nachos and wings, and the price is reasonable."

"Well," said Nick, checking his watch under the front entrance lights of the National Baseball Hall of Fame and Museum, "it's only 8:30 PM. We've got lots of time to get the carpets and showcase windows done and catch a little of the party."

Andrew pulled out his keys and unlocked one of the big red doors that yearly saw hordes of tourists and baseball fans pass through on their way to visit the thousands of artifacts that tracked the history of baseball from its roots and paid homage to the greatest players of all time.

The brothers brought the carpet vacuum inside and, as was their custom, immediately saluted the pair of life-sized, painted wooden statues depicting two of the most magnificent hitters that ever lived, Babe Ruth and Ted Williams. They had been carved and painted by artist

6

Armand LaMantagne in the 1980s and were so lifelike it was eerie. One would never know, until a close inspection, that the Babe's baggy pinstriped uniform or Teddy Ballgame's Red Sox cap were once a hunk of timber.

"Say," said Nick, "you're getting a little thick around the waist, just like the Babe. Maybe a New Year's resolution to drop a few pounds, bro?"

"You're one to talk. I heard you wheezing just rolling the steamer up the steps outside."

Both brothers laughed. Confirmed bachelors, they lived in Milford, the next town over from Cooperstown - thus avoiding the summer "Induction" craziness - in an old Victorian they'd fixed up after moving upstate from New Rochelle to "enjoy life in the country." Their enterprise, Golden Glow Corporate Cleaners, took care of a lot of the local businesses and municipal buildings, as well as a number in the nearest city, Oneonta. The Hall of Fame contract, which they'd bid on and won the previous year, was a feather in their cap, and was used to promote their company in this corner of the Catskills. *The Pros Go with Golden Glow* was plastered on the side of their truck, in fact.

The problem was that this region, as compared to New Rochelle downstate, was pretty stagnant socially, and desirable single women were kind of scarce. And so the Florios did the guy thing - beers and apps at The Dugout and other establishments in the environs surrounding the "Birthplace of Baseball." There was always a game on the bar's TV and the camaraderie of similar roughhewn local yokels to enjoy. Unfortunately, hard as they worked, the brothers had packed on quite a few pounds since their move. The winters, which were brutal up here, caused them to stay indoors even more, as neither was a hunter or fisherman. On this night, the Florio boys were both tipping in somewhere north of 250 pounds. Not a good thing on a five foot-eight frame.

That was why the Hall of Fame gig was so sweet. Not only was each floor of the facility accessible by gently pitched ramps, there was an elevator large enough to accommodate the carpet cleaner.

The brothers, as they'd done at the end of every month, proceeded through the main lobby past the gift shop entrance into the heart of the

Hall of Fame, the vaulted-ceilinged Plaque Gallery, where rectangular bronze likenesses of the game's immortals, arranged by year of induction, graced the blonde wood-paneled walls.

At the base of the first ramp, which led to the level featuring the research library and the "Baseball at the Movies" exhibit, Andrew opened the switchbox to flick on the lights to the upper levels, which cast a muted twilight effect onto all the exhibits. Then they split up. Andrew decided to lug the glass cleaner, rags and squeegees to the third floor, which housed the ballparks room, grandly named "Sacred Ground," and World Series displays, while Nicky would start on the first floor carpets outside the Grandstand Theater, which featured stadium seating and a wraparound painted crowd mural that gave the Hall's patrons a sense of really being at a game as they watched a twelve-minute multimedia production called "The Baseball Experience." Here, if one entered another corridor, he could trace the history of the game from its origins as far back as Egyptian times, through the advent of the pro game in the late 1800s, to the Dead Ball Era that preceded Babe Ruth, both World Wars, the Golden Age of the 1950s and beyond, right up through the steroid period from which the game was still recovering. The story was told through hundreds of display cases and interactive exhibits, the latter which were constantly rotated for the benefit of those fanatics who made a yearly pilgrimage to their baseball mecca. Thousands of bats, balls, gloves, uniforms and ephemera were on display, and the maintenance of the climate-controlled cases was an ongoing labor of love for the museum's curators and support staff. Many of the sport's relics, all donated, were priceless, and were afforded the same respect and care as the Crown Jewels of England in the Tower of London. And it was up to Andy and Nick to make those thick glass cases sparkle and suck up every speck of dirt tramped in by the daily armies of visitors - not that there was too much to handle. Except for snacking toddlers dragged along by their parents, most people tended to treat the Hall's environs like their local house of worship.

By 9:30 PM Nick had finished steam cleaning the rooms housing artifacts through 1950 and was on to the turbulent 1960s and groovy 1970s, the era of multicolored polyester pullover uniforms and bushy hair. He never failed to chuckle at the green and gold double-knit monstrosities the Oakland A's, of owner Charlie Finley, sported on their way to consecutive world championships from 1972-1974. But mostly he paid no attention to the contents of the cases, even when he was doing the glass. The goal tonight was to get in and out - and hopefully make it to The Dugout under the Glimmerglass Inn before all the wings were gone.

He was just wiping his mouth after straightening up from a water fountain near the restroom when he heard a tap-tap-tap. He thought maybe the steam vacuum, which he'd turned off to go to the bathroom, was just ticking down, but when he stooped over to give a listen, no such sound was forthcoming.

"Huh," he said to himself, and started up the machine again. A minute later he found himself before the floor-to-ceiling case dedicated to the great Roberto Clemente. It was strange; as much as Nick was oblivious to the history surrounding him, the Clemente display never failed to creep him out.

Back around 1970, as a prank or tribute, he didn't know which, someone had apparently created a life-sized mannequin double of the Pittsburgh right fielder, dressed it in the Hall of Famer's famous Pirate home white double-knit number 21 with black and gold piping, and put it in the trainer's room at Three Rivers Stadium where players and staff, after flicking on the lights, never failed to do an abrupt double take. There the mannequin was standing, next to an original locker room chair from Forbes Field, the Pirates' home park that preceded the concrete doughnut of Three Rivers Stadium built in 1970.

Nick flipped the STEAM switch and began the mechanical forward-and-back motion of the vacuum. But then, out the corner of his eye, he caught a quick movement in the Clemente case. He turned and peered into the glass box. There was Clemente, one arm raised as if in greeting, the mannequin's face expressionless as always. *Now wait a minute* he thought. *Isn't he supposed to have both arms at his side? Did they change it?* He couldn't remember. Oh well.

He bent to his task and began again. But then - BANG! He jumped, whirling to find what had caused a sound so loud the vacuum couldn't drown it out.

Clemente's arms were both down.

9

"H-hold on here," said the cleaning man, breaking into a sweat. He took a step back, trying to slow his thudding heartbeats, and then squinted hard at the mannequin again. "C'mon, *move*," he challenged in a shaky voice.

That's when it got weird. The Clemente-mannequin face started to morph into something lopsided and milky, and Nick could even make out traces of the skull underneath. He closed his eyes - hard - and held them shut, gripping the steam vacuum's handle for dear life.

Okay, I'm going to count to three and open my eyes again and this will all be normal, he thought. *One, two...*

He snapped his eyes open and was greeted with the sight of not one, but TWO Clementes, the one in uniform and another in casual dress standing right behind, a hand on the ballplayer's uniformed shoulder. Except that the other Clemente was only about three quarters solid, his expression a mixture of confusion and wonder.

Now Nick was hyperventilating, and sharp pains were shooting down his right arm. The room started spinning and he hit the ground with a thud. Fighting to stay conscious, he managed to muster enough strength with his left arm to yank the extension cord to the vacuum from the outlet across the room. "Andy!" he called, faintly. Then with all the power he could summon, "ANDY!"

His voice reverberated in the empty Museum as he started to slip into unconsciousness. Within a matter of seconds Nick heard the heavy footfalls of his brother pounding down the main staircase from the third floor, heard Andy's labored breathing as he flopped down on the freshly-steamed carpet and cradled Nick's head in his hands.

"Nicky, Nicky!" Andy cried, half-sobbing. "Hold on! I'll call 9-1-1!" Andy fumbled in his utility vest for the cell phone and had just located it when Nick gripped his shirt front and pulled him down towards his ghastly gray face. His breath misted in the strangely chilly room.

"Clemente... here," he gasped before closing his eyes for good.

Andy looked up into the case. The statue of Roberto Clemente stared straight ahead, impassive and inscrutable.

Chapter Two

Another bleak, brutally cold February morning was dawning in the Civil War town of Gettysburg, Pennsylvania. Terri Darcy crept up the stairs to the second floor of the Victorian where she lived with her husband Mike and adopted daughter LouAnne on Seminary Ridge, the scene of desperate fighting on the first day of the battle of Gettysburg in July of 1863.

But the conflicts of bygone history were not important to Terri Darcy; she was waging her own war in the here and now. Taking a deep breath, she cautiously rapped on her daughter's bedroom door. "LouAnne, can I come in?" she asked gently.

"Sure," came the faint answer from within.

Terry eased open the heavy old door and leaned in. The room itself was gaily decorated with canary yellow paint, its walls and shelves festooned with trophies, ribbons and certificates recognizing the triumphs of her daughter's high school track career to date. Over her bed were two enlarged photographs. One was an antique daguerreotype of the girl in Civil War era dress, her blonde hair pulled back in a bun, surrounded by two boys in Union uniforms, looking quite serious. One of the boys had the wholesome good looks of a young Paul McCartney, his longish Beatle haircut peeking out from under his forage cap. The other sported bushy curls that almost covered his thick glasses. The accompanying photo featured the same threesome, this time in tropical attire on the beach, their arms casually thrown over each other's shoulders. They were all sunburned and smiling.

"Honey, you're going to be late for school," said Terri with only a

11

hint of her immense frustration. "You missed the bus, but I can drive you."

"Not today, Mom, okay?" the girl replied, a lilt of defeat and despair in her voice.

Terri made her way over to the bed and carefully sat down. Her daughter lay covered up to her chin despite the temperature setting in her room being close to sweltering. LouAnne's face was wan from weight loss and her eyes expressionless. "Honey," Terri reasoned, "it's the second time this week. You're going to fall way behind in your school work. And what about spring track? Coach Morgan has already begun indoor practices -"

"I can't, Mom, not today," said LouAnne with an air of finality. "Tomorrow, I promise." She turned in her bed and faced the wall.

There was nothing to do. Neither Terri Darcy nor her husband could lift the veil that had descended upon their daughter. Terri sighed and rose from the bed, heading for the door. As she reached it the girl said, "And leave the lights off, please."

Chapter Three

Ozzie Mantilla was a bundle of nerves. Here it was, March, with Opening Day not far off, and he'd been plucked from Spring Training camp in sunny Bradenton, Florida to come to the Hall of Fame. He'd been asked to address a small audience in the Bullpen Theater adjacent to the first floor Library Research Center in recognition of the loan of his Silver Slugger award from last season. He'd flown into New York with his Pirates manager, Hoss Wilborn, and his agent, Scott Samuels, earlier that morning, then connected on a small jet that took the three men as far as Albany. From there it was an hour's SUV limo ride over the still-icy roads of upstate New York to the small village of Cooperstown, nestled in the Catskills by Lake Otsego.

But neither the bumpy flight nor the treacherous mountain roads terrified Ozzie as much as public speaking, which was funny because he routinely performed at a high level in pressure situations before thousands of sometimes hostile fans. In fact, the previous season he'd put up prodigious numbers for the third place Buccos: 44 homers, 128 RBI and a .340 average, barely missing the Triple Crown because Albert Pujols of the Cardinals had out-homered him by two.

Ozzie, stocky and muscular with a matinee idol smile that made him millions in endorsements of everything from sports cars to shaving cream, was nevertheless apprehensive about presenting himself to what would probably be a healthy contingent of fawning fans. Maybe it was because his English wasn't perfect, and that when he was nervous his Spanish accent was more pronounced. Or maybe it was the fact that he'd achieved his lofty status in part because of his use of performance

13

enhancing drugs like HGH that he'd had shipped from the Dominican Republic, which he'd been able to mask with other chemicals in the random drug test he'd taken last August. It actually wasn't a moral dilemma for Ozzie; he would do *anything* to stay off the island and away from the poverty from which he'd come. If he had to risk a suspension, so be it. Even Scott Samuels, who made millions off him in brokering his current five-year deal with the Pirates, had no idea of Ozzie's transgressions.

As the Hall's tech crew was adjusting the podium microphone for a sound check, Ozzie approached Hoss Wilborn, who was deep in conversation with the Hall's president, Bob Simmons. "Uh, Skip, I think I need a breath of fresh air," he interrupted.

Immediately Samuels was at his side, ever mindful of protecting his golden goose. "You okay, Ozzie?" he asked in an almost motherly way. "Was it something you ate on the plane?"

"Nah, I don't think so," he replied, forcing a smile. "I'll be all right. How long 'til this thing starts?"

Wilborn looked at his watch, a memento of an All-Star game appearance he'd made as a player back in the 1970s. "Got a good half-hour before they let the people in, podna. Why don't you take a walk upstairs? It's too cold outside the building."

"Yeah, good idea," said the outfielder. "We went through the Museum so fast when we got here, I'm sure I missed a lot."

Wilborn clapped him on the shoulder. "Atta boy. Go clear your head and be back at seven-thirty. You'll do fine."

"You want me to come with you?" inquired Samuels.

"No, that's okay. I'd rather be alone. My first time here, you know?"

"But not your last," said the agent. "Trust me on that."

Ozzie accepted the compliment with a weak grin, stuffed his hands in the pockets of his Armani suit, and shuffled out of the theater and up the ramp to the second level. In reality, baseball history meant little to him, as was the case with the majority of modern players. The fact that he was a part of it paled in comparison to his desire for the wealth and fame he derived from it. Not that he didn't love the game - it was his passion, and he worked very hard at his craft, year-round. The PED's were just a little insurance for the dog days of summer when ballplayers, who were all nursing bumps and bruises by the All-Star break, needed a little pick-me-up to keep grinding it out through the stretch run in September.

There was, however, one exhibit he'd blown past earlier that he wanted to revisit - that of the Latin ballplayers and their impact on the American game. Called "Viva Baseball!" it was interactive in nature; with the push of a button the visitor could watch videos and hear interview clips from such all-time greats as Orlando Cepeda, Juan Marichal, and Ozzie's father's idol, Roberto Clemente. He spent a few minutes there, gazing at the Caribbean map which highlighted the birthplaces of notable Latin players, as well as selected artifacts from their careers. A horizontal display compartment, which lay empty, would tomorrow house his Silver Slugger Award bat.

He remembered playing catch with his father in the deserted lot behind their shack just outside Santurce, where Clemente had played winter ball for the local team. Their baseball was wound with electrical tape; his cheap, second-hand glove was ripped and tattered. The whole time, his father - whose roughly callused farm laborer's hands needed no glove for protection - would extol the virtues of The Great Clemente, rattling off his lifetime statistics and rhapsodizing about his fluidity on the diamond, especially while patrolling right field. "Strong and true like a rifle," was how he'd portray Clemente's legendary throwing arm. And then of course he'd add the tragic circumstances of the ballplayer's death, in a plane crash on a humanitarian mission to Nicaragua to deliver supplies to earthquake victims. It had elevated him to godlike status on the island and earned for him almost instantaneous induction to the Hall of Fame. The fact that his body was never recovered from the wreckage of the cargo plane only added to the mystique of the man.

Suddenly, Ozzie felt a bit lightheaded, and he was definitely getting chills. Had they shut off the heat up here? Maybe he *had* eaten some spoiled food on the plane. He looked at his Rolex; still fifteen minutes before he was due back. He decided to move on to the Clemente case he'd seen earlier which had at first startled him, maybe take a picture on his iPhone and send it to his aged father back home. Yeah, his father would get a kick out of that. It was annoying, though. As successful as Ozzie had become, as much money as he'd made, Orestes Mantilla - who now lived in a villa on a hill thanks to his son - never gave Ozzie his due. "Maybe someday you will attain the greatness of Clemente," Orestes was fond of saying, which vexed Ozzie to no end.

"But I hit forty-four homers last year alone!" he'd cried during his recent Christmas visit. "Your Great Clemente never hit more than twenty-nine in the season!" His father had responded with an infuriating dismissive wave.

He now found himself in front of the case, still a bit out of sorts and cold, his gaze boring into the likeness of Clemente. Frowning, he fished his iPhone out of his jacket pocket and snapped the photo, then checked his watch. Seven twenty-five. He had no sooner turned for the exit to the main staircase when a rather high-pitched voice called, *"Para lo que estás haciendo. Es una vergüenza. ¡Recuerda que tú representas Puerto Rico!"*

Ozzie stopped short, the words piercing him like arrows. Who would dare accuse him, the great Ozzie Mantilla, of being a disgrace? Who could possibly know about his dirty little secret? He wheeled around, the motion inducing yet another wave of dizziness, to face his accuser. What he saw stunned him. There, in the case behind the statue, stood Roberto Clemente, his eyes aflame with anger, a wagging finger pointing his way.

Ozzie ran from the exhibit to the main staircase, bounding down the steps two at a time, and headed for the rear entrance to the Bullpen Theater, which was beginning to fill. He flung open the door and encountered Wilborn, Simmons and Samuels, who were about to take their seats on stage.

"Holy cow, Ozzie," said the manager, alarmed at the sight of his terrified slugger. "You're as white as a ghost, son. What's going on?"

"Roberto...Clemente..." he panted, bracing himself against the wall for support.

"Clemente?" said Wilborn. "What about him?"

"What *about* him? He's come *back!*"

Chapter Four

T.J. Jackson finished his practice swings in the on-deck circle, grabbed his aluminum Easton bat by the top and rammed it down into the still-hard earth, dislodging the weighted plastic doughnut from its barrel. He gripped the barrel at the trademark with his left hand, strode to the batter's box, then held up his right hand to signal the umpire for time until he had dug in his back foot properly with his spikes.

"Comfy, Hollywood?" the New Canaan catcher cracked, looking up at him from his crouch.

"That'll be enough, catcher," said the umpire. "You ready, batter? I'm getting cold back here."

"Ready, Blue," said T.J., already cocking his back and locking onto the pitcher.

It was late March and still chilly, despite the fact that it had been a mild winter. T.J. was wearing his home white number 21 jersey, trimmed in blue and red, and a spandex turtleneck underneath to keep the heat in. The ground was thawing, which made the skin parts of the infield and around home plate a muddy mess that had to be doused with Diamond Dust to absorb the moisture. His Nike spikes were caked with it.

T.J.'s team, the Bridgefield High junior varsity, was in its third preseason scrimmage, and the centerfielder was having a rough go, all because of a TV show. The previous summer, T.J., his best buddy, Bortnicker, and his adopted cousin, LouAnne, had been invited to the vacation paradise of Bermuda by The Adventure Channel to film what was supposed to be the pilot episode for a series called *Junior Gonzo Ghost Chasers*, a spinoff of the wildly successful paranormal program

17

hosted by their friend Mike Weinstein. Their tumultuous week on the island had seen the teens discover the identity of a sunken pirate warship, come face-to-face with the ghost of a slave-trading buccaneer, dig up his earthly remains, and more or less get thrown off the island by the Bermuda National Trust for uncovering some rather unsavory aspects of that country's history.

But ghost hunting was only a part of the excitement. T.J. felt that his tricky relationship with LouAnne had taken a step forward, albeit a small one. And Bortnicker, long-time class nerd of the Bridgefield school system, had fallen head-over-heels for a beautiful island girl who seemed to return his affection.

Unfortunately for Mike Weinstein, who had brainstormed the spinoff idea, The Adventure Channel saw *Junior Gonzo Ghost Chasers* as an occasional TV special rather than a series, but that didn't stop them from throwing a gala premiere party in New York City in mid-October at a swanky restaurant. Mike and some higher-ups from The Adventure Channel were in attendance for the VIP screening, as well as T.J. and his dad, Bortnicker and his mom, and LouAnne, who'd come up from Gettysburg with her parents. It was great for the gang to be back together, and the Darcys had stayed over for the weekend at the Jackson home so T.J. and Bortnicker could show LouAnne around Fairfield. The trio of teens had been inseparable, and though T.J. wished there'd been a little time to be alone with his adopted cousin, he didn't mind. The weekend had culminated with a grand barbecue on the Jacksons' spacious flagstone patio, with the kids satisfied that the TV special would be a success.

And it was. Promoted heavily on The Adventure Channel and its sister cable stations, *Junior Gonzo Ghost Chasers: The Bermuda Case* was a ratings sensation, and Mike relayed the feeling from The Adventure Channel brass that this might not be the only one.

Of course, much of what happened on the island was left on the cutting room floor, most notably the sordid details of Sir William Tarver's treatment of the slaves who toiled on his palatial tobacco plantation. But what really irked the team was that the groundbreaking electronic voice phenomena (EVP) recording they'd elicited from Tarver - in which he'd recounted the story of his pirate life and his own murder during a slave uprising - was under lock and key at the Bermuda National Trust headquarters, where it would remain forever.

Overall, though, their investigation made for great TV, especially the scuba diving sequence in which they'd discovered the coral-encrusted brass bell of the *Steadfast*, Tarver's pirate vessel. The find itself was historic. Jasper Goodwin, the divemaster who'd taken the team out to the reefs that day - and whose lovely daughter was the object of Bortnicker's ardor - had become an instant island celebrity, which led to a boom in his dive shop business as well.

But nothing in life was perfect. T.J., who'd dealt with adversity as a child when his young mother had died of cancer, had learned that all too well. The TV show brought instant celebrity to the two boys at Bridgefield High. T.J., always leery of the spotlight despite his charm and good looks, tried to play it off as best he could, even deflecting the advances of a number of girls in his sophomore class - and older - who figured his looks, athleticism and newfound fame made him a "must-have." The fact that he still pined for LouAnne provided self-justification for his behavior, which was sometimes misinterpreted as aloofness by the spurned females.

Bortnicker, on the other hand, had embraced celebrity status. Most girls still viewed him as somewhat of a kook, but that hadn't fazed him at all. In fact, he'd kept up his friendship with Ronnie Goodwin throughout the winter via emails and the occasional Skype, and he wasn't averse to flashing her photo around when the other students started ragging on him.

But the biggest test of T.J.'s mettle was not the come-ons from females who longed to be near him - it was the jealous, snide remarks of some of the guys around school. They said the whole show had been staged, claiming that it was probably even stunt doubles that'd been doing the scuba diving that he and Bortnicker had worked so hard to learn during an intense training course the previous spring.

It was even worse in these early preseason games, where bench jockeys from the other teams ragged him constantly and generally made his life miserable, no matter how much Coach Pisseri complained. The guys from New Canaan had taken it to a new level today, their pitchers throwing up and in toward his head, making him spin out of the way in self-preservation. But T.J., though sometimes nagged by self-doubt in his athletic endeavors, refused to back down. The first time he'd been "dusted" today he'd picked himself up and promptly rifled a single back through the box that nearly took the New Canaan pitcher's hat off. The next time, with men on second and third and two out, he'd stepped back into the batter's box after an inside fastball that made him "skip rope" and lined a slider on the outside corner past the lunging first baseman into right field for two RBIs. As was his habit, T.J. had taken his turn around first, and then retreated to the bag, offering a single understated handclap to signal his pleasure. Of course, his teammates, Coach Pisseri, and especially his pal, Bortnicker, who kept the team's stats (though he insisted on wearing a uniform, his bushy hair sticking out in all directions from under his cap) were all up and cheering with each successive hit, vexing the opposition to no end.

This time the game was on the line: last ups, bases full, two down in a tied game. A single would win it.

T.J. scanned the field. They were playing him straight away. With no reason for them to hold the runners he lost the very inviting opposite field hole through which he'd singled his last time up. The New Canaan relief pitcher, a burly, crew-cut guy who reminded him of Roger Clemens - he was even chomping what appeared to be tobacco - sneered as he rubbed up the ball, which was by this time in the game discolored and a little out of round.

"You n'me, Hollywood," he called out, toeing the pitching rubber.

"Bring it," was T.J.'s curt reply.

The pitcher, with no reason to fear a stolen base attempt, went into a full windup. His fastball cut the plate up around the numbers.

"Ball one!" cried the ump.

Working quickly, the pitcher rocked and dealt a curveball that caught the outside part of the plate.

"Stee!" said the ump, giving the strike signal.

T.J. called time and backed out of the box. He picked up some dirt and rubbed it on his hands, enjoying the sensation. He was the only guy on the team who eschewed batting gloves, even in cold weather, when a ball off the bat handle sent shockwaves up your arms to your shoulders. This pause apparently annoyed Clemens Jr.

"Get back in there!" he challenged, which made T.J. move even slower.

Everybody was into it now, both sides exhorting their man in this one-on-one duel.

The next pitch just missed inside, which clearly upset Mr. Crew-cut, who snapped his glove at the return throw from his catcher.

T.J. waited, wagging his bat ever so slightly, his hips gently rocking as the pitcher wound up again and blazed one on the inside corner that T.J. turned on and smoked, barely foul, outside third base.

The New Canaan hurler now realized that T.J. had his number. He'd thrown his best fastball and the Bridgefield glamour boy was *on it*. Flustered, he served up a sloppy curve that his catcher had to lunge at to prevent a passed ball. Full count.

"No place to put him!" sang out Bortnicker, in a piercing falsetto, his eyes dancing behind his Coke bottle glasses. "Oh dear, what should I *do?*"

"Jeez Louise, Bortnicker," muttered T.J. under his breath, "could you just shut up?"

Sure enough, the pressure and the razzing got to the pitcher, who grunted as he unleashed a wicked fastball, which bore in on T.J. so fast he could barely react. The ball caught him just over the earflap of his batting helmet and ricocheted some 30 feet in the air as T.J. went down like he'd been shot. He didn't lose consciousness because he could hear both the pitcher cursing at himself and Coach Pisseri screaming at the other team's manager, whose name apparently was Frank. Almost immediately the catcher, the umpire, and Bortnicker were leaning over him.

"You all right, son?" asked the ump, his mask tipped back on his head.

"I...think so," he replied, woozily feeling around for his helmet, which had tumbled off when he'd hit the ground.

"You want me to call it here, or do you wanna touch first base and make it official?" he asked concernedly.

T.J. got to his knees and shook his head vigorously. Things were going in and out of focus, but he wasn't about to wimp out. "My helmet," he said to Bortnicker, who had it waiting with a wry smile. He took the helmet, eased it onto his aching head, stood and half-jogged to first, where he touched up and then fell full on his face.

Chapter Five

"Is everybody here?" asked Bob Simmons. He settled into his seat at the head of the conference table in the board room of the Hall of Fame office building, adjacent to the Museum on Main Street.

To his right were Bryan Davis, supervisor of exhibitions and collections, and Sarah Martin, director of exhibits and design. On his left were Pete Alfano, director of security, and Simmons' right hand man, Dan Vines, the senior vice president. They constituted the core of the Hall of Fame's staff and had all been with Simmons for at least five years. He trusted them implicitly, which was why they were included in this top secret meeting.

"Okay, people," he began, "hope you had a great weekend, but now it appears we have a problem to start the week, one we have to deal with immediately. I need you all to realize that what is said in this room today stays here. Agreed?"

After a bewildered glance at each other, the board members nodded their assent.

"All right, then. What I'm going to tell you might seem way out there -"

"Even for you, Bob?" asked Vines, trying to lighten the mood. But Simmons wasn't smiling.

"Even for me, Dan," he said evenly. "So please, take this seriously. I'll start at the beginning.

"Back on New Year's Eve the cleaning guys were in to do the carpets, as you might remember. It's pretty common knowledge that one

23

of them, Nick Florio, suffered a heart attack on the second floor. By the time his brother called 911 and the EMTs showed up, Nick was gone. Now, this man was in pretty bad physical shape to begin with, but when I spoke to the brother the next day he swore that Nick had been literally scared to death."

"Scared to death?" queried Martin. "By what?"

"Not exactly a *what*," answered Simmons. "Let me explain. Apparently Florio collapsed in front of the Clemente case on the second floor. You know, the one with the life-sized statue. His last words to his brother were, and I quote, 'Clemente…here'."

"That makes sense," reasoned Davis. "They were right in front of the display, no?"

"Of course they were, Bryan," said Simmons patiently, "but why say *that* to his brother?"

And uneasy silence fell over the group.

"Let me continue," said Simmons. "So, as you know, we are having a series of events this year celebrating Latin baseball to coincide with the 40th anniversary of the death of Roberto Clemente. Well, a couple weeks ago we had Ozzie Mantilla of the Pirates come up from Spring Training to donate his Silver Slugger Award to the Viva Baseball! exhibit. The Bullpen Theater was packed with members of the Friends of the Hall of Fame, and some people from MLB.

"Well, the night went off as planned, pretty much, but what you don't know is that we had to delay the ceremony for about a half hour -"

"Because of a power outage, correct?" cut in Alfano.

"That's what we *told* everyone, Pete. The truth is, Ozzie Mantilla had come running downstairs in a panic, sweat pouring off him, claiming that he'd seen *a second* Roberto Clemente in the case."

"What!" the staff members cried in unison.

Simmons held his palms out. "Easy, everyone," he cautioned. "I know this is a lot to swallow, and nobody's more skeptical about this stuff than me, but this guy was dead serious. He even said Clemente tried to communicate with him, though he wouldn't divulge the exact words."

"And he's sure it was Clemente?" asked Martin.

"Yes, in street clothes. I took down his description before Ozzie left that night. Needless to say, I don't think he'll be back anytime soon.

Now, I was able to check, in a roundabout way so as not to alarm anyone, especially his family, as to what Clemente was wearing the night he died on that flight to Nicaragua. Mantilla nailed it."

"How do you know Mantilla isn't down in Florida blabbing this to anybody who'll listen?" asked Vines, his expression indicating he was already considering the repercussions.

"He won't, and neither will Hoss Wilborn or his agent, Scott Samuels. The last thing they want is for the Pirates' star player to be thought of as Looney Tunes."

"But still, Bob," said Alfano, "all you've got going so far to prove Clemente was there is based on hearsay."

At that very moment the door to the conference room cracked open and a twenty-something, studious-looking man poked his head in. "I've got it, Mr. Simmons," he whispered.

"Then come in, Jody," said the president, "and close the door behind you."

The bookish assistant seated himself at the table, and the others nodded at him. "Folks," said Simmons, "this is Jody Rieman, one of our interns working with the restoration and preservation department. He has something to share with all of us. Jody?"

"Okay, Mr. Simmons," said the intern politely. "Uh, Miss Martin, isn't it true that all of the glass cases in which artifacts are displayed are kept at a climate-controlled, low humidity level at all times?"

"Why, yes," she replied confidently. "That would account the barely discernible hum that is omnipresent in the Museum. The cases are periodically aired out and the artifacts inspected for deterioration."

"Exactly. And if I do say so myself, ma'am, you and your staff do a thorough job. But after the Mantilla incident, Mr. Simmons had me do an inspection of the Clemente case. I opened and entered it from the back and was immediately overwhelmed by a strange smell -"

"Of what?" she interrupted.

"Well, it was kind of swampy...sea-weedy, if you will. So, I checked the air duct leading into the case to see if a mouse had died in there, or if there was any mold or whatever. It was clean as a whistle. But I did find something." He reached into his inside jacket pocket and removed a small tan archival envelope. Carefully he opened the flap and shook out a tiny object onto the conference table. Everyone leaned in for a look.

"A shell?" said Vines. "A *shell* was in the duct work?"

Rieman shook his head. "No, sir, it was on the floor of the case, behind the statue. It's so small I almost missed it."

"Well, son," said Vines, "we *are* near a rather large lake."

"No, sir," the intern countered gently. "With permission from Mr. Simmons, I brought the shell over to the Marine biology department at SUNY Oneonta. One of the professors took it to their lab and did a complete analysis, and I'm just back from picking it up."

"And?"

"Well, the truth is, without getting too technical, this is a saltwater species native to the Caribbean. It can't possibly be from Lake Otsego, or any other lake in the Catskills."

The board members sat back in their seats, stunned.

Simmons, who knew all of this from Rieman's excited cell phone call from earlier that morning, nodded. "Thanks, Jody. Great job."

He leaned forward on his elbows and addressed his lieutenants. "Well, there you have it, folks. To me this all points to one conclusion: the ghost of Roberto Clemente is here, at the Hall of Fame. One would think that this 40th anniversary thing might play into his reappearance, but who knows for sure?" He turned to his director of security. "Now, Pete, think hard. Have there been any problems with any of the motion sensor alarms lately?"

Alfano furrowed his brow. "Now that you mention it, yes," he admitted. "The past few weeks it's been set off a few times, but I suspected a short in the wiring system."

"Did you have someone in to take a look at it?" said Simmons, an eyebrow raised.

"Yeah, Bob. It all came up negative."

The president of the Baseball Hall of Fame and Museum sat back and crossed his arms on his chest. "Okay, then. If you look at our spring calendar of events related to the 40th anniversary observation, we've got a Viva Baseball! extravaganza weekend scheduled for late April. Every living Latin Hall of Famer and their families, as well as a number of notable retired non-Hall of Famers, is invited. This situation, as I see it, has to be dealt with by then. Some of those gentlemen and their wives are elderly, and we can't have anyone else dropping dead from fright.

"Now, if you remember, we had one of those paranormal TV shows come in here a few years back and do a sweep of the Hall, as well as the Otesaga Hotel by the lake where all the Hall of Famers stay during Induction Weekend. Frankly, we agreed to it because visitorship was down due to the bad economy. And it was all right, though in retrospect it wasn't one of my best marketing decisions. Of course, they found nothing going on.

"But now we've got a real problem on our hands, and I've got someone in mind to look into it who might be just what the doctor ordered. Anyone here against a serious investigation the first week of April?"

The Board solemnly shook their heads. "Okay, then, let me make a call. But remember, loose lips sink ships. Don't breathe a word of this to anyone. I'll keep you posted, but not through emails or anything that will leave a paper trail. Does anyone have a question before I let you go?"

Vines cleared his throat. "So, uh, Bob," he said, "do *you* really believe Clemente's come back?"

"I do, and you don't know how much I hope I'm wrong."

Chapter Six

"Hey, handsome, are you awake?" asked the middle-aged nurse, flipping open one of T.J.'s eyelids.

"Yes, ma'am," he replied with a yawn. "What time is it? Have I been sleeping?"

"Yes indeedy," she said, reading his chart. "We had to keep you up all night while we were checking your noggin. You took a pretty good thunk on your batting helmet. Did you know you cracked it?"

"Uh, no," he said, scanning the room.

"Well, I can tell you that you're fine. The doctor will be in in a few minutes. And you've got some visitors in the hall"

"Send them in, please."

"Will do." She patted him on the cheek and went out as Bortnicker, his dad and Coach Pisseri entered.

"How's it going, Big Mon?" said Bortnicker, pulling up a chair as T.J. sat up in the hospital bed. "Word on the street is that some of the young nurses are all aflutter over you."

"Yeah, right. When can I get out of here?"

"They ran a lot of tests on you, son," said Thomas Jackson, Sr., dressed as always in khakis and a button down shirt. "Checking for concussion and whatnot. The doc should be by shortly to see if they'll be releasing you."

"But you never lost consciousness, right?" asked Pisseri.

"No, I was just a little disoriented. And jogging to first probably wasn't the best idea."

"Well, Big Mon," said Bortnicker, "you sure impressed the heck out of those New Canaan guys. I even heard the pitcher say to his catcher, 'That guy showed me something by getting up. Maybe he isn't such a pansy after all'."

"Comforting."

Just then the doctor came in, an Indian man named Mathur. He carried a clipboard and was all business. "How are you feeling, T.J.?" he asked in clipped English.

"Better, doc. Just a little leftover headache."

Dr. Mathur flipped through the pages on his clipboard. "Well, fortunately there was no concussion. We did every possible test for that. However, I am always one to err on the side of caution, so it is my recommendation that you engage in no strenuous physical activity for the next two weeks, especially contact sports. If, during that time you experience any symptoms of lightheadedness, nausea or fatigue, I must be alerted immediately. Understood, young man?"

"I guess so," he said dejectedly.

"Look at it this way, T.J.," said Pisseri, ever the optimist. "We only have one more scrimmage next week. The week after that is Spring Break and there are no games at all. What's important is that I have you out there in center for the beginning of the regular season."

"Sure, Coach," he replied, forcing a smile.

Mathur left after speaking briefly with Mr. Jackson.

"Okay, T.J.," said Pisseri, "I've gotta get moving. Hey, you two are still coming to my team get-together tomorrow, aren't you? I'm putting out lots of food."

"We're there!" cried Bortnicker.

Pisseri shook his head. He enjoyed having Bortnicker as team statistician, but everyone knew the kid could be a bit much at times. "I told the guys to show up about 1:00 PM. That should be okay on a Sunday. If it's all right with you, Mr. Jackson?"

"No problem, Coach. I'll run the boys over to your house. Just get ready for the onslaught. These guys can *eat*."

"No big deal. We'll have some chow and talk some baseball. The perfect afternoon." Pisseri left, rushing off as always.

"Maybe he's got a date," said Bortnicker. "It is Saturday night, after all."

"It was nice of him to come," said Tom Sr. "He cares a lot about his players." He checked his watch. "Hey, T.J., mind if I go downstairs and grab a cup of coffee before we leave? By that time they should be ready to release you."

"No problem, Dad," T.J. said.

"I'll come with you Mr. J.," said Bortnicker. "I could use a soda myself - and maybe a sandwich."

They left together, and T.J. got out of bed to fetch the clothes his father brought from home. He opened the hospital room closet; then his cell phone rang.

"Hello?" he said tentatively.

"Cuz?" came a familiar, faraway voice.

"LouAnne? Hi, Cuz, what's up?"

"Your dad called about your injury. You got beaned?"

"Yeah, but not too bad. I've got to take two weeks off, is all."

There was a long silence on the other end. LouAnne?"

"Oh, sorry. Well, I'm glad you're feeling okay. I was worried."

"No problem. Hey, uh, Cuz, can I ask you something?"

"Sure."

He took a deep breath. "Something's been kinda bothering me. Why didn't we get together at Christmas like we talked about?"

Indeed, after their happy reunion at the TV premiere the two families had made plans for the Jacksons - accompanied by Bortnicker and his mom - to visit Gettysburg for a couple days. It would have been the first return for the boys since their memorable summer trip in 2010, in which they'd conducted their initial paranormal investigation and came face-to-face with the ghost of a Confederate cavalier.

"T.J., you know I had the flu, like, that whole week. We couldn't have you all come down here and get infected." She sounded fairly convincing, but T.J. could sense a slight hitch, a hesitation in her response. Could she have found a boyfriend? He'd tried not to consider it, but it was only normal that a knockout like LouAnne had to have boys chasing after her all the time. That's what sucked about this long distance relationship thing - if there *was* a relationship. He wasn't so sure anymore.

"Uh-huh. Well, have you given any thought to Spring Break? I was

30

hoping -"

"Give me a couple days on that, Cuz, all right?" she asked, and he could hear something disquieting in her voice. It didn't sound like the supremely confident LouAnne Darcy he knew. "I, uh, gotta make sure my schedule checks," she added somewhat awkwardly.

"Yeah, no problem," he said warily. "Call you in a couple days?"

"You know it. Feel better."

"Okay."

He hung up, but he didn't feel better.

Chapter Seven

"Glad you're back to normal, Big Mon," said Bortnicker as he and T.J. shoehorned their way out of Tom Sr.'s Jaguar XJS sports car, which Tom Sr. was breaking out for the first time this spring.

"Thanks. Hey, Dad, don't worry about picking us up," said T.J. "It's just a twenty-minute walk, and it's a nice day. Take the Jag and give it a good run."

"I was hoping you'd say that," smiled the elder Jackson, who was sporting his aviator sunglasses and black driving gloves. "Make sure to help Coach clean up if he needs it. And try to leave a little food for him."

"Okay," said T.J., shutting the passenger door. Tom Sr. gunned the Jag's motor and took off, as the boys turned toward the door of their coach's house. The split-level had belonged to his parents, who had retired to Florida a few years before. Now Pisseri had the whole house to himself and his legendary baseball memorabilia collection, which the boys had only seen one other time the previous spring, their first year with the JV baseball team. It was Pisseri's custom to have a "spring training" get-together with his players to help strengthen the feeling of camaraderie and get them into total baseball mode because some of them, like T.J., had played other sports earlier in the year due to the limitations of tiny Bridgefield High's talent pool. T.J. loved running cross country and the opportunities for self-contemplation and personal challenge it afforded, but there was something to be said for the team aspect, everyone pulling together for a common cause.

This year's JV squad was a good mix of sophomores and freshmen, with T.J. firmly established as the centerfielder and number two hitter in the lineup, a position that utilized his ability as a right-handed hitter to "go the opposite way" with a man on first to move him into scoring position. In the field, he covered a lot of ground with his graceful stride and was able to track and run down almost everything hit in the gaps. His arm wasn't the strongest, and he needed to work on getting rid of the ball quickly, but he was extremely accurate in throwing to all bases, usually on one hop. He had also, in his second season, felt more comfortable in "taking charge" in the outfield, calling off the corner fielders to make putouts.

Moreover, the other guys had been supportive of him over the whole TV thing, and if there was any jealousy, he hadn't picked up on it. One of his pitchers had even buzzed an opposing batter in a previous scrimmage after their pitcher had tried to intimidate T.J. It elicited a halfhearted rebuke from Pisseri, who they knew was inwardly glad to see his players taking up for each other and following the ancient codes of the game.

As for Bortnicker, well, he helped Pisseri with all the equipment and fed him balls during fungo drills, computed the most accurate stats this side of the Majors, and never failed to have a quip or observation that kept everyone on the bench loose, even in the tightest situations. Indeed, the varsity coach, whose own team was dreadful this year, was eagerly awaiting both of the boys. Bortnicker rang the doorbell and was greeted almost instantaneously by Nathan Yokoi, the team's Amerasian catcher, who was hefting a man-sized hunk of sandwich. "Coach, the *Junior Gonzos* are here!" he woofed over his shoulder.

"Very funny," said Bortnicker. "Hey, Nathan, you might want to pick up that wad of salami you just spit on Coach's carpet." The boys breezed into the house and were greeted by their teammates, who good-naturedly ribbed T.J. about his encounter with a rising fastball the previous day.

"Grab some grub and a Coke and we'll go down to the Man Cave," called out Pisseri. "I've got a preseason game on the wide-screen, Yankees versus Braves from sunny Florida!"

T.J. and Bortnicker made their way into the kitchen and the dining table, taken up mostly with the six-foot sub sandwich - now half gone; side salads, and bowls of chips. Bortnicker fished a couple of ice-cold

Cokes out of Coach's fridge while T.J. hacked off brick-sized chunks of sandwich.

"Glad to see the headache didn't affect your appetite," cracked Bortnicker.

"A guy's gotta eat," he replied with a shrug.

"That's what I'm *talkin'* about!"

They descended the stairs into what resembled a mini-museum. Unlike the mishmash of clutter one might expect from a jock, Pisseri had stylishly decorated the spacious room from ceiling to floor, utilizing every square inch of display space. Framed photos of ballplayers, many of them autographed, adorned the walls, one of which featured a hanging bat rack of game-used clubs for its entire length. What was really cool to T.J. were the seats from torn-down ballparks, some wooden, some plastic. Each had a brass trophy plaque affixed to its top slat.

"Wow, Coach. Ebbets Field?" Bortnicker said, pointing to a straight-backed navy blue box seat. "That's where the Jackie Robinson Dodgers played, right?"

"You got it," Pisseri said proudly. "And that grey one with the orange iron stanchions is from the Polo Grounds, home of the New York Giants."

"Cool!"

Pisseri had set aside a small closet for his binders of Topps baseball cards, arranged by year on built-in bookshelves. "I have complete sets going back to 1970," he said, shaking his head. "I'm starting to run out of space."

"What's gonna happen when you get married?" asked Nick Isabella, their scrappy second baseman.

"Well, I guess she's going to have to like baseball," was the answer, which drew a round of applause from the team.

Some of the players plunked themselves down on the carpeted floor in front of the flatscreen, checking out the Yankees game, while others like T.J. flipped through the plastic pages of the card binders, careful not to spill any food or drink on the cherished pasteboards. All in all, the gathering accomplished exactly what the coach had hoped for: a sense of team building and togetherness.

Gradually the food evaporated and the conversation wound down.

Sensing that the afternoon was nearing its end, Pisseri called the team together for a little pep talk.

"Fellas," he began, "our season started in the frigid cold of early January when you demonstrated your dedication by showing up at the batting cages on Saturday mornings. Then it was fielding drills on the basketball courts in the gym at school, and all the running you've done in between.

"We've had three scrimmages so far, and I think we're shaping up as a team. I know the fields have been sloppy, but we've got to tighten up our defense a little, especially on the left side of the infield. As for our hitting, I'm very encouraged over what I've seen, although a few of you have to work the count a little more; be a bit more patient until you get your pitch.

"And one other thing," he said, glancing briefly at T.J. "We had an incident yesterday with a pitcher coming up and in on T.J. I know he's been hearing some garbage from the other teams because of that TV show, but we can't allow ourselves to be drawn into trading beanballs or talking trash. From now on, if there's an incident, I'll handle it with the other coach -"

"You mean, like, kick his butt?" broke in Yokoi, an expectant look in his eyes.

"No, Nathan," he answered patiently. "I'll tell him to control his team or I'm pulling you guys off the field till he does.

"Now, we've got one more scrimmage this week against Westport, which T.J. will be sitting out as a precaution. Then, you have a week off for Spring Break before we open the regular season. I'm gonna ask you guys, no matter where you are that week, to do some running and also a lot of stretching to stay loose. And if you're near a batting cage, try to get in some swings. I'm looking forward to a great season, and I don't mind telling you that the varsity coaches have their eyes on some of you already."

As the boys thanked Pisseri and drifted out, T.J. and Bortnicker stayed behind to help clean up. It was while tying the ends of an oversized kitchen bag that T.J.'s cell phone rang. When he saw the caller ID his eyes widened. "Bortnicker," he hissed, "it's Cooperstown, New York. Don't know of anything up there but the Hall of Fame. Why would they call *me*?"

"Can't imagine," his friend replied, draining a half-empty soda can into Pisseri's sink. "I don't think it's your election notice 'cause you haven't played in the Majors yet. Why don't you just ask them?"

T.J. frowned at his friend's sarcasm and picked up. "Hello?" he said tentatively.

"T.J. Jackson?" inquired the voice on the other end.

"Speaking. Who's this?"

"T.J., I'm Bob Simmons, president of the National Baseball Hall of Fame and Museum, and I need your help. Got a minute?"

"Sure, Mr. Simmons," he said, taking a seat at the kitchen table. By this time Bortnicker had whispered to Pisseri that the Hall of Fame was on the phone. The coach stopped making kitchen noises and gently pulled up a chair next to the boys.

"T.J.," said Simmons, "forgive me for calling you out of the blue."

"No problem, Mr. Simmons," he replied smoothly, easing into his trademark diplomat mode. "As a matter of fact, I'm at my baseball coach's house right now for a team get-together."

"Well, how appropriate. Didn't know you were a ballplayer."

"Yeah, centerfield, and I bat second. I'm on the JV."

"Fantastic. Anyway, I got your number from Mike Weinstein of the *Gonzo Ghost Chasers*."

"Mike?"

"Yes, I spoke to him via cell phone on location in Vancouver, British Columbia, where his team just arrived to film a show at an abandoned fort from the French and Indian Wars. Listen, there's a lot for me to tell you, but I'll just cut to the chase. We've got what we believe to be, what you describe as, a *paranormal manifestation* at the Hall."

"Really. Any idea who it might be?"

"Well, I can tell you, but I can't express how important it is that this is kept quiet. Ah, who's there with you, T.J.?"

"My coach, Mr. Pisseri, and my buddy, Bortnicker."

"From the TV show?"

"One and the same, Sir. And you can trust them both."

"Okay. Well, son, I'll come right out with it. We think it might be…Roberto Clemente."

"From the Pirates? Who died in a plane crash?"

"That's him. Supposedly we've had two separate sightings. And you might not be aware, but this year marks the 40th anniversary of his tragic death. We have a series of events planned to commemorate the anniversary, one of which has been marred already. I can't take the chance of this happening again.

"Now, I have to tell you that you weren't exactly my first choice in this case. As I said, I contacted Mike, but his team is going to be tied up in Vancouver for the week before moving on to Jamaica to investigate the plantation house of some maniac mistress from the 1700s. Fortunately, Mike didn't hesitate to recommend you and your junior team for a possible investigation. He said that if you agreed to do it, he'd have The Adventure Channel ship whatever equipment you need to Cooperstown so you could do a thorough job. He even said something about this becoming another TV special for you all. After speaking to him I was able to find a DVD of your Bermuda show and I have to tell you, I was impressed. And the fact that you're a ballplayer yourself makes me even more confident that you'd be perfect for the job." Simmons was so persuasive that T.J. had no problem understanding why he was the president of such a prestigious institution. But that didn't mean he was sold on the idea.

"Gee, Mr. Simmons," he said, "Bortnicker and I would like to help you out…" He waved at his friend, who was practically levitating out of his chair with excitement, to calm down. "…but it would be tough."

"How so?"

"Well, first, there's school."

"But don't you have a spring vacation coming up?"

"Well, yeah, but that's not for two weeks."

"That wouldn't be a problem. In fact, it would give your ghost hunting team a little time to brush up on Clemente and his career, and for the equipment to be shipped here."

"Yes, sir, that's okay, but we'd have no way of getting up there, and if we did, I don't know who would be able to accompany us. My dad's supposed to be away on business in Arizona that week, and -"

From the corner of his eye T.J. saw Coach Pisseri, looking like a shy third-grader, raise his hand slowly. Bortnicker immediately pointed at the coach, nodding madly.

"Okay, T.J.," said Simmons pleasantly. "Here's what I was thinking. You would be guests of the Hall of Fame. We'll send an SUV limo for your team and bring you up here. I believe it's a four-hour ride from Fairfield. We'll put you up at a bed and breakfast in the center of town. Meals at local restaurants would be on us."

"How about my cousin, LouAnne? Would she be allowed to take part?"

"Most certainly. We have as many as four rooms at our disposal at the B&B, for as long as a week, if necessary. It's kind of the off-season, anyway, but like you said, we'd want a chaperone to escort you."

"And did Mike say anything about whether we were actually making a TV show out of this?"

"He intimated that the final decision would rest upon you."

"He trusts us that much?"

"Apparently. Look, the main thing is that we resolve the situation at the Hall. The TV thing is secondary, to tell the truth."

"And you really enjoyed the Bermuda show?"

"Every minute of it, and I was impressed by your maturity, thoughtfulness and professionalism. And by the way, my niece is a big fan, particularly of your friend, Bortnicker."

T.J. rolled his eyes as his friend tipped back his chair, put his hands behind his bushy head of hair and flashed his trademark crooked grin, his eyes sparkling behind the Coke-bottle glasses.

"T.J.? Are you there?" asked the president.

"Sure thing, Mr. Simmons," he answered. "Tell you what. Let me speak to my dad and my cousin and a few other people on this end and I'll call you back sometime tomorrow. If that works for you?"

"Of course. And if you have any questions or there's anything else you would need from the Hall of Fame, just ask. You have my phone number locked in?"

"Yes, Sir," T.J. answered respectfully. "Thanks for the opportunity. I'll speak with you tomorrow." He hung up and looked at Bortnicker and Coach Pisseri, both studying him anxiously.

"Well, Big Mon?" asked his friend, breaking the silence.

"Jeez Louise, I don't know," he replied. "On the one hand, you're talking about a bigtime operation here, the Hall of Fame, although I'm kinda feeling we were a second-round draft choice. And this ghost is a famous person. So it's a dream investigation, but there's more pressure.

"And also...I just don't know if I'm up to going through the whole TV investigation deal again. Cripes, we've taken so much grief over the last one. I don't want people to think I'm some sort of glory hound, Bortnicker. Do you?"

His friend removed his glasses and started polishing them with his tee shirt. "Actually, I like to bask in the glory of our accomplishments. But, I see what you mean. And Roberto Clemente...that's kind of raising the bar for us."

"You guys want my input?" asked Pisseri.

"Sure, Coach," said T.J.

"Okay, then. Hear me out. Roberto Clemente was one of the greatest, ever. Yeah, you might look at his career statistics as compared to today's steroid era guys and say, 'Jeez, he only hit around 250 homers and barely got to 3,000 hits over a fairly long career.' But I gotta tell you, fellas, this guy was a *ballplayer*. Hustled his butt off every day he was out there, won batting titles and an MVP award, and I believe was MVP of a World Series. But, man, you have to see videos of him in the outfield. T.J., *nothing* got by him; he could go get 'em and make it look easy. And he had one of the most awesome guns of any right fielder ever. He was like a lock for a Gold Glove every year.

"But even more so, he was a pioneer for the first wave of Latin players in the late 1950s and early 1960s. Today we see all these stars from the Dominican Republic or Puerto Rico or even Cuba and it's no big deal. Well, Clemente was like Jackie Robinson for these players. They all looked up to him, and in Puerto Rico, where he was from, he's still regarded with reverence. And if that isn't enough, the way he died was almost mythical."

"How so?" said T.J. with deepening interest.

"Well, like I said, he was a huge celebrity in all the Caribbean and South American countries that played baseball, and he was always doing charitable work in the off-season, not like some players today who spend their winters playing golf and counting their money."

"Or getting arrested," cracked Bortnicker.

"Or getting arrested," repeated Pisseri. "Well, there was this huge earthquake in Brazil - no, wait, it was Nicaragua. Thousands of people died, and the country was so backward there was no way they could handle the devastation and disease that resulted. Clemente personally organized the collection of tons of supplies for shipment to Nicaragua, but a lot of it wasn't getting through because the corrupt government there was confiscating it for their own use."

"No way," said Bortnicker.

"I'm not kidding. So he decided to go over there himself on a mercy flight in a cargo plane that apparently was overloaded. It crashed into the Atlantic shortly after takeoff. They found some wreckage later on, and I think a couple bodies, but his was never recovered.

"As I said, he was like a god to a lot of people in the Caribbean. Many refused to accept the fact that he could be dead. There were even rumors later on that he'd survived the crash and was spotted in different countries."

"Like an Elvis thing?" said Bortnicker.

"Yes, more or less, but of course, this wasn't the case. The area where the plane went down is infested with sharks."

"Oh, man," said T.J.

"But when you have no body, even if you hold huge memorial services like they did in Puerto Rico, there's always this kind of mysterious aspect to his death, know what I mean?

"And another thing, the Hall of Fame made an exception to the induction rule where a player has to be retired for five years before he can be voted in. He was put in with that year's class; something like that hadn't happened since Lou Gehrig, who died of ALS."

"So Coach," said T.J., "what you're saying is, it's, like, an honor to be asked on to this case?"

"Exactly. And, know what? It's more appropriate for two guys who are connected to the game rather than some other group who comes in cold and doesn't know Roberto Clemente from 'My Darling Clementine'." He paused and got himself under control. "Whew, sorry guys," he said, "but the way I see it, this is fate at work here. You can't pass up this opportunity. And tell you what. If you can't get your parents to chaperone, I'm in. We don't have any games or practices scheduled, anyway, that week."

"Coach," said T.J., "you'd really do it? How about if I'm able to talk my cousin LouAnne into it?"

"If your parents - and hers - are okay with it, I'd be happy to help you in any way I can. There's just one thing, ah…"

"What is it, Coach?" asked T.J.

He regarded them earnestly. "I'm afraid of ghosts." That broke the tension, and Pisseri shared a laugh with his boys.

"Look at it this way," said Bortnicker optimistically. "The first two ghosts, Major Hilliard and Captain Tarver, we didn't know if they'd kill us or something. This has *got* to be better."

* * * *

As the teens walked home, Bortnicker could see that his best friend was doing some serious pondering. "So what's the issue, Big Mon?" he asked while tight-roping atop the curb.

"LouAnne. Something's up with her. Yesterday I asked if she was coming for Spring Break and she was hemming and hawing. My gut tells me she wouldn't be gung-ho for another investigation…or to see me at all."

"You think there's another guy?"

"Maybe. *Something's* going on down there. She just doesn't sound like herself."

"Yeah, I know what you mean. Like, we still text each other with Beatles trivia and all, but it seems kinda forced lately. And what happened to us going to visit her at Christmas? *That* didn't exactly pan out."

"I know. She claims she was sick the whole week, but seriously, who's in better physical shape than her? It just doesn't add up. I'm afraid to even ask her about doing an investigation."

"But you *have to*, Big Mon," said Bortnicker. "She's a part of the *team*. Maybe this would be the thing to snap her out of whatever funk she's in. Besides," he added with a mischievous smile, "I'd like to meet this big fan of mine up in Cooperstown. She might be a fox!"

"And what about Ronnie?" asked T.J., recalling the exotically alluring island girl who'd been his friend's companion in Bermuda.

"Ah, Veronique," Bortnicker sighed dramatically. "Well, a man can have two admirers, can't he?"

"The perks of stardom," said T.J., with more than a hint of sarcasm.

Chapter Eight

"Have a good day, honey," said Mike Darcy as his daughter opened the passenger door of his Dodge Durango outside Gettysburg High School. Darcy, a Ranger at the National Battlefield Park, had decided to drop her off this morning on his way to the Visitor Center and Museum where he started each day, for two reasons. First, he didn't want her freezing at the school bus stop for her habitually late ride; second, it was the least he could offer as a show of moral support. If only she'd talk to him in her old, endearingly sassy manner.

"I will, Daddy. Love you," she replied, swinging the door closed.

It's like she's walking the last mile, he thought as LouAnne made her way up the long walk to the front entrance. He paused a few seconds after she slipped inside, sighed deeply, and dropped the Durango into DRIVE.

* * * *

Overall, it wasn't looking like a bad day. LouAnne met her friends for a bagel in the cafeteria and then went to first period biology, where she got a unit test back - an 88% - before moving on to phys ed, leading her pickup team to victory in volleyball. After participating in a spirited discussion in English class over Poe's "The Raven," she hustled to her locker to drop off her books before rerouting to home ec, where they were supposed to learn the basics of making focaccia bread today.

The words, big and bright in red Sharpie, made her stop short, like a slap in the face. She reached out to touch the unspeakable slurs plastered on the beige metal, as if to confirm that they were real. Then she was

43

running, not with the graceful stride of the cross country champion she was, but with an anger and desperation befitting a condemned criminal fleeing an angry mob.

* * * *

That evening, just after the dinner she'd barely touched, the phone rang. She checked the caller ID and picked up.

"Hey, Cuz," said T.J. "how ya doin'?"

"Okay," she managed. "How about you?"

"Fine. My head's pretty much cleared up. Uh, LouAnne," he labored, "I've gotta ask you something, but I've gotta tell you up front, just hear me out before you say anything. Okay?"

"Uh-huh."

"I got a call yesterday about an opportunity for us to maybe do a new ghost investigation -"

"I'm there."

There was a heavy moment of silence on the other end. "What?"

"I said, 'I'm there,' T.J., is that clear enough?"

"Yeah, sure, Cuz," he stammered, "but don't you want to hear about it first? Like the details?"

"Sure," she said patiently. "I'm sorry. Tell me all about it."

He began slowly, cautiously, with the phone call at Coach Pisseri's party, the discussion with Bob Simmons, and a summary of Pisseri's biography of Clemente.

"Yeah, I've heard of him," she said. "Remember, Pittsburgh is in Western Pennsylvania, so in this state you're either a Phillies fan or a Pirates fan."

Feeling adventurous, T.J. pressed on. "So, the Spring Break thing isn't a problem?" he asked hopefully.

"Well, my dear cousin, if I remember correctly you wanted to get together, anyway. Connecticut, New York, what's the difference? My folks'll be okay with it. The main thing is that I get away from...here."

He decided to go for broke. "Would you like to tell me about it?"

"About what?"

"About what's *wrong*, Cuz."

Now it was her turn to be silent for a moment. After what seemed like forever she said, "I'll tell you what, Cuz. We'll have a long talk up there in the mountains. What I will tell you is this: I miss both you guys, terribly, and I...really *need* you, T.J."

He felt himself tearing up, encouraged, but utterly powerless at the same time.

Chapter Nine

The next week was filled with phone calls, emails and preparations for the Cooperstown trip. First and foremost was T.J.'s call to Bob Simmons, as promised, the evening after their initial conversation.

"So, it's a go? Excellent!" said the Hall of Fame's president with an air of relief. "Shall I ring the Glimmerglass Inn and make reservations for four rooms?"

"That won't be necessary," T.J. replied. "Bortnicker and I will share one, if it has two beds."

"That's fine. And who will be the chaperone?"

"My baseball coach, Mr. Pisseri. All our parents are okay with it. He's a teacher and a pretty responsible guy."

"Hmmm," said Simmons. "Tell me, T.J., do you have any specific duties planned for Coach Pisseri regarding the investigation?"

"Not really," said T.J., "And I feel kinda bad about that. Besides riding up with us and back and checking in to make sure we're okay, he won't have much to do. He's not exactly big on the whole paranormal thing."

"Well, then, I think I have a solution. The week you're coming up we are staging an adult fantasy camp, both at Doubleday Field and the Clark Sports Center nearby. A handful of Hall of Famers are nominally in charge, guys like George Brett and Ozzie Smith, but we usually recruit local high school or college coaches to run the drills and such. Think he'd be interested?"

"Are you kidding? Mr. Simmons, Coach P. is gonna be in heaven. Hanging out with famous ballplayers and coaching at the same time?

Sign him up. I can't wait to tell him!"

Simmons chuckled. "That's the great thing about baseball, T.J. It brings out the boy in all of us. Now, back to business. Have you contacted Mike Weinstein about The Adventure Channel shipping your equipment?"

"I'm just about to. Shouldn't be a problem."

"All right, then. So when will we expect you?"

"We should be there mid-morning on Monday of next week."

"Fine. Let's set a time of 11:00 AM for a meeting of your people and mine in the Museum's conference room. We'll go from there. But if you don't mind, keep a lid on this. Only a few people up here know what's going on. I'm not even mentioning it to the Hall of Famers doing the fantasy camp. Please do the same on your end."

"No problem. See you next Monday, Mr. Simmons."

* * * *

T.J. finally tracked down Mike Weinstein as his team was wrapping up their Vancouver investigation.

"Dude, so good to hear your voice!" he boomed. "Man, it's cold up here! But we got some awesome results at the fort. A definite shadow figure and a load of EVPs. Of course, I'm still trying to catch up with you guys. Man, you go on two investigations and you actually *meet* two ghosts! You know, Dude, I'm starting to think you're sensitive."

"About what?"

"No, T.J. When someone in the paranormal community says you're 'sensitive' it means that you attract, and are open to, communication with spirits. Let's face it, Dude, you're two-for-two. And I've got a feeling you're about to hit the trifecta with Roberto Clemente. You're cool with setting up all the equipment?"

"Well, Bortnicker's the tech wizard, actually. He'll figure it out."

"Okay, so we are sending you a couple terminals with four DVR remote cameras you can set up, and handheld video, EVP, and thermal imaging recorders. Walkie-talkies and flashlights. Extra batteries, too, if an entity drains your first set. That should do. If you need anything else, just call this number. We are about to move on to Jamaica, and boy do we need it. Caroline and Josh got sick up here, and the warm weather

47

will be like medicine."

"Like Bermuda?"

"Exactly, Dude. We could all use a little beach time. Good luck up in the mountains. Come back with enough cool stuff for another show!"

"We'll try," said T.J. halfheartedly.

* * * *

As they had done before the Bermuda trip, Tom Sr. and the boys visited their local hangout in Fairfield, Pizza Palace, for a good-luck Saturday night dinner. And, as last time, they took the Jag out on the town. The teens always enjoyed the looks Tom's oyster metallic XJS got, especially from girls. Applying for their driving learner's permits was only a year or so away.

"So," said the senior Jackson, passing around a basket of Italian bread as they waited for their pasta dinners, "have you guys boned up on Clemente? With only one week, you had to cram."

"Yeah, Mr. J. It wasn't easy, what with school and all," said Bortnicker, buttering his piece. "But the library had some great videos, including the *ESPN Sports Century* documentary. So we learned a lot."

"What sticks out the most is how underappreciated the guy was, even in Pittsburgh, for most of his career," said T.J. "And that's with all the awards he won. I mean, if he had played in New York he'd have been a megastar. But what got me the most is how some of the sports writers kind of mocked his accent, made him look like he wasn't intelligent. They'd never get away with that today. It's almost like Clemente had to die to really get respect."

"I have a question, though," said Tom Sr. as their heaping plates of macaroni were served. "That first time in Gettysburg, you guys figured out that Major Hilliard came back because his bones had been dug up inadvertently from the battlefield, right?"

"Yup," said Bortnicker, leaning in to his ravioli.

"And with Sir William Tarver, the trigger was Jasper Goodwin discovering his sunken pirate ship on the reefs."

"That's right," said T.J., sprinkling parmesan over his penne ala vodka.

"So, what's made Clemente come back? Is it the anniversary of his death? The Hall of Fame's celebration? Or what?"

"Dad, we can only guess at that 'til we actually speak to him - hopefully."

"One other thing, guys: LouAnne. I know that Coach Pisseri is going to be around, but make sure you watch out for her. You know how protective Uncle Mike is."

"Don't worry, Dad," said T.J. "By all accounts, Cooperstown is a pretty dull place. I mean, I've heard there's only one traffic light in the whole town. How dangerous could it be?"

"That's what you said about Gettysburg," mused Bortnicker, popping a ravioli into his mouth. "*And* Bermuda."

Chapter Ten

The Jacksons, junior and senior, along with Bortnicker, waited anxiously on the dark, chilly platform of the Fairfield train station for the 9:15 out of Grand Central.

"Is it on time?" asked Bortnicker, munching on a vending machine chocolate bar.

"So far," said T.J., "but remember she had to take Amtrak from Philly to New York first, so you never know."

"Well, Metro-North's running on time, and besides, we would have heard from your cousin by now if there was a problem," assured Tom Sr. "Just be a little patient."

Minutes later the Metro-North local ground to a halt and the doors slid open. The boys craned their necks to look over the top of the first passengers exiting the cars. And then a girl, her Phillies ball cap pulled down over her blonde locks, emerged, towing a small suitcase. She looked a little thin and there were faint traces of circles under her eyes, but even on her worst day LouAnne Darcy was stunning. Upon glimpsing her friends her face lit up. T.J. could feel his heart begin to melt. She gave a small wave, and then they engulfed her.

T.J. waited until Bortnicker and his dad had administered hugs, and then pulled her close.

"Missed you," she murmured in his ear, her eyes suddenly misty.

"Back atcha," he replied, holding the embrace perhaps a second too long. But as much as he longed to keep her in his arms, T.J. thought he'd felt an involuntary flinch on her part when he'd put his arms around her. She didn't even hug him back. Just stood there like a sack of potatoes.

He moved her back to arm's-length and for a moment regarded her quizzically, but her face was impossible to read, save for the wetness in her eyes. *Am I imagining this?* he thought. *Am I looking for stuff that isn't really there?*

Bortnicker, sensing the consternation on his best friend's face, decided to lighten the mood. "Okay, my dear," he said dramatically, "first question of the trip. Which Beatles song is about a train station?"

"'One After 909'," she said smartly, snapping back into the old LouAnne and handing him her suitcase.

"Foiled again!" he wailed.

Tom Sr. chuckled and shook his head. "It's kind of late, honey," he said to her, "but we could stop at the diner or Starbucks if you want something."

"No thanks, Uncle Tom," she replied wearily, "I had something to eat at Grand Central Station, and my mom packed plenty of snacks for me. Right now I just need a good night's sleep."

"No problem, Cuz," offered T.J. "We have the guest room all set up. Let's get you home and in bed; the limo is coming for us at 6:00 AM sharp, and we're picking up Coach P. on the way. We can talk about the investigation on the ride up, because it's like four hours."

"Sounds like a plan."

T.J. slid into the front seat of his father's Explorer while Bortnicker and LouAnne stowed her suitcase and got in. They had barely left the parking lot when LouAnne listed toward Bortnicker's shoulder and started dozing. In the past, when both boys were vying somewhat for her attention, this would have elicited a smirk of triumph from the scraggly-haired boy, but now he shared the look of concern from T.J. that was reflected in the car's rear view mirror.

* * * *

After leading the groggy LouAnne to the Jackson guest room, the boys said their good night at the front door.

"Something's up with her, Big Mon," Bortnicker said, confirming T.J.'s fears.

"But what?"

"Don't know." He yawned in the frosty darkness. "I guess the

Clemente investigation isn't the only mystery we'll have to solve up there. See you bright and early. Adios."

They fist-bumped and Bortnicker ambled off across the street, whistling "I'm Looking Through You". Though T.J. was considered by some a dead ringer for the young Paul McCartney, he was only a casual Beatles aficionado. But even he understood the significance of Bortnicker's choice of song. Because after the song's first line title, it's followed by the lead singer (McCartney) questioning what happened to the girl he knew, if he ever really knew her at all.

Chapter Eleven

"What time is your flight, Dad?" asked T.J. as he poured milk over his cornflakes. He slid the container over to his cousin, who seemed rejuvenated - and ravenous - this new day.

"Ten this morning. The car service will be picking me up not long after you guys take off. Now, I'm going to be in Scottsdale the whole week, but I want constant updates. Call me or text if anything goes haywire."

"We will, Uncle Tom," promised LouAnne as she dug into her cereal. "As they say, 'this isn't our first rodeo'."

"I understand that, honey," he replied, "but let's face it, what you guys do isn't exactly 'normal'. The first two cases were pretty different, and last year's was unpredictable at every turn."

"That's for sure," said T.J., remembering. "Who ever thought we'd be digging up a dead pirate?"

"Or talking to his ghost?" added LouAnne.

"So you can understand my concern," concluded the elder Jackson.

"Got it," said T.J.

"Hey, Cuz, you bringing your running stuff?" asked LouAnne, an eyebrow raised, "or are you totally into baseball right now?"

T.J., inwardly pleased, replied, "Nope, I'm bringing my stuff. Coach wants us to stay in shape during the break, and running's the best thing. But I'm packing my glove, too. Want me to bring one for you, too? I'll need someone to have a catch with, keep my arm loose."

"That won't be necessary," she said. "I've got my softball mitt with me that I use for phys ed. Derek Jeter model."

"I thought you were a Phillies fan."

"I am. But how can you not like Jeter? Besides, he's kinda cute, even for an old guy."

He smiled. It would be good to go running with his cousin again. Besides the obvious competitive nature of their runs, which had come to a head in Bermuda the previous summer during a 5K teen race, LouAnne had been forced to withdraw due to leg cramps, but the time they spent practicing afforded the teens an opportunity to talk about things. Maybe she'd open up on a morning jaunt in Cooperstown.

The doorbell rang and Tom Sr. let in Bortnicker, looking as disheveled as always, dragging the same olive green duffel bag he'd lugged down to Gettysburg during their first case. He pulled up a chair and poured himself a load of cereal. In his best Liverpudlian accent he said, "Well then, is everyone ready for the Magical Mystery Tour?" Then he turned to Tom Sr. and innocently asked, "Hey, Mr. J., got any coffee?"

"You know I'm not supposed to give you that, Bortnicker."

"Dad, c'mon," admonished T.J. "He drinks a cup every morning at school."

"Okay, okay," surrendered the elder Jackson. "I was just trying to be a responsible parent."

"Don't worry, Mr. J. I won't rat you out," smiled Bortnicker, slicing bananas over his cornflakes. "We're all men here. Except LouAnne, that is."

She punched him lightly in the shoulder.

Within minutes a large black SUV had pulled into the driveway. "Your ride's here, guys," said Tom Sr., waving acknowledgment through the kitchen window. "T.J., you'll promise to keep in touch?"

"I'll make sure he does, Uncle Tom," assured LouAnne.

"And Bortnicker, don't forget to call your mom, either," said Jackson. "She doesn't make a big show of it, but she worries about you."

"Will do, Mr. J.," promised the boy, downing the rest of his coffee in a big gulp.

The teens grabbed their bags and went outside into the cool dawn. Their driver, a middle-aged man who identified himself as Richard, took their bags and stowed them in the back. He wore a black suit and silk tie and looked quite official.

"Not exactly another Chappy," cracked Bortnicker, referring to the Afro-Bermudian driver on their last case who had become a friend and confidant during their stay.

"It's just as well," said T.J., sliding into one of the back seats next to his cousin. "This is all supposed to be hush-hush."

They pulled away from the curb, waving to Tom Sr. standing at the front door, coffee cup in hand. Within minutes they stopped at Coach Pisseri's house, where he awaited them with a suitcase, a bat, glove, and a pair of spikes bundled together.

"How cute!" said LouAnne. "He looks like a kid about to go to summer camp."

"And probably just as excited," added T.J.

"Morning, everyone," greeted Coach Pisseri as he took a seat next to Bortnicker. "You must be LouAnne," he said, offering his hand for a polite shake. "I'm Todd Pisseri, but you can call me Coach like the guys do, if that's okay."

"That will be fine," she replied sweetly.

Richard, the driver, interrupted the pleasantries to inquire as to which route the group would like to take to Cooperstown.

"What are the options?" asked T.J.

"Well, sir, we could take I-84 to I-87, which is the New York State Thruway, and follow that all the way to exit 21, then cut over to Cooperstown, which is more direct; or get off I-87 at exit 19, which is Kingston, and take Route 28, which meanders through the Catskills. It's a much more scenic drive, but a little longer."

"We're in no hurry," said T.J. "Why not take the scenic route?"

"Very well, sir. I'll be putting up the glass partition to give you in the back some privacy. If you need me or want to make a stop, just buzz me on the intercom."

"Pretty fancy," said Pisseri, impressed.

"All in a day's work for the *Junior Gonzo Ghost Chasers*," joked Bortnicker.

Soon they were breezing along on I-84, which connected their home state of Connecticut to New York. It was a fine spring morning and there was an air of excitement and anticipation in the limo.

"LouAnne," said Pisseri, his round, boyish face gleaming beneath a fairly recent buzz cut, "T.J. tells me you're quite the athlete. Cross country, is it?"

"Well, ah," she began, blushing.

"C'mon, Cuz, tell him how good you are," prodded T.J.

"Well, Coach, since my cousin here insists, I'm in my junior year, and this fall I made the All-County team."

Pisseri whistled through his teeth. "All-County as a junior? Not too shabby. Are you thinking about running in college?"

"That's a possibility," she acknowledged with a faint smile. "Might not able to afford it otherwise."

"By next year the colleges will be knocking your door down," Bortnicker predicted.

"Well, we'll see," was her response; very *un*LouAnne-like, noted T.J. "But what about you, Coach? Did you have a career in baseball?"

"Yeah, Coach P.," said Bortnicker. "I've never gotten the whole story on your baseball days."

"It's not really much to speak about," answered Pisseri. "Wouldn't want to bore you with my past."

"Tell us, Coach," said T.J. "We're all interested."

"Okay, if you insist." He took a deep breath, and it was clear that although Todd Pisseri was adept at teaching high school science and coaching baseball, he was awkward at talking about himself. His eyes took on a kind of faraway look as he began to reminisce. "Let's see, where to start…well, my first memories of baseball were kind of classic. I was just getting into the game, Little League and all that. My dad would get home from work, he was an accountant who sat at a desk all day, and we would eat dinner and then play catch out back. And even then, he'd tell me I had a smooth motion when I threw, good technique.

"I was better than the kids my age. Not much bigger, just better. I picked up the nuances of the game easily, like bunting and cutting the bases when I ran them. But pitching was my deal. I could really bring it, as early as fifth grade. I threw a four seam fastball and a cutter that hitters couldn't touch. So, I was always getting moved up the All-Star squads and whatnot.

"Dad was real proud of me but he wasn't your typical Little League overbearing parent. He never second-guessed the coaches or spent hours pointing out my flaws. He might give me a gentle hint if I was tipping my pitches or not following through, that kind of thing, but it was never 'You stunk it up today. Let's go in the backyard and work on it.' And at the same time he got me interested in the history of the game and encouraged me to read books on it. So if you want someone to blame for that out-of-control memorabilia collection of mine, I guess you can attribute it to him as well." He chuckled fondly.

"Anyway, I got to Bridgefield High and my success just built. We made the state playoffs every year, and I really started getting attention when I threw back-to-back one-hitters my junior year. That, and my coach Dave Carol -"

"Mr. Carol, our athletic director?" cut in T.J.

"One and the same. He was my coach back then, and he touted me to anyone who would listen. By the time my senior year rolled around, I was being scouted by both colleges and the pros, who considered me a mid-range prospect because I was only about six feet tall at the time.

"I had a real good senior year, and we won our conference, which hasn't happened since, by the way. But I'd pretty much decided I wanted to go to college before trying for the pros, so I turned down some pretty enticing offers to stay close to home at UConn. As it turned out, UConn was a great choice. Despite playing in the Northeast, which is a pain I don't have to tell you two guys about, we had some really competitive teams and even got to the regionals of the College World Series my senior year. But we got knocked out by Maine. The thing is, I was pitching in that elimination game, cruising along with a shutout for four innings, when I felt something strange in my throwing shoulder. Not a snap or anything dramatic - but it just didn't feel right." He frowned, looking out the car window at the passing scenery, then continued. "My coach figured I was just tiring because I'd pitched so much that season down the stretch. So he pulled me, and we ended up losing, 3-1. But the pro scouts had seen enough to satisfy them, and I got drafted by the Tampa Bay Rays in the middle rounds. I wasn't but three weeks removed from graduation at UConn when I found myself at their Single-A affiliate in Vero Beach, Florida."

"Where the Dodgers used to train?" asked Bortnicker.

"Yup, the former Dodgertown. But it was still being used by the Dodgers at the time, though they were well into their season in Los Angeles by the time I reported. Still, training in that park, where historic players like Jackie Robinson and Duke Snider and Sandy Koufax had played, was very cool. And Holman Stadium was top notch for a Single-A facility.

"Of course, I never told anyone about my shoulder. I didn't want to scare the scouts off, and besides, there was a little part of me that was sure it would just go away, work itself out. But I was just kidding myself. I got through the short season with an 8-4 record and an ERA under 3, but I was doing it with smoke and mirrors. And the mornings after I pitched it was a struggle to even comb my hair, the pain was so bad."

"Jeez Louise," was all T.J. could offer.

"You said it. What made it worse was that I met a girl down there. Listen, it's not uncommon. You've got a bunch of young guys, most just out of high school or college, and they're always scanning the stands for pretty girls. Well, one night around midseason this man brought his family to a game, and I was pitching. The guy was maybe in his 50's, but his eldest daughter was just...stunning. They were sitting behind our dugout, and an inning ended when a batter... I think it was Fort Myers we were playing...hit a line drive back at me which I gloved chest high before it bored a hole through me. So, real cool, I jogged off the field, remembering as I crossed the foul line that I had this ball in my glove. Then I saw her standing there, applauding, and I casually tossed her the ball before I went down the dugout steps. When I came out for the next inning she called out, 'Hey, Two-Six' - that was my number - 'would you sign this for me?'

"'After the game, okay?' I called back. Sure enough, her family waited around and I autographed it. Turns out her dad was the owner of one of the biggest car dealerships in Vero Beach, one we advertised on our outfield wall. I signed the ball and we took photos and whatnot. She had me sign it 'To Cindi', so I knew her name at least. Our next home game she was there again, and I asked her for a date."

"Way to go, Coach!" cried Bortnicker.

"You're interrupting," chided LouAnne.

"Oops, sorry, Coach," he apologized. "Keep going."

"Why thank you, Bortnicker. Anyway, we hung out for the rest of the season. Her dad was always throwing lavish parties at their house, which was right on the ocean. I can't tell you how much fun it was down in Florida the rest of that season. She even came to visit me up here in Connecticut for Christmas. But at the same time I had real worries about my shoulder. So I finally broke down and called my manager, Chris Sileo -"

"The guy who used to play for the Indians?" asked Bortnicker.

"Yeah, that's him. This was his first managing gig, and he didn't want to be responsible for a prospect like me screwing up his arm, so he contacted the Rays' front office and they sent me to a noted orthopedist to try and figure out why I was having the shoulder fatigue. He gave me every test imaginable but they all came up negative. His final prognosis was complete rest until the next year's training camp.

"So, I rested the shoulder and did lots of running, and reported to Vero Beach raring to go. But the shoulder never came around. By my third start I was getting shelled and aiming the ball. They sent me for more tests...all negative. Finally they just threw their hands in the air and gave me my release."

"What about Cindi?" asked LouAnne.

"She kind of gave me my release, too," he answered wistfully. "So, I went back to school at UConn, got my teaching certificate, and was hired by my former coach, Mr. Carol, at Bridgefield High as a science teacher and baseball coach, which is how I was given the opportunity to work with you fine young men," he said with a sarcastic wink. "Any more stuff you need to know?"

"Did you ever hear from Cindi again?" asked T.J.

"Nah. I think she just wanted to find a ballplayer on the fast track to the Majors. I wasn't him."

"Wow," said Bortnicker. "That really sucks, if you don't mind me saying."

"Well, you live and you learn," said Pisseri. "And I learned a couple things. First, don't trust girls who just like you because you're wearing a uniform. And second, I learned that baseball is a very fickle passion. You may love her madly, but she doesn't always love you back."

"Well, Coach," said LouAnne, "Major League Baseball's loss - and Cindi's, I might add - is these two coconuts' gain. They're lucky to have you as their coach."

"I knew I liked you the minute I saw you," he replied with a laugh. "Even if you are just a long distance runner."

* * * *

After a pit stop at the Plattekill rest stop on I-87, the limo made the turn at exit 19 and entered the Catskill Mountains via Route 28. The four-lane highway gave way to two-lane winding roads that took the foursome up steep inclines and down through lush valleys. Farms and forests alternated, with a picture-postcard villages like Meredith and Andes every ten miles or so.

It was in one of those verdant valleys of Catskill State Park that Bortnicker suddenly pounded on the glass partition and called to Richard to stop the car. Before them was a small steam train on a siding, with people boarding for a sightseeing tour. As T.J. and LouAnne knew, their friend was a model railroading fanatic, and loved the old steam locomotives and cars. T.J. couldn't count the number of times Bortnicker's mother Pippa had taken the boys up to the quaint Connecticut town of Essex, where they'd ridden the famous Essex steam train.

"Bortnicker," cautioned T.J., "I know what you're gonna say, but we have no time for this now."

"Arghh," he replied, crumpling from his seat to the floor.

"Enough with the dramatics, Bortnicker," ordered LouAnne. "Maybe we'll do it on the way back."

"Promise?" he pleaded like a heartbroken child.

"Promise," his comrades pledged in unison.

Bortnicker gave his trademark crooked smile and pressed the intercom button. "Richard, you may proceed back to the road now," he sang out, his strategy having worked to perfection.

They made one more stop at a gas station in Delhi, and then it was on to Oneonta and Cooperstown. By the time they'd passed the last dairy farm and reached the outskirts of the town, billboards started popping up, advertising the vicinity's various attractions.

"It's kind of like being at home," observed LouAnne, whose hometown of Gettysburg was one of the country's foremost tourist destinations, and who was already looking forward to its personal mega-event: the 150th Anniversary Battle Commemoration in July 2013.

"Except there's no haunted battlefield," said T.J. "And instead of five or six museums, Cooperstown proper only has one - the Hall of Fame."

"Two, if you count the Farmer's Museum just outside of town," added Bortnicker.

They passed a huge baseball complex called Field of Dreams, where many Little League and softball tournaments were held during the warmer months, and some chain hotels that had grown outward on Route 28 to dwarf the few mom and pop 1950s style motor inns that remained.

And then the SUV passed over a set of railroad tracks and proceeded down a leaf-canopied street bordered by 1850s Georgian and Victorian houses, until they came upon the one and only traffic light at the top of Main Street. Richard eased the SUV into a right-hand turn and they crept along the three-block long main drag bordered by cars parked on an angle, their noses to the curb. It seemed that every storefront in this old town was either an eatery or some sort of a sports memorabilia shop. At one point they passed the entrance to a fairly good-sized blacktop parking lot, with the red brick façade of Doubleday Field looming in the distance. At the midpoint of Main Street, marked by a stately flagpole, Richard took a left past the tiny Village Green and turned into the driveway of the Glimmerglass Inn, a red-brick three-story building with maroon awnings over each window which could easily have been placed in Gettysburg's Historic District. Just to the left of the steps leading up to the front door were descending steps to a restaurant aptly named The Dugout.

Richard helped the travelers up the stairs and into the inn with their bags then bid them goodbye. At the front desk LouAnne gave a small call-bell a couple taps.

"Coming!" trilled a voice from upstairs. Within seconds an elderly woman with bouffant hair was sweeping down the staircase. "Ah, the guests of the Hall of Fame have arrived!" she sang out." Welcome to the Glimmerglass Inn Bed and Breakfast. I'm Clara Frank, the proprietor.

My husband Nat's around somewhere, doing his handyman chores. And what are your names?"

"T.J. Jackson," said the group's leader, extending his hand with a winning smile, followed by LouAnne, Bortnicker and Coach Pisseri.

"You'll be the chaperone, I take it, Mr. Pisseri?" she asked with an arched, penciled eyebrow.

"Yes ma'am," he answered. "You have a lovely establishment here."

"Why, thank you. We try. Bob Simmons is a dear friend, and whenever he has a small group visiting he puts them up here. Not as ostentatious as the Otesaga Hotel down by the lake where all the Hall of Famers stay for the induction festivities, but more centrally located, and quiet. Come, let me show you to your rooms!"

Trailing their wheeled suitcases behind them, they negotiated the narrow stairway to the second floor, which featured three rooms off the same hallway.

"Mr. Jackson, Mr. Bortnicker, you two will share the larger room, with two single beds. Ms. Darcy, you and Mr. Pisseri will have the two single rooms across the hall, which are fairly identical. All rooms have their own full bathroom. Call me if you need anything else. Breakfast is served downstairs in the dining room between 7 and 9 AM. As you probably noticed on your way in, there are many places to eat in town, from casual to fancy, though a few are still closed because the tourist season doesn't get into full swing for another couple of weeks. But our own Dugout below street level is a cozy place for lunch or dinner. The Hall of Fame is a half block away, left at the flagpole. You can't miss it. Ta-ta!" With that, Clara Frank sashayed back down the stairs, singing to herself.

"Interesting woman," quipped Pisseri. "Okay, guys, why don't we all take a few minutes to unpack in our rooms and then we'll go over to the Hall. It's only ten-forty and we're not expected until eleven."

"You got it, Coach!" said Bortnicker, who threw open the door to the room he'd be sharing with T.J. and flopped on the closest bed. T.J. put his bag near the other bed and then crossed the hall to where Todd Pisseri was stowing his clothes in an antique dresser.

"Coach? Got a minute?" he asked, peeking into the room.

"Sure, T.J. What's up?"

The teen closed the door behind. "Listen, Coach," he began, "all the guys on the team know you played minor league ball and all, but you didn't have to tell us all the other stuff back there in the car. How come you did?"

"Well, it seems like you guys wanted the whole story."

T.J. fixed him with an appraising look. "But it *wasn't* the whole story, was it?"

Pisseri frowned a little and shrugged his shoulders. "You're a perceptive kid, T.J.," he said. "It's one of the reasons you're such a good leader." He sat on the edge of the bed and absently picked up his baseball glove, then started tightening the laces. "You want the truth?"

"I guess."

"Okay, T.J. The truth is that getting released devastated me. I mean, it was my lifetime dream being snatched from me right before my eyes, and I was powerless to stop it. And on top of it, I got dumped by a girl who I really thought loved me.

"So what did mature twenty-four-year-old Todd Pisseri do? I went home to Fairfield with my tail between my legs and sulked and drank beer. *Lots* of beer. Day after day I rolled out of bed around noon, looked around my room at all my trophies and awards, got even more depressed, and either went fishing or hit the local pool hall until late in the day when I found my way to one of the bars in town, watched ballgames and ate stale pretzels, and pretty much acted like a jerk. There's still a couple places today in town where I'm not welcome."

"Gee, Coach, I don't know what to say."

"What *can* you say, T.J.? It was the Todd Pisseri pity party, and I was the guest of honor. I got fat and out of shape, and had no idea what I wanted to do with my life.

"Then, as I told you, Coach Carol called me and got me back on track, thanks to my dad cluing him in about my state of mind. It was Coach Carol who gave me the talking-to I needed, told me to get off my butt and be a man. And so, I got my teaching certificate back at UConn, and here I am."

"LouAnne's right. We're lucky to have you."

"Well," said Pisseri, pulling the glove's web lacing tight, "she seems like a sweetheart. But now I have to ask *you* something, Two-One." He tossed the glove aside and locked eyes with his player. "What's the deal with you and her?"

T.J.'s eyes widened. "What do you mean?" he stammered.

"Oh, c'mon, man. She might be your cousin, but you sure don't *look* at her like she's your cousin. There isn't something weird going on here, is there?"

Shaking his head vigorously, T.J. blushed and said, "No, no, Coach. Actually, we're only cousins by adoption. We don't share the same blood or anything."

"Whew," said Pisseri. "I feel a lot better now, although it's still kind of out of the ordinary. And she's quite the athlete, huh?"

"You've got no idea, Coach," chuckled T.J. "When I got to Gettysburg two years ago, I tried to impress her that I was going out for cross country at Bridgefield High. Then she tells me she's already on the varsity at her school - as a freshman! See, we're the same age, but she's a year ahead of me in school 'cause she skipped a year of Pre-k. Anyway, we'd run in the morning around the battlefield, which is huge, and she'd just blow me away. It was embarrassing. But I kinda got her back last summer in Bermuda. There was a 5K road race for teens and I did pretty well, posted a good time. Unfortunately, LouAnne had to drop out around midway with leg cramps. We'll probably run in the mornings up here."

"But that's *all* that you'll be doing, right?" Pisseri asked with a raised eyebrow. "Remember, T.J., I'm in charge of you guys."

"No worries, Coach. I'd never want to put you in a bad position. Besides, something's going on with her. You don't know my cousin too well, but I can tell you that she's not herself. Tell you the truth, I think she's got a boyfriend back home or something."

"Well," Pisseri said, placing a fatherly hand on his centerfielder's shoulder, "if there's anything you can learn from me it's that moping around over a girl is a colossal waste of time."

He looked at his watch just as LouAnne hammered on the door and called, "Hey you guys, we're gonna be late! And I had to wake Bortnicker up. He fell dead asleep in there!"

"Let's get after it, then," said T.J. "On to the Hall of Fame!"

Chapter Twelve

It had turned into a fine spring day as the group made its way a couple hundred feet to Main Street and turned left at the flagpole. The teens all wore their *Junior Gonzo Ghost Chasers* golf shirts that Mike Weinstein had issued them in Bermuda underneath a light jacket, so as to look professional at the meeting - T.J.'s idea - and Todd sported a brand-new "Bridgefield Baseball Staff" crewneck pullover and carried his baseball equipment.

They passed a five-and-dime department store on the right and there it was, in all its regal splendor: the red brick façade of the National Baseball Hall of Fame and Museum. Its main entrance, accessible by both granite steps and handicapped accessible ramps, with black wrought iron railings featuring inlaid crossed gold bats, was imposing. A series of huge doors led to the reception area that included ticket desks and a highlighted display dedicated to the players of the Hall of Fame Class of 2012, Barry Larkin and Ron Santo.

"I can't believe we're actually here," marveled Pisseri with boyish wonder.

"The adventure begins," added Bortnicker in a dramatic tone.

Almost immediately they were approached by a thirtyish woman with chestnut hair and a Hall of Fame Legends Camp sweatshirt. "You must be the group to see Mr. Simmons," she said with a smile. "I'm Debbie McCray, and I help run our Legends Fantasy Camp." She looked Pisseri over with polite interest. "You have to be Todd," she smiled, extending her hand. "Ready to coach some out-of-shape middle-aged kids?"

"Sounds great to me," he answered, shaking her hand warmly.

"Super. Our base of operations is a couple blocks away at the Clark Athletic Center. We'll be meeting the campers today and getting everyone acclimated. Our Hall of Famers are already there, along with the local coaches helping out. I'm glad you brought your stuff, but of course we'll be issuing you a uniform and whatever else you need equipment-wise. Lunch will be served at the facility, and we'll have you back at your hotel for dinner. Sound okay?"

Pisseri looked like a five-year-old on Christmas morning. "Just lead the way," he gushed. "See you later, guys." And with that, the two fantasy camp staffers departed.

"Did you see Coach P. giving her the eye?" asked Bortnicker slyly.

"I think it was mutual," agreed LouAnne.

T.J. rolled his eyes. "Enough of that, please. Let's find Mr. Simmons." He inquired at one of the ticket desks that was manned by a sprightly senior citizen in a Hall of Fame man-tailored shirt.

"Well, hi there, young fella," she beamed. "Mr. Simmons said to send you next door to the Hall of Fame offices upon your arrival. Did you have a good trip?"

"It was very scenic," smiled T.J. "Do we just go in the front door?"

"Oh, yes. His office is the first one on the right." She reached under the desktop. "Here are three passes for your group that will give you access to the Hall and its ancillary buildings for the duration of your stay. We've put them on lanyards for you." She handed the laminated cards to T.J., who distributed them to his mates. "Let any of our staff know how we can be of help. Enjoy your stay in Cooperstown."

The teens exited the main building and entered the smaller attached office facility next-door. "So far, so good," said Bortnicker. "Hey, by the way, do I look okay?"

"Since when do you care what you look like?" asked T.J.

"Since he found out he has a fan up here, that's when," joked LouAnne. "Bortnicker, I wouldn't get too anxious. I hardly think she'll be included in the planning meeting."

"You never know," he smiled, brushing his unruly mop away from his glasses.

T.J. shook his head and knocked on the door marked *President.*

"Come in!" boomed Bob Simmons as he came from around his desk to personally greet the threesome. His silvery hair was cut stylishly, and he wore a navy blue suit with a red Hall of Fame logo tie. T.J. judged him to be around sixty, and quite fit. It looked like he'd maybe played some ball himself along the way.

"T.J., it's so good to finally meet you," Bob said amiably. "LouAnne, you're just as beautiful as on TV," he said, shaking her hand lightly. Then he turned to Bortnicker. "Son," he said, "I got such a kick out of you on that program. You helped keep everything light."

"Why, thank you, Mr. Simmons," he replied, taking a page from the T.J. Jackson diplomacy handbook. "I just try to keep us on track when things get crazy." His teammates had to suppress the urge to offer a snappy comeback.

"How was the trip?" inquired Simmons, removing a manila folder from his desktop.

"It was a great ride," said T.J. "Although Bortnicker wanted to detour for a Catskill Steam Train ride."

"Which we'll do on the way back," the boy reminded.

Simmons laughed. "Well, folks, what I have planned for us this morning is an organizational meeting to make sure we're all on the same page. It will be attended by selected members of my staff, a trusted group who has been sworn to secrecy on this. I'm confident that everyone will lend their full support to your investigation." He handed T.J. a credit card. "Please feel free to use this during your stay at any restaurant in town. It's got the Hall's logo on it, and the local proprietors have been alerted to your presence. I take it your coach has already been whisked away to the fantasy camp by our Miss McCray?"

"Yes, sir," said T.J., accepting the card gladly.

"A fine young lady." Simmons looked at his watch. "Oops, we're late. Please follow me to the board-room. Can I get you a beverage before we start the meeting? A bottled water or -"

"Coffee for me, please," said Bortnicker with an air of maturity that made his colleagues want to bust out laughing.

"Water would be fine," said LouAnne.

"Me too," chimed T.J.

"I'll buzz my secretary. On to the meeting." They entered the plush board-room whose walls were tastefully decorated with original paintings of Major League Hall of Famers including Jimmie Foxx, Willie Mays and Bob Gibson. Around the table sat the same group of staffers whom Simmons had assembled previously, including the up-and-coming Jody Rieman, who had distinguished himself with his Caribbean seashell discovery. After introductions all around, Simmons buzzed his secretary to order the teens' refreshments and hold all calls. T.J., who sat at one end of the rectangular cherry wood table flanked by his friends, got a very positive vibe from everyone in the room - except Dan Vines, Simmons' second in command. He was frowning slightly as the president started things. T.J. thought he resembled a Buddha with indigestion.

"Good morning, everyone. Now that we all know each other, let's remind ourselves of the situation and formulate a plan whereby our visiting ghost hunting team can maximize the use of the Hall during the night this week.

"As we know, there have been two incidents at the Hall in the past couple months, one that unfortunately resulted in a fatality from a heart attack. In both cases an alleged sighting of Roberto Clemente - or his ghost - was involved. We need to get to the bottom of this, so it was agreed upon to call in professional help, which we now have in the form of T.J. Jackson and his team. Am I on track so far?"

Vines, who had obviously been waiting for an opportunity to offer his two cents, spoke up immediately. "With all due respect, Bob," he began, "I was okay with all of this when you contacted the Michael Weinstein team, who seem to have a proven track record in the paranormal community, if that's what we even call all this hooey. But, forgive me, what I see across the table here are three high school kids -"

"Who have been on two cases so far, Mr. Vines," cut in Bortnicker, "and have interacted with two ghosts. Which, in baseball parlance, means we're batting a thousand."

After administering a swift kick to his friend's shin under the table, T.J. coolly took up the baton. "Mr. Vines," he said evenly, "while it's true that Mike Weinstein's team was the first choice, he did recommend us to Mr. Simmons. And, as Bortnicker says, we're two-for-two. If you watched the TV special I'm sure you'd agree that we conducted ourselves pretty competently -"

"And how do I know that's not just a by-product of Hollywood special effects?"

"Now wait a minute here," began Bortnicker - until LouAnne, smiling sweetly, delivered yet another kick to his shin.

"Mr. Vines," she said pleasantly, "I really don't think it's your intent to question our integrity or seriousness, is it? We took time from our spring vacation to come all the way up here and help out the Hall of Fame."

"Young lady, I wasn't trying -"

"We could just get back in the limo and go back to Connecticut."

Now both boys were staring at LouAnne, but neither had the guts to kick *her*. Thankfully, Simmons stepped in to quell the uprising. "Whoa, whoa, whoa," he cautioned gently. "Dan, the kids here are our guests. I know you have the best interests of the Hall at heart, but you're making it sound like we didn't think this through enough. Well, I'm here to tell you that we did, and T.J. and his friends are welcome to stay for as long as it takes to get it done."

"Thanks, Mr. Simmons," said T.J. "Mr. Vines, you have to understand that the same thing kind of happened to us in Bermuda. The National Heritage Trust invited us to do the investigation there, but one key member -"

"Mrs. Constance Tilbury, to be exact -" interrupted Bortnicker before T.J.'s glare silenced him.

"As I was saying, one key member did her best to throw roadblocks in front of us at every turn. All we were trying to do - as we are trying to do here - is solve a case and help you out."

The matter temporarily resolved, Simmons said, "Let's move on," as his secretary discreetly entered through a side door and placed water bottles and a cup of coffee on the table before easing out again. After passing them along to the teenagers he continued. "T.J., the equipment hasn't arrived yet, hopefully by tomorrow afternoon. Could you tell Pete, our director of security, what you'll need from him?"

"Sure, Mr. Simmons. Mr. Alfano, could you please disarm the security system between the hours of 10 PM and 3 AM each night that we need to use the Hall?"

"Everything?"

T.J. thought hard. "Would you be able to keep the motion sensors active in certain areas?"

"We can't do that. However, I could show you guys on the grid downstairs how to manually get the lights on and off."

"Perfect."

Sarah Martin asked, "Would you need access to any of the cases?"

"Perhaps the Clemente mannequin display. And do you have any other Clemente memorabilia we could look at?" T.J. unscrewed the top to his water bottle and took a sip.

"There are some artifacts in storage," Martin said.

"Where would that be?" asked Bortnicker, adopting a more civil tone as he stirred his coffee.

"A rather secret place," was her reply. "But I can take you there. How about tomorrow morning?"

"That sounds great, Ms. Martin," said T.J.

"I think a visit to your library archives would also be helpful," offered LouAnne. "Remember how much the librarians in Gettysburg and Charleston helped us on the first case?"

"Good point," agreed T.J. "Is the library open tomorrow morning?"

"Yes indeed," said Simmons. "Jody, why don't you meet them there at, say, ten o'clock, to give them a hand? In fact, I'm thinking you could be the Hall's unofficial liaison to their team during this investigation."

"You mean it?" asked the intern excitedly.

"Yes. You've earned it for all the hard work you've been putting in."

"Wow, thanks, Mr. Simmons," he gushed.

"Okay, then," said Simmons with an air of relief. "We have a plan in place, at least for tomorrow. The team will visit both the storage vault and the library, beginning at 10 AM. I'd also suggest following that up with an afternoon walking tour of the floors of the Hall in daylight so as to familiarize ourselves with the layout for tomorrow night. Hopefully the equipment will arrive and you'll be able to set up after the Museum closes at 9 PM."

"I guess that leaves us a free afternoon today," said T.J. "My idea was that we poke around town and see the sights after a little lunch."

"Great idea," said Simmons. "You can obtain an illustrated street map at the Visitor Information kiosk on the Village Green right next to the Glimmerglass Inn. Hope you've found the accommodations to your liking."

"It's charming," said LouAnne. "I live in an old Victorian back home and it has that same feel."

"Excellent."

Bryan Davis, who had kept silent during the entire meeting except for a few awkward throat clearings during the testy exchange between Bortnicker and Dan Vines, suggested they stroll over to Lake Otsego and Doubleday Field.

"We passed that on the right coming down Main Street, correct?" asked T.J., sipping the last of his bottled water.

"That's it. Just walk through the parking lot out front and into the main entrance behind home plate. It's always open." Davis smiled, happy to finally contribute to the discussion.

"Is Doubleday Field part of the Hall?" asked Bortnicker, draining the last of his coffee with a noisy slurp.

"Actually, no," said Simmons, "though we maintain a close partnership with the town, who keeps it up. We schedule many events there. In fact -"

Suddenly, the sound of two female voices arguing came blasting through the closed doors to the conference room. At first the words were unintelligible, but as they came closer and grew in decibel level, the teens could make them out:

"You *cannot* go in there! They are in a meeting!"

"Who died and made *you* boss? The only person around here who can order me around is Uncle Bob, and he said to come down so I could meet him!"

"Meet who?"

"*Bortnick*er! Uncle Bob told him all about me!"

Bortnicker gave T.J. a sly smile and wiggled his eyebrows. LouAnne looked alarmed.

Simmons was only halfway out of his seat when the door flew open.

"I'm sorry, Mr. Simmons," called a distraught voice from behind. "I tried to stop her, but -"

Simmons weakly waved off his secretary because his niece had already crossed the threshold. She stood there defiantly, feet spread to shoulder width, fists ground into her hips, her thick oval glasses slightly askew and wild, tousled hair billowing out and around to shoulder length. The adults all seemed to be cowering in their seats, though the girl couldn't have been more than twelve years old. The president, thoroughly embarrassed, cleared his throat and said, "T.J., LouAnne, Bortnicker, allow me to introduce my niece, Fiona Bright."

LouAnne reflexively put her hand to her mouth; whether it was to muffle a scream or a laugh was uncertain.

The object of Fiona's search sat wide-eyed, gripping the edge of the table for dear life.

"Jeez Louise, Bortnicker," whispered T.J. out the corner of his mouth, "you never told me you had a sister."

Chapter Thirteen

As the attendees of the Board meeting filed out hurriedly, Bob Simmons led his niece over to the far end of the table. "As you can see," he began with a nervous chuckle, "Fiona has been awaiting your arrival. I have a little business to attend to in my office, so I'll let you guys get acquainted." He escaped out the side door, leaving the teens with the scowling adolescent.

"How ya doing Fiona," said T.J. "Your uncle said you really liked the Bermuda special."

"Yeah, it was pretty cool. But I have *two questions* for Bortnicker," she announced.

It was all T.J. and LouAnne could do to not fall out of their chairs. This girl was using Bortnicker's famous line on him!

Their friend, realizing the irony here, managed a crooked smile. "Let's hear 'em," he offered.

"First, did you really find that ship's bell on your very first dive? It seems quite unlikely." Her tone was challenging, though only mildly nasty.

"Actually, it was the second dive of the day, but it was our first day out on the water, so yeah, it was pretty incredible."

"Okay, here's the second one. When you actually saw that pirate guy in the house, did he look solid, or was he see-through?"

"He kinda went in and out," was Bortnicker's reply. "Almost like a light bulb during an electrical storm when you think there's going to be a brownout."

Fiona, not in the least a shy type, pulled up a chair next to LouAnne so she could face Bortnicker. An awkward silence followed.

"Do you live in town, Fiona?" asked T.J., trying to make conversation.

"Nah. I'm actually from Massachusetts. But when I heard you guys were coming to Cooperstown, I kind of made my dad drop me here for a few days. He didn't have a problem with it."

I can see why, LouAnne's expression revealed as she glanced at T.J. This kid was scary.

"Well, do you know exactly why we're here?" asked Bortnicker.

"To ghost hunt at the Hall, *obviously*," was her answer. "But my uncle didn't get specific."

Pleased that the girl wasn't in on the Clemente aspect of their visit, T.J. breathed a sigh of relief. He looked at his friends, then at the girl, whose eyes were locked on Bortnicker. "Well, uh, Fiona," he said, "we were gonna take a walk around town, maybe grab a bite to eat. Would you like to join us?"

"*Of course* I would," she said haughtily. "But I just want you to know that I'm allergic to all manner of tree nuts and I'm lactose intolerant."

"Can you eat a burger and fries, with a Coke?" asked Bortnicker, whose own stomach was grumbling.

Fiona fixed him with her own crooked smile. "That sounds *smashing*, Bortnicker. Let's go!"

They exited the room, with Fiona in the lead. "*Smashing?*" LouAnne whispered in her cousin's ear. "Who says that?"

"Sshh," answered T.J., barely containing himself.

They left the office building and ventured across the street. "Want to try The Dugout?" asked T.J.

"Fine with me, Big Mon," said Bortnicker. "I'm so hungry I could eat a moose."

"Me, too," piped Fiona, at Bortnicker's side.

The group descended the stairs underneath the Glimmerglass Inn to a cozy, wood-paneled eatery that contained a bar, circular dinner tables with checkered tablecloths, and walls decorated with photos of Cooperstown village scenes reaching back to the late 1800s. They seated themselves and the waiter took their order. Predictably, Fiona ordered the same thing as Bortnicker. T.J. went for the turkey club with fries but LouAnne, surprisingly, only wanted a salad. "That's all you're going to eat?" asked her cousin.

"Yeah, not that hungry," was her disquieting reply. T.J. had always known his cousin to have a voracious appetite, which never affected her figure because she was a calorie burning machine. But so far today, after a fast start she seemed a little sluggish, and the light lunch she desired gave him still more cause for concern.

"So, Fiona," asked Bortnicker as they dove into their lunches, "what are you, ten years old?"

"*Eleven*," she snapped with a mouthful of burger. "I'm halfway through sixth grade."

"Really. How you liking middle school?"

"Middle school? It *sucks*. Dopey boys, and mean girls who talk behind your back, or even worse, act like you're not even there."

"I know the feeling," he replied, his solemn expression harkening back to the tough times at Bridgefield Middle School when it seemed T.J. was his only comfort.

As if reading his mind, T J. asked, "So, who's your best buddy there?"

"Well, I have this one friend, Jamie Bell, but she's kinda been avoiding me lately, trying to get in with the cool girls. And she was my bunk mate at camp last summer. What a backstabber!"

"Fiona, what made you like the show?" said LouAnne, trying to switch gears.

The girl paused, burped, and then popped a French fry between her braced teeth. "Hmmm," she mused. "Well, I've always been interested in paranormal stuff and ghost stories, but what I liked about your show was how close you guys were, how you helped each other out when things were going against you. I felt... I wouldn't mind having friends like you when I got older."

The teens glanced at each other. After some of the garbage they'd been dealing with at school over the show, the thought that they might actually have a positive effect on other kids never occurred to them. Bortnicker seemed particularly moved.

"Well, tell you what, Fiona," he said, polishing off the last of his burger. "I'd like to have you as a friend *right now.*"

"Me too," said T.J., and LouAnne smiled her assent.

"Cool!" said the girl, brushing the bangs from her eyes. "So, this means I'm helping out on the investigation?"

T.J., thinking quickly, said, "Well, we can't have you take part in the night stuff that's going to be filmed, Adventure Channel rules and such, but I have an idea. Last year in Bermuda there was this girl from the island, what was her name again?"

"Ronnie Goodwin, I believe," said Bortnicker, playing along.

"That's it. Anyway, she kind of helped us out behind-the-scenes. So, if you want to, meet us over at the Hall tomorrow morning at ten o'clock when we do some research. Are you okay with that?"

"Way cool!" yelped the girl, turning many heads in the restaurant. "I can't wait to tell Uncle Bob! See you guys tomorrow!" She gathered her stuff, paused by Bortnicker's chair, gave him a quick peck on the cheek, and literally skipped out.

"Well, wasn't that sweet," said T.J. sarcastically as his best friend blushed.

"What can I say, guys?" he replied. "I'm irresistible."

LouAnne bounced her used napkin off his forehead as T.J. paid the check. "It can't hurt to let her think she's involved, guys," she reasoned.

"The poor kid just needs a friend," observed T.J.

"Don't we all, Cuz."

* * * *

"Well, where to, Big Mon?" queried Bortnicker as they ascended into the afternoon sunlight.

"Let's do what Mr. Davis said. I'll grab a street map at the kiosk right here and we'll take a walk." He returned within seconds with an unfolded map. "It looks like if we just keep going down Pioneer Street we'll hit the lake. Come on!"

They proceeded down the incline of Pioneer, past a Victorian funeral home and some private residences. Suddenly Lakefront Park and Lake Otsego itself opened before them in a stunning panorama.

There were really two sections to the recreation area. To the left was a green space with picnic tables and a huge bronze statue depicting characters from local native James Fenimore Cooper's novel *The Deerslayer*. The right hand section, much more spacious, held the boat docks at which pleasure craft both large and small, as well as tour barges, rocked gently in the breeze. At the point, there was a distinctive lighthouse, painted white with red stripes, and a ramp for launching boats near the Lakefront Motel, whose deck featured a few hardy souls taking their lunch on this relatively mild spring day.

The lake itself seemed to go on forever, framed by majestic forested mountains on both sides. Seagulls gracefully careened overhead. "I think I see a picnic here in our future," noted T.J., and his mates readily agreed.

From there the teens made their way up to Lake Street and hung a right. A couple blocks later they stood before the formidable Otesaga Hotel and resort, where the Hall of Famers and other baseball dignitaries were billeted each summer during Induction Week.

"They've got their own golf course here," said Bortnicker. "You always see it in the background when the Hall of Famers are getting interviewed. Pretty ritzy."

Following the map, the threesome went up Chestnut Street past the James Fenimore Cooper Inn, which was fairly impressive itself. They came again to the traffic light at the top of Main Street. "Not much to this place, is there?" asked T.J.

"Nope," answered Bortnicker, "but that could end up being a plus. Let's work our way to Doubleday Field."

After inhaling the heavenly aromas emanating from the corner bakery, the ghost hunters strolled down the main drag, noting the various establishments they would later have to video as "local color" if the investigation would make it to TV.

"It seems like you either have some kind of restaurant or a memorabilia shop," observed LouAnne as they popped in and out of baseball-themed stores selling every imaginable kind of related item, from team hats and jerseys to bats, yearbooks and baseball cards. After entering three or four, one of which was housed in the former Smalley's Movie Theater, T.J. said, "Jeez, it's just like Gettysburg, Cuz. The same kind of shops selling all the same stuff."

"You got that right," she agreed.

Halfway down Main they turned into the half-full parking lot to Doubleday Field, but at that point LouAnne stopped them. "Hey, guys, you mind if I quit here for today?" she asked. "I'm kinda tired and I want to be awake for dinner later. You can fill me in on Doubleday and anything else."

"You feeling sick?" asked T.J. concernedly.

"Nah. I just want to lie down for a bit, that's all."

The boys looked at each other quickly. "Sure, that's fine, Cuz," said T.J. "Call you around six for dinner?"

"Sounds great. See ya."

The boys watched LouAnne go, her blonde ponytail swishing behind her.

That's not like her, thought T.J. *My cousin usually runs rings around us.*

"Something's amiss, Big Mon," said Bortnicker, reading the concern on his face. "And did you see what she had for lunch? *A salad.* What's up with that?"

"Don't know. Oh well, let's go check out Doubleday. It's only two o'clock."

"Wow, what a beautiful park," said Bortnicker reverently as they approached the brick façade of Doubleday Field. Its arched entrance highlighted a three-paneled rectangular wall that stretched halfway down the foul lines. Eye-level windows with green panes matched the green restroom and maintenance doors on its flanks. The grandstand's outer shell was crowned by a simple peaked green roof, and the words Doubleday Field in white were set against a red background curving over the entrance.

The boys walked inside under the cool darkness of the grandstand, then ascended one of the matching inner ramps to the seating area behind home plate. Simple, gray-painted wooden benches with matching numbered backrests, maybe twelve rows high, followed the curve of the foul-line-to-foul-line grandstand. The dugouts, which were at field level, were tucked into the brick wall just past home plate. Down the right field line, aluminum bleachers were protected by a low cyclone fence. The left-field stands, a small portion of which were covered, featured similar aluminum benches built into a more substantial concrete pavilion.

Centerfield, which didn't seem all too far away, displayed aluminum bleachers beyond a green concrete wall. Trees from private residences, as well as a towering church steeple, could be seen past the modest electric scoreboard down the third base line. The playing field was manicured to perfection, a true diamond in every way.

The boys settled into the wooden bench seats behind home plate and put their feet up.

"What I wouldn't give to play just one game here," sighed T.J.

"Maybe you will someday, Big Mon."

"Hey, want to try to walk on the field? There is a gate where the grandstand ends down the first base line."

"And I was just getting comfortable. Let's check it out."

They hopped off their seats and descended one of the ramps, exited the park from the front and found their way to the side gate, which was unlatched.

"After you," said Bortnicker politely.

They tentatively ventured onto the field to home plate, where T.J. stood in the batter's box, scanning the ballfield. "Man, I can feel the history, Bortnicker. Think of all the great players who came through here."

"Help you, boys?"

They whipped around to find a man, surrounded by rakes and other maintenance implements, leaning casually against the brick wall below the net backstop protecting the box seats.

We must've been so taken in with the field we didn't even notice him, thought T.J. embarrassedly. "Uh, sorry, Sir," he stammered, "we didn't mean to mess up the field, but the gate was open and -"

The man held up one hand to infer no harm had been done, then motioned with the other for them to approach. "What brings you here?" he asked somewhat guardedly.

"I'm T.J....T.J. Jackson, and this is my friend, Bortnicker. We're kind of on assignment for the Hall of Fame. Do you work here?"

"I watch over the field," said the man with a placid smile. "Name's John Goodleaf. You boys don't have to worry, it's all right being here."

John Goodleaf was an imposing figure. He stood about six-foot five in his work boots and jeans. A red and black checked lumberjack jacket was rolled to his elbows. But what made Goodleaf even more striking was his jet black hair, combed straight back from his forehead and gathered in a short ponytail at the back. That and piercing black eyes set in a ruddy face dominated by a Roman nose.

"Do you know a lot about the history of this park?" asked Bortnicker.

"The history?" Goodleaf replied. "Well, let's see. These grounds have been used for baseball since 1920. Before that it was a farm belonged to a man named Elihu Phinney. They put a wooden grandstand on it in 1924, then replaced it with this steel, concrete and brick building in 1939. Up until a couple years ago they played the annual Hall of Fame game here as a part of the Induction Week celebration. Expansions over the years have raised the capacity to around 9,800. The dimensions are 296 feet to left, 390 feet to the dead center, and 312 to right.

"Now this Elihu Phinney was by trade a printer who moved up here from Connecticut -"

"We're from Connecticut!" interrupted Bortnicker.

"How about that?" said Goodleaf coolly. "Anyway, he did well for himself in the printing business and later bought this land. Of course, he wasn't the original occupant."

"Who was?" asked T.J.

"This was all Indian territory, T.J.," said Goodleaf. "For hundreds of years before Elihu Phinney or William Cooper, for whom the village is named, or any other white man showed up."

"Mr. Goodleaf," said Bortnicker uncertainly, "are you Ind - I mean, uh, Native American yourself?"

John chuckled. "You won't hurt my feelings by calling me an Indian, son," he said. "It's all the same to me. And yes, I am. My friends call me Chief, in fact."

"Really?" said T.J. "And you're okay with that?"

"Sure. They don't mean it in a derogatory way. Leastways, I hope they don't." He took a long look around the field. "God, this is beautiful country," he said with appreciation. "It's kind of a magical place, actually, if one is to believe the old legends."

At those words T.J.'s mind began to work. "J-uh, Chief, are you pretty knowledgeable about these local legends and such?"

"You could say that."

"Well, would it be okay if me and Bortnicker run some stuff by you while we're up here?"

"Stuff about what?"

"Some things that might be...related."

"Sure, T.J. You boys know where to find me."

"Thanks, Chief."

From there the teens pressed on to traverse what was left of both sides of Main Street. By this time all the parking spaces were full and cars were cruising up and down waiting for someone to pull out. T.J. and Bortnicker found themselves weaving in and out of tourists sporting hats and jerseys from virtually every MLB team, and took note that except for New York, no two consecutive license plates on parked cars were the same.

They worked their way past the F.R. Woods sports memorabilia shop, the oldest in town, crossed the street at the post office directly across from the Hall of Fame, and ducked in and out of more shops. Since neither boy was a huge baseball collector, much of it left them unaffected.

"Wait till Coach P. gets a chance to do some shopping," T.J. cracked. "This stuff is right up his alley."

"Hey, Big Mon," said Bortnicker, trying on a Red Sox ball cap in a Mickey Mantle-themed shop, "what did you think of the Chief back there?"

"Seems like a friendly guy," he answered, hefting a wooden Louisville Slugger. "He sure keeps that park in pristine shape. Wish our home field was that nice. I think he might end up being a good resource on this case."

Bortnicker gave up on the fitted cap he was trying - his bushy hair made it pop off - and went to a larger size. "Why do you say that? How is he gonna help us inside the Hall?"

"That's just it. I'm getting the feeling this investigation might go beyond the walls of that building."

"How come?"

T.J. was now shuffling through a pile of baseball cards from a large cardboard box. "It's hard to explain," he said, "but a couple times as we've been walking around I got a feeling… like a certain place was special."

"Such as?"

"For one, the lake. I got a weird vibe there."

"And let me guess - the other is Doubleday Field."

"Yup."

"The question is, how do we hit all those places?"

"Well, we either do it together, which will take more time, or split up, for which we might not have enough equipment. We have to see what The Adventure Channel ships to us. Of course," he added with a grin, "we could always have you and Fiona team up."

"Don't even," warned Bortnicker, replacing the larger cap on the shelf. "Although to tell ya the truth, I'd feel really guilty about just blowing her off. I hope you were serious about letting her tag along tomorrow morning."

"Sure. I mean, what's the harm, right?"

"Can I ask you a question?" asked Bortnicker, suddenly serious.

"Yeah, what?"

"Was I…that…*difficult* in sixth grade?"

T.J. thought for a second. "You still are," he smiled. "Let's go back to the inn and relax a little before dinner."

"Sounds good. I've got a mild baseball overdose going."

They climbed the steps to the second floor and Bortnicker unlocked their room's door and went in. T.J. was about to follow him when he heard a faint sound from across the hall. He listened more carefully. It was coming from his cousin's room. After looking up and down the hallway he tiptoed to LouAnne's door and listened. What he heard was both shocking and heartbreaking: the jagged sobbing of the girl he loved.

Chapter Fourteen

"Yo, wake up, Big Mon," prodded Bortnicker. "It's time to get spiffed up for dinner."

T.J., somewhat disoriented in his new surroundings, managed a "Wha-what time is it?" and yawned.

"Coming up on six o'clock. You've had a good snooze, and meantime I've been in and out of the shower. In fact, I ventured downstairs and ran into Clara, the owner, and guess what?"

"What?" he replied, sitting up groggily.

"She wants me to help cook breakfast for all of us tomorrow. Just like with Aunt Terri in Gettysburg!"

T.J. shook his head and chuckled. During their ghost hunting trip to Pennsylvania his friend had discovered another passion to go with model railroading: culinary arts. He and LouAnne's mother had whipped up memorable breakfasts every morning, from fluffy omelets to fruit-laden waffles, and this interest had stayed with him to the point where he was now a more-than-competent chef.

"I figured, while you and your cousin are out for your morning run I'd help old Clara serve up some good eats. That is, I'm assuming, that you two will be doing your customary workouts?"

"I hope so," said T.J., who'd decided not to share his experience at LouAnne's hotel room door with his friend. "To tell you the truth, I don't know what to expect from her anymore," he confessed.

"Oh, and by the way, Coach got back from the Legends camp and he's in the shower right now. Sounded pretty jacked up when he came in so I guess he had a good day. That Debbie McCray suggested we try this

Italian restaurant, Maria Amelia's, on Main Street near the drugstore, so I called and made us reservations for seven."

"Well, you've sure been a busy beaver."

"Just coordinating, Big Mon. BTW, the dress code there is casual but neat, so nothing raggedy. I'd advise we lay off the *Junior Gonzo* attire, though."

"Yeah, Bortnicker, we wouldn't want to get interrupted during our meal by autograph seekers or paparazzi," chided T.J.

"I'll respond with one word, Big Mon: *Fiona*."

"Point taken. I'll jump in the shower. Tell LouAnne about dinner, okay?"

"I already have. Remember, I'm coordinating here."

T.J. paused. "And...how was she?"

"Seemed fine to me. I guess the nap did her good. Now get cracking!"

* * * *

"Wow, guys, pretty fancy place," said Todd Pisseri. "And you say the Hall is picking up the tab?"

"You got it, Coach," said T.J. "Though I'm sure we won't abuse it. Right, Bortnicker?"

"Are you accusing me of being a glutton?" he countered in mock horror.

"Yes!" his three comrades replied before dissolving into laughter.

T.J. was happy to see LouAnne had fixed herself up, decked out in a sheer black turtleneck sweater and dress jeans. There was only the slightest trace of redness in her eyes from before.

"I especially like the framed photos of Frank Sinatra," said Bortnicker. "It's a little fancier than Pizza Palace."

"Yeah," said T.J., "but remember last summer when we went to one of the better Italian restaurants in Bermuda? It was cute, but Pizza Palace blew it away, food-wise."

"True," he replied as a waiter in black vest and tie approached their table.

Eschewing a glass of wine in deference to his younger friends, Pisseri ordered an iced tea with his seafood ravioli. The boys went with their standard penne ala vodka, and LouAnne - thankfully - ordered a plate of fettuccine Alfredo.

As they awaited their food, they passed around a basket of breadsticks and rolls. The crowd was light this evening, so there was no rush, and much to discuss.

"So, tell us about your day at the Legends camp, Coach," began T.J., sipping a Coke.

"Oh, man, guys, it was so great," he replied. "That girl Debbie drove me over to the Clark Center, where I met the Hall of Famers. Get this: we had Carlton Fisk working with the catchers, Phil Niekro and Dennis Eckersley with the pitchers, Jim Rice with the outfielders, Ozzie Smith running the infield, and George Brett is the batting coach! Talk about your baseball cards coming to life. And they couldn't have been nicer to the staff coaches and the campers. I kind of thought a couple of them might big-time us a little, but they actually helped out with the drills and didn't step all over us when we were trying to do fundamentals, which is all we had time for today. It was like a 'getting to know everybody' kind of day. And listen to this: we all got uniforms, which look like Yankees pinstripes with the Hall of Fame logo on the chest, and our own lockers."

"Cool!" said Bortnicker, while motioning the waiter to bring more breadsticks. "What are the campers like? Is it a lot different from coaching high school?"

Pisseri chuckled. "Guys, it's a whole different atmosphere. First, I'd say the age range is like from forty to sixty years old. Most of the guys are in decent shape, and some played in high school, but the majority of them are just baseball nuts who were given this week as a gift from their families. They don't have much ability, but they sure love the game.

"Today we just got them into their uniforms, did a meet-and-greet with the Hall of Famers and showed them how to stretch before breaking up for very basic drills. Even so, I bet there will be a lot of sore campers tomorrow morning.

"What's cool for them is that they're staying at the Otesaga with the Hall of Famers, so they get to hang out with them for dinner and drinks."

"Another reason there may be sore campers tomorrow," quipped LouAnne.

"You might be right about that."

The food arrived and they dug in. "So, how was your first day of the investigation?" asked Pisseri as the waiter sprinkled Parmesan cheese on his ravioli.

"There really wasn't much investigating, Coach," said T.J. "We had a meeting with the board, who all seemed pretty supportive of us being there except for this guy, Dan Vines, who's like second in command. The equipment won't get here until tomorrow, so we just kind of scouted the town. Coach, you've got to visit all the memorabilia shops, you'll go crazy. Anything to do with baseball, you'll find it here."

"Can't wait."

"Anyway, we checked out the lake, which is only a block down the street, and Doubleday Field -"

"Real old-timey," interjected Bortnicker. "You'd love it, Coach."

"Well, as it turns out, guys, the campers will be playing their intra-squad game there at the end of the week, so I'll actually get to go on the field," he beamed.

T.J. turned to LouAnne. "By the way, Cuz, we met a real interesting guy over at Doubleday. He's like the groundskeeper, and his name is John Goodleaf. But what's cool is he seems to be an expert on local Native American history -"

"He's Native American himself," cut in Bortnicker.

"And he kinda gave the impression that this whole town might be full of spirits."

"That's promising," she said, working her way through the fettuccine, which pleased her cousin. "Do you think he'll end up helping us?"

"You never know. He seems like a cool guy." T.J. flashed a devilish look and said, "Speaking of help, it seems like Bortnicker here has an admirer who's pledged her assistance in the investigation."

"Really?" asked the coach, cutting up his last ravioli. "What's she like?"

"Picture a female Bortnicker, around 11 years old, who's head over heels in love with him."

"You're exaggerating," Bortnicker harrumphed, wiping up vodka sauce from his plate with some bread.

"Oh, Bortnicker," LouAnne trilled in a dramatic falsetto, "you're so

86

smashing!"

Even he had to laugh at that one. "Yeah, that was kind of cool, wasn't it?"

* * * *

T.J. took care of the bill and they exited into the pleasantly brisk evening. It was only 8:30 PM, but the streets were virtually empty.

"I think I'll turn in early, guys," said Pisseri. "Debbie is going to be picking me up at eight tomorrow morning to run me over to the athletic center."

"Oh, so now we're on a first name basis, Coach?" joked Bortnicker. "That didn't take long."

"Cool your jets, Mr. TV Star," he replied. "She's just a nice lady."

"Uh-huh," said T.J. with a wink.

"Whatever," Pisseri called out over his shoulder. "See you tomorrow at breakfast."

"Don't be late!" warned Bortnicker. "I'm cooking it!"

The coach gave a weak wave of acknowledgment.

"Well, guys, what about us?" asked T.J. "Anyone up for a walk?"

"Not tonight, Cuz," begged off LouAnne. "It's a little cold, anyway. But we're running tomorrow morning, right?"

T.J. brightened. "You know it. How's 7 AM?"

"Make it 6:45. We'll need to get a good stretch. Besides, I wouldn't want to miss Bortnicker's gourmet breakfast."

"I'll be going back, too, Big Mon," said Bortnicker. "All this adulation has put me in the mood to Skype Ronnie over in Bermuda."

"You aren't going to tell her about Fiona, are you?"

"Heaven forbid. What happens in Cooperstown stays in Cooperstown. C'mon, LouAnne, I'll walk back with you."

T.J. watched them disappear around the corner down Pioneer Street, alone in the chill with his thoughts. Before he knew it, his feet were pointed in the direction of Lake Otsego, and within minutes he was standing at the shoreline, the gently lapping waves nearly reaching his Timberlands. The moon was partially obscured by some scudding clouds, and there was only the hint of a breeze. The smell of water and pine trees mingled in his nostrils and he felt fortunate to experience such a moment. He wondered about his cousin, whose mood swings were unnerving, and his best buddy. Would they be able to pull this off? In Gettysburg they were freelancing, and in Bermuda they had Mike Weinstein for support; now there were expectations, from Bob Simmons, The Adventure Channel, even Mike. But something was here, he just *knew* it. As he turned back up Pioneer Street he had a feeling that the next day it would all begin to unfold.

* * * *

Though the Glimmerglass Inn was only a block away from Maria Amelia's, Bortnicker suddenly felt panicky. He hadn't been alone with LouAnne for a long time, really not since Gettysburg two years ago; T.J. had always rounded out the threesome. Sure, they'd talked on the phone, texted and emailed, but this was different, and the girl seemed content to stroll in silence. He had to break the ice somehow.

"Okay, I've got one for you," he challenged. "We're on our way to the inn. Which Beatles song begins with the word *in*?"

"That's too easy," she sighed. "'In My Life'. And by the way, are you really going to Skype Ronnie in Bermuda?"

"Yeah," he replied uncertainly. "Is there a problem with that?"

"I hope you aren't just leading the girl on, is all," she said airily. "I'd hope you aren't doing the typical guy thing."

Wounded, he followed her up the steps and through the front door. "Hold on a minute," he said. "Don't you think that's a little unfair? She meets new guys all the time in her job. I'm sure over all these months she hasn't just sat at home looking at the wall. Why are you picking on me all of a sudden?"

"Because I think this TV stuff has gone to your head, that's why," she snapped, looking him dead in the eye.

Bortnicker gaped at her; it was like he was talking to a stranger. And then the words tumbled out of his mouth before he could take them back: "You know, T.J.'s right," he spat. "Something's come over you."

"What do you mean by *that*?" she fired back, her voice rising.

"I mean, you're not yourself! Don't you know how weird you're acting lately?"

She was trembling now, and wagged a warning finger in his face.

"Don't...you...*dare* try to tell me who I am or what I should act like. And don't you drag my cousin into this."

"That's easy for you to say," he called after her as she bolted up the stairs, beginning to cry. He caught her at the top just outside her room. "Don't you know you're driving him crazy? Don't you realize how much he -"

"Is everything okay here, guys?" asked Coach Pisseri, cracking his door open with concern.

"Yes!" they both yelled, and he retreated quickly.

In the silence after the door snicked shut, they again faced each other, breathing heavily. Finally, Bortnicker whispered, "I'm sorry."

"It's a little late for that, don't you think?" was her icy reply. And with that, she unlocked her room, went in and slammed the door.

"Shoulda gone with T.J.," he said to the empty hallway.

Chapter Fifteen

T.J.'s eyes cracked open and he checked his portable alarm clock: 6:15 AM. He didn't know if he'd awakened because of anticipation of his morning run with LouAnne or Bortnicker's prodigious snoring. He thought back to the previous night and his friend's somewhat odd behavior. When he'd returned from his walk to the lake, Bortnicker reported, somewhat indifferently, that he'd tried to Skype Ronnie but she had been out. Then, instead of his normal gabbing that would keep T.J. up until all hours, he'd turned in, claiming exhaustion. Giving thanks for small favors, T.J. called it a night as well and was soon sound asleep.

He wasn't much of a dreamer, but this night the lake had crept into the threadless string of events at various times, reinforcing his belief that it would be somehow important in the scheme of things on this trip. T.J. used the bathroom and then quietly pulled on his Bridgefield red and gray tracksuit and New Balance 1226s. He was just lacing them up when there came a familiar *tap-tap-tap* at the door, followed by a whispered, "Hey, Cuz, you ready to rock?" The words were barely out of her mouth when he eased open the door and slipped into the hallway beside her.

"Sleep good?" he asked as they padded downstairs to the lobby.

"Not bad," she replied, zipping up the top to her Gettysburg High School tracksuit of blue and red. "How about you?"

"Okay, I guess. Had some weird dreams, but they were all kinda jumbled together. I only remember bits and pieces."

"How about Bortnicker?"

"Slept like a rock, snoring up a storm. He was out cold while I was still getting undressed."

"Did he get in touch with Ronnie?"

"He said she wasn't home."

"Anything else?"

"Nope."

They exited the front door and descended to the sidewalk, where they did some stretches. The streets were empty and there was a decided frost in the air as the sun began peeking over the mountains. "Which way do you think we should go?" she asked, easing forward into a hurdler's stretch.

"Well, I looked over that street map from yesterday, and I figure that if we go down to Lake Street like yesterday and make a left, we can follow Lake to Chestnut, which will take us completely across town. Then we make a left on Walnut down to River Street, up Main and back to here, a great big circle. It should be a good half hour, I'd estimate."

"Seems about right," she answered. "But let's not overdo it, okay?"

T.J. was somewhat taken back. It was not like his cousin to express trepidation about anything concerning running. In the past it was always he who had to ask her to dial it down a little. "Uh, sure," he managed. "We'll go a nice easy jog. My baseball muscles will thank you."

They rose from their stretches on the cold sidewalk and started off down Pioneer toward the lake. As they turned left on Lake they were treated to an eerie sight, the dense mist rising from the dark waters of Lake Otsego.

"Very cool," said LouAnne. "Nothing like that near Gettysburg, I can tell you."

The teens made another left on Chestnut just before the Otesaga Hotel and eventually crossed Main Street, again catching a whiff of the bakery on the corner. "We've gotta check that place out at least once before we leave," said T.J.

"Sounds good to me. I think I smelled cinnamon buns."

Farther down Chestnut they found themselves in a residential area of impeccably neat, modest-sized homes that all seemed to have been built in the first half of the 20th century. Not much passed between them conversationally. T.J. wasn't about to bring up hearing LouAnne crying in her room the previous day. Likewise, the girl stayed away from her contentious encounter with Bortnicker. This run was too pleasant to ruin.

91

There was even the faint smell of chimney smoke that gave the village a comfortable country feel. However, by the time they'd passed the hospital at the corner of River Street, LouAnne was beginning to slow down. They were approaching Christ Church when she asked if they could walk for a bit.

"Sure, why not?" said her cousin. "Hey, let's go into the graveyard here, Cuz. I read some neat stuff about this place when I was researching the town."

The burial ground of Christ Episcopal Church was definitely old. Fancy monuments mingled with smaller tombstones, some of which had seen years of exposure to the elements erode their inscriptions.

"Of course," began T.J., "the most famous people here are Coopers." It didn't take long for them to find the monuments for the town founder, William, and his famous son, the author, James Fenimore. "Hey, Cuz," he said, "are you up for a ghost story this early in the morning?"

"Sure."

"Okay. As the story goes, back in the 1980s a young girl and her friends pay a visit to this cemetery, right? So one of her friends, showing some disrespect to the grounds, casually leans up against one of the gravestones. What happens? The tombstone topples over, directly on one of her legs, pinning her to the ground. Her friends run to get help and they finally get the tombstone off the girl. That's when they notice that the birthdate of the dead Cooper matches the girl's! Pretty cool, huh?"

"Not bad."

"Here's another one you might like. One of the Coopers was named Hannah -"

"Wait a minute! I can see her stone from here," said LouAnne. She led her cousin to the weathered, lichen-stained marker where he continued his tale.

"So, anyway, this girl Hannah was beloved by everyone in town. Totally virtuous and admirable, the whole bit. But when she was in her early 20s, she tragically died after falling off a horse."

LouAnne spat on her hand and wiped the stone. "In 1800," she said.

"Right. Well, there was this guy, Richard Cary, a colonel in the U.S. Army who'd served in the Revolutionary War under George

Washington. Even though he was a lot older than Hannah, the two were friends.

"A few years after her death, Cary himself became seriously ill. On his deathbed, he made a request to the Cooper family that he be buried as close as possible to Hannah. Apparently, he felt like he'd led a regrettable life, and that if he could be buried near this girl he could kinda ride her skirt-tails into heaven."

"Interesting. What did the Coopers say?"

"They were so convinced of his sincerity that they agreed." T.J. pointed to the right of Hannah Cooper's stone. "And there he is."

T.J. smiled at a story well-told and was therefore alarmed to see his cousin staring at the girl's tombstone, tears rolling down her cheeks. *What was this about?* "Hey," he said gently, "I didn't mean to upset you. I thought you'd like the story." He considered putting his arm around her but thought better of it.

"No, no, T.J., it's a beautiful story," she said, quickly wiping her eyes the on sleeve of her tracksuit.

Trying to play off her discomfort, he said, "I think it's a good idea being buried next to a virtuous woman. You're gonna have to reserve me a spot someday. I'd like that."

"Would you? Really?" was her enigmatic reply. Her words hung in the still air of the cemetery.

"Let's start walking to the inn," said T.J., deflated. "Remember, Bortnicker's fixing breakfast."

Not a further word was spoken.

Chapter Sixteen

"Welcome to Chez Glimmerglass," said Bortnicker with a sweep of his hand as T.J. entered the inn's dining room. The large mahogany dinner table was set for four; in the middle were platters piled with bacon, sausages, and toast, and each breakfast plate was covered with a copper warming dome.

"Pretty fancy," said T.J. "I didn't realize how hungry I was until I was in the shower. That early run got my appetite going."

"How far did you go?" asked Coach Pisseri, who was pouring himself a mug of steaming coffee.

"We did a couple miles, all told," he replied, taking a seat. "Nothing major."

Seconds later, LouAnne appeared, her freshly washed hair falling beneath the shoulders of her *Junior Gonzo Ghost Chasers* golf shirt. Upon viewing the dining room table she broke into a wide grin. "A Bortnicker feast," she mused. "The perfect way to start your day." Both boys secretly exhaled. It appeared the girl's roller coaster was on the upswing for the time being.

"Oh, he was so helpful!" sang Clara, entering with a fresh pitcher of orange juice. "All I had to do really was show him where the ingredients were, and he took it from there."

"What about me?" voiced a compact, dapper gent past her shoulder.

"Allow me to introduce my better half, folks," joked Clara. "This is Nat. He doesn't say much, but he's a help. He personally squeezed the oranges for your juice this morning."

"Hi, Nat!" the group said in unison.

"Nice to meet you all. If you'll excuse me I'm off to Oneonta to pick up some replacement light fixtures. Have a good day." He gave his wife a peck on the cheek and ducked out.

"As I told you, he's a man of few words," said Clara. "But he's a dear. Well, enjoy your breakfast. If I don't stop gabbing it will get cold!"

All at once the foursome lifted their warming domes to find fluffy spinach and feta cheese omelets, still steaming. "Wow," said Pisseri, "I sure don't eat like this at home. Thanks, Bortnicker."

"No problemo, Coach," the boy replied. "It's what I do."

As they passed around the platters family-style, T.J. took over. "All right, so this morning we're doing research. I think that Jody guy is going to meet us at the museum. We've all got our golf shirts on, which is good, but it might be smart for us to keep our jackets over them when we're not filming so we don't attract attention. That is, if our equipment's arrived."

"It has, Big Mon," said Bortnicker, loading his fork with egg and sausage. "Bob Simmons called over while you guys were running. Early delivery from UPS. A big crate, apparently. He's had it moved to an exhibit room off the Plaque Gallery which they've closed off temporarily."

"Great," said T.J. "What I think we should do first thing this morning is check out whatever Clemente items are in the storage archives and get familiar with whatever gadgets The Adventure Channel sent."

"We should also see what's in the files at the library," added LouAnne, buttering a slice of whole wheat toast. "These eggs are delicious, by the way." She gave Bortnicker a thumbs up, which somewhat eased his pain from the night before.

"It's the whipped butter and milk I add," he said proudly. "Gives 'em that fluffy texture."

T.J., redirecting the conversation, said, "Then I figure we'll close out the morning with a walking tour of the Museum, grab some lunch, and spend the afternoon doing 'local color' sound bites around town. You know, the stuff you see in the first few minutes of a typical *Gonzo* episode. Mike had us do a lot of them in Bermuda. We'll flash the shirts for those."

"Sounds good, Cuz," agreed LouAnne.

Pisseri checked his watch. "Whoops, gotta go, guys," he said, taking a last gulp of coffee. "Debbie's meeting me outside. Great breakfast, Bortnicker." He gathered up his glove and spikes from the hallway. "Any thoughts for dinner tonight?" he called out.

"Probably The Dugout," said T.J. "Nothing fancy. If all goes according to plan, we'll be setting up our stuff after dinner for the first investigation, so we can't eat too late."

"Oh," said Pisseri. "Well, then, if you guys don't need me, would it be okay if maybe I took in a movie in Oneonta with Debbie afterwards?"

Bortnicker shot his mates a wink. "That's fine with us, Coach," he said with mock seriousness, "as long as you're home at a reasonable hour."

* * * *

As the teens approached the Hall's main entrance on this crisp morning they met with a familiar sight: that of Fiona Bright, splayed out on the front steps as if she'd slept there all night. "'Bout time," she grumbled. "What took you so long?"

"It's only nine-thirty," answered Bortnicker gently, offering his hand to help her up. "We'll have a lot of time to do what we've gotta do."

"Which is what?" she questioned, following them inside.

"All kinds of neat stuff."

At that point the girl backed off, obviously not wanting to annoy her hero.

Awaiting the group in the main lobby were Sarah Martin and Jody Rieman. "Good morning, all," said Martin. "What would you like to do first, visit the storage archives or check out the equipment you've been sent?"

"Why don't we split up?" suggested T.J. "LouAnne and I will do the archives; Bortnicker and Fiona will inventory the equipment."

"Fine," said Martin. "Jody, you are more tech savvy than I. You can show Bortnicker and Fiona to the Halper Gallery while I take T.J. and LouAnne downstairs."

"Sure, Miss Martin," said the intern. "Follow me, people." They breezed past the ticket desks, now clogged with morning patrons, and proceeded past the grand staircase toward the Halper Gallery, named in honor of the famous collector of baseball memorabilia. It had been closed temporarily to serve as a secret command center for the ghost hunters.

"All right, you two," said Sarah Martin. "Ready to visit the vaults?"

"Sounds mysterious," said LouAnne.

"Oh yes," said Martin, leading them through the Plaque Gallery and up the ramp to the first floor. "We'll access the vaults via the elevator in the Giamatti Library Research Center." They passed the Bullpen Theater and entered the incredibly neat library, where Sarah introduced them to Tom Fentz, the head librarian. "Tom, these young people will be stopping back in a bit do some research on Roberto Clemente," she said. "Would you be so kind as to have your people pull whatever files you have so they're ready when they visit?"

"Consider it done," said the scholarly-looking librarian. "There's quite a bit to go through."

"Well, there are three of us, Mr. Fentz," answered T.J. He thought for a second. "Maybe four. I think we can handle it."

Martin led them down a short hallway behind the research tables to an elevator. As they stepped inside she said, "The old storage room used to be in what was the basement of the main building. What you had basically was rows and rows of industrial-type metal shelving crammed with boxes containing uniforms, gloves, and whatever else. Other shelves were loaded with trophies and awards. You see, for many years beginning in the late 1930s the Hall accepted any and all donations from players and their families. A player would pass away and his family, instead of throwing away his effects, would send them to us. And we happily took them.

"This was, of course, before the sports memorabilia collecting craze of the 1980s and onward. Today, auction houses do a big business of liquidating the estates of deceased players or players who simply want to sell off their stuff, either because they need the money or their houses are jammed with it, and they're fearful of losing it to theft or fire. This makes it hard for the Hall to acquire items via donation. We don't pay for any item, although today's players will gladly loan items to us from historic games or record-setting events. If a player, his family, or just a passionate collector wants to permanently donate something nowadays, it has to be submitted for consideration to a committee here at the Hall to determine its worthiness as a display item or historically important artifact."

The elevator slowly descended a floor beneath the library and opened onto a brightly lit, climate-controlled modern facility.

"Wow, Miss Martin, this is impressive," marveled T.J.

"How big *is* this place?" asked LouAnne.

Martin, obviously experienced in her capacity as tour guide, proudly explained, "Well, when we decided to take the plunge and enter the modern era as a museum, we realized we needed to store somewhere upwards of 30,000 items, including uniforms, balls, bats, gloves and other textiles, in addition to various art objects from paintings to statues, and ephemera such as player contracts and letters. We also had to make sure that the facility would support a collection growth rate of 400 new objects yearly over a ten year period. The solution you see before you is a custom-designed, high density mobile system."

"What does that mean, exactly?" asked T.J., eyeing what appeared to be rows of connected cream colored metal doors with wheel-type handles.

"Well, they're called mobile shelving because we can move them in and out, depending on what we're looking for. Built into these eight-level shelves are customized racks for our hundreds of bats, lateral art racks that can safely store many paintings, 4D shelving with museum cabinets, and rolled textile storage. This helps us eliminate all the wasted space you need by having aisles between the shelves. And the shelves we have are cantilevered, which simply means they can be pulled out for easy access. Let me show you."

She led them to one of the end storage sections which appeared to be around three feet across and turned the handle, which made it easy to slide away from the rest of the block. This section was around 50 feet long and 24 shelves per side, with pullout drawers for uniforms and cubbyholes for hats and batting helmets.

"Amazing," said LouAnne.

"Is there much Clemente stuff here?" asked T.J.

"Unfortunately, no," Martin replied, gently pushing the unit back into place. "Much of Clemente's personal equipment, what little there is, lies in the hands of private collectors or his family. There is the display in the museum featuring his mannequin, which we discussed at our meeting, wearing a Pirates 1970 double-knit uniform. However, though this uniform is authentic and team-issued, there's no documentation attesting that he actually wore it in a game. Let me show you what we do have down here."

Martin led them to yet another mobile shelving block and maneuvered it out for inspection. This one held bat racks. "Ah, here it is," she said, picking out a specific knob. "Let me put on some gloves. You'll have to as well." Martin passed out thin white cotton gloves to the teens. "You have to wear these whenever you handle the artifacts. Oils from human hands can seep into the bats, gloves and uniform material quite easily."

They pulled them on and Martin drew from the rack a tan-colored Louisville Slugger model that showed some wear from game use. "This is one of Clemente's bats circa 1965-1968," she said, gently handing the club to the teens for inspection. T.J. held the bat head and LouAnne the handle. "It's 36 inches long and weighs 35 ounces. The model number, U1, has been stamped into the knob, and the clubhouse man for the Pirates added Clemente's number 21 in black marker over it."

"How can you tell it's the real thing?" asked LouAnne.

"Good question. Well, with a Louisville Slugger, you have to check a few things. First, if the player's signature on the barrel of the bat is in script, that means he had a contract with the manufacturer, Hillerich and Bradsby. If not, there would be CLEMENTE MODEL in capitals. Then, the code has to be right. Louisville Slugger made personal bats for the pros according to their desired specifications of length, weight, and handle thickness. If you were the first one to request a bat with a previously unused set of specs, the code for that that would be the first letter of your last name and the number one. The next guy with different specs would be the letter and number two, and so on. They kept files on each player, so when he or his ballclub put in an order they'd just look up his code number, find his specs on file, and hand-turn the bat accordingly.

"As we can see here, Clemente liked a model that was used by another player who came before him, a guy from the 1934 Cubs named Frenchy Uhalt, believe it or not. So, he requested that player's code, U1, and had his own signature, *Roberto Clemente*, burned into the barrel.

"Finally, most if not all Louisville Sluggers will display the *Powerized* logo designating it as a professional model, next to the famous oval Louisville Slugger trademark on the barrel. This very trademark has varied over the years, so that's another way to help date the bat."

"Pretty scientific," observed T.J.

"But even with all that, you can get fooled," said Martin. "Unfortunately in today's sports memorabilia market, forgeries are prevalent in everything from autographs to uniforms to bats. Unscrupulous people will go to great lengths to fake a piece of equipment and try to pass it off as authentic. That's why any item donated to the Hall has to undergo a rigorous panel examination by our experts. And even then, there's the chance of a misstep. Therefore, the greatest help in authenticating items is what we call *provenance* - the actual documentation or credible account by the donor as to how the artifact came into his or her possession. In this case the bat was given by Clemente to a Pirates official, who willed it to the Hall. We have a signed affidavit from him and a photo of Clemente handing him the bat as a gift. That's what we call rock-solid provenance."

"And how much is it worth?" asked T.J.

"Well, we don't deal in monetary values," said Martin, "but on the open market I'd say anywhere from five to ten thousand."

"And this is all you have from Clemente?" questioned LouAnne.

"Yes, outside of some old documents, a weather beaten hat and a pair of crusty spikes. But no uniform."

"Would that be worth more than the bat?"

"Much more, as would a glove. A player might go through a dozen bats over the course of the season, cracking them and whatnot, but in Clemente's day you were only issued two sets each of home and away uniforms. And in Clemente's era, players were not allowed to keep their uniforms."

"What happened to them?" asked T.J.

"They were sent to the team's top minor league affiliate and then passed down through the system from season to season until they finally fell apart.

"A glove is even rarer, because a player might use the glove for five or ten years until it, too, disintegrated. But he'd usually start breaking in a new one if the end was near for his 'gamer'."

"That would mean a Clemente uniform or glove is valued as -"

"Priceless," was her answer.

"Hmm," said T.J. "I had no idea. So I guess it would be silly to ask you if we could use any of these items as a trigger mechanism to bring out Clemente's ghost?"

"That's a good guess," said Sarah Martin, smiling sweetly.

* * * *

Meanwhile, in the Halper Gallery, Bortnicker was conducting a tech session. The huge wooden crate that had arrived had been dismantled, revealing two black steamer trunks with GONZO GHOST CHASERS stenciled in white on the sides. Carefully, he and Jody Rieman had removed a pair of black computer terminals and keyboards, as well as stationary DVR video cameras and tripods, from the first one; the second trunk contained all manner of handheld devices, along with walkie-talkies, packed in cushioned covers.

"Look at all this stuff," marveled Fiona. "Do you really need all this to hunt ghosts?"

"Well," said Bortnicker, "let's just say they threw the kitchen sink at us. Depending on the nature of the entity, one device might be suitable while another's useless."

"I have two long tables set up here for you to lay out everything," offered Rieman.

"That's great, Jody. Why don't you hook up the computers and make sure they work, and I'll go through the handhelds."

"I'm on it," said the intern.

"Okay, Fiona," Bortnicker began, "you hand me an item and I'll tell you what it does. Sound cool?"

"Definitely," she answered, brushing hair out of her glasses. The girl unwrapped a black device the size of a blackboard eraser and passed it to him.

"Uh-huh. This is what we call a K2 meter. See those five small lights across the top? If there's a paranormal entity close by, those lights will start blinking. And sometimes, if the entity is what we call 'intelligent,' the meter might light up in response to simple questions we ask. Hand me something else."

She rummaged through the trunk and came up with another black unit shaped like a small hairdryer.

"Now, this baby is a thermal imaging camera. You point it at something and it will show you, by colors, if there is a heat source, namely an entity, occupying that space. You can even determine its shape, if it *has* a shape. It will also give you a readout on the room's temperature or any cold spots, which could be another kind of tipoff that you have a spirit in your midst. Cool."

"What about these?" asked Fiona, handing over what appeared to be a normal camcorder.

"All right. This is a full spectrum camcorder which takes both video and still photos. It picks up stuff not readily visible to the human eye."

"Like ghosts?"

"We hope," he smiled.

"So, why do you need those computers and stuff over there?" she asked, pointing to Jody Rieman, who was methodically connecting wires and checking switches.

"Well, what we're gonna do is set up this table, probably right here because it's closed off and quiet, and then position a bunch of what's called DVR cameras at various points around the museum which will be set on RECORD while offering a view of that area to whoever's manning the computer. The screen here will be divided into squares, each of them a feed in real time from a different camera. This way you can watch what's going on at a bunch of different places simultaneously. We'll have to set those up tonight after everyone's left the building. Then, the next day we go through all the video and see if we caught movement or shadows or whatever."

"Is that something I could help out with?" she asked hopefully.

"That's a possibility."

"Thanks, Bortnicker. But how about just hearing voices?"

"Look in the trunk again," he said. "There should be one more item."

"Found it!" she cried triumphantly. "You have a few of these packed together." Fiona unwrapped a handful of devices the size of a granola bar.

"Yup, here we go. These little beauties pick up EVPs. That stands for electronic voice phenomena, sounds the human ear can't normally hear. In Bermuda, we first heard from Captain Tarver on one of these. We were asking questions out loud, and when we played it back, there was his voice responding. We just went wild over that.

"Of course, later on he showed up as a full-bodied apparition, but that's another story. We actually ended up with an audio of him telling his life story, but the Bermuda National Trust confiscated the tape."

"What nerve!" she exploded.

"Well," said Bortnicker sheepishly, "we were kinda trespassing on their property at the time, so they had us. But that doesn't change the fact that we *did* get a ghost's voice on tape and it *can* be done. Maybe we'll get lucky again tonight."

"But, who are you looking for?" she innocently queried.

"Anyone who shows up," was his enigmatic reply.

Chapter Seventeen

"How's it going in here?" asked T.J. as he and LouAnne entered the Halper Gallery and quickly shut the door behind them to shield their command post from the prying eyes of the hundreds of Museum goers now circulating in the building.

"Great," said Bortnicker, surveying the dazzling array of ghost hunting instruments laid out on the table. "They sure didn't spare any expense. Jody hooked up all the computer stuff and will be back this afternoon to give us the grand tour of the Museum. Fiona's been a big help with sorting out the small stuff."

LouAnne offered the girl a high-five, which was heartily returned.

"How about you guys? Find anything cool in the secret vaults of Cooperstown?"

"Nothing that will help us terribly," answered T.J., purposely remaining vague around Fiona. "Maybe we'll find something in the library."

"Yuck. I hate libraries," mumbled Fiona.

"Unfortunately, research is a big part of what we do," said T.J. patiently. "It played a really big part in our first case in Gettysburg."

"I suppose," she replied, "but when are you going to get down to some serious ghost hunting?"

"Not till tonight," said Bortnicker. "Lots to do before then."

"And you're sure I can't help out?"

"Like I said, Fiona," answered T.J., "it's against Adventure Channel policy." He thought for a second, then snapped his fingers. "Tell you what. How would you like to meet us here tomorrow morning to review

104

the videotapes from the DVRs? With another set of eyes, it'll go a lot quicker. You might even be the first to catch a ghost."

"I guess so," she relented. "I'm kinda tired, anyway, from getting up early and doing all this work with Bortnicker."

"Well," said LouAnne, "by helping him, you freed up some time for us to hit the library. It's only 10:45, guys. We'd better get moving."

"Sounds good," said T.J. "So, Fiona, meet us back here tomorrow morning around 10:00. Okay?"

"Sure, T.J.," she replied. "But if you need my help later on, just call Uncle Bob."

"Will do."

She high-fived Bortnicker on the way out and closed the door behind her. "Man, she sure took that well," he observed. "I thought she'd put up a fuss for certain."

"You're right," said LouAnne. "That was just too easy."

"We can't worry about that now," said T.J. "On to the Research Center?"

"Let's hit it," said his cousin.

They made their way discreetly through the crowds of Museum goers and entered the blessedly quiet library, where they were immediately greeted by the affable Jim Fentz. "Welcome, folks," he said, handing out the same white cotton gloves as Sarah Martin. "We've got six folders on Clemente, chock-full of information. There are two copy machines over there under the portrait of Mr. Giamatti if you need them."

"We are especially interested in the events surrounding his death," said T.J. "Not that the other stuff isn't important, but we've researched his baseball career pretty much."

"Understood," said Fentz, "though you'll find a lot of material you haven't seen because our archives are pulled from not only The States, but the Caribbean and South America. Do any of you speak Spanish?"

"I do, a little bit," said Bortnicker. "I mean, I should...I've been taking it since sixth grade."

"What about you?" joked LouAnne to her cousin. "Didn't you go to the same school?"

"I took French, and after 'je m'appelle T.J.' I'm pretty lost."

Fentz laughed. "Well, call me if you need anything. Good luck."

The teens sat at a long table with two folders each, the contents of which ranged from news clippings to magazine articles. Bortnicker took the 1955-1965 folders; LouAnne followed with 1966-1970, and T.J. tackled the sad business of his death and the aftermath.

Bortnicker was the first one to comment after an hour amidst the sound of flipping papers. "This guy was a machine, a .300 average or above year after year."

LouAnne chimed in: "Yeah, and Gold Gloves from 1961 onward. All-Star team almost every year, too."

Bortnicker: "Four time National League batting champ."

LouAnne: "But only one MVP in all that time. Strange."

Time passed. News clippings riffled. Finally, T.J. sat back and held the bridge of his nose while he exhaled. "Man, my eyes are tired," he remarked. "This crash stuff is pretty grim."

"Can you summarize it?" asked Bortnicker, polishing his glasses.

"Well, the night the plane went down, they started scrambling boats and aircraft from the U.S. Coast Guard Rescue Center in Old San Juan, but since they didn't have an exact location, it was like trying to find a needle in a haystack. In the dark.

"People on land heard what happened and started showing up on the beach in droves, looking for some kind of sign. The Governor immediately declared a three-day period of mourning, but many refused to accept it. Rumors flew. A lot of people just expected him to come walking out of the surf. Psychics were called in, saying they'd heard from him. His poor wife just prayed they would find a piece of him."

"Oh, my God," whispered LouAnne.

"Listen to this," continued T.J. "His Pirate teammate, Manny Sanguillen -"

"Catcher," interjected Bortnicker.

"He came in from Panama and wanted to help in the search. Sanguillen literally stripped down to his bathing suit and joined a group of volunteer divers who were exploring a nearby reef, looking for snagged bodies.

"Eventually you had boats, planes, and helicopters in on the search. Some debris came to the surface, along with the wallet of another guy who'd been on the plane.

"They had a memorial service for him even as others were claiming to have seen him wandering, dazed, through the streets of waterfront villages near Old San Juan.

"Finally they found the body of the pilot, but just about every one of his bones was crushed. Doctors figured the force of the crash must've been horrendous."

He sighed.

"And then the sharks took it from there."

* * * *

At Bortnicker's suggestion they bought sandwiches at the Baseline Deli and took them down to the lake, but the fresh air failed to lift their spirits. They spent the time filming sound bites with a camcorder they'd brought and trading anecdotes about the man they sought, merely picking at their food.

"Man," said Bortnicker finally, "I know we all wanted to find Major Hilliard and Captain Tarver, but I really *want* to meet this guy."

"Same here," said LouAnne, wrapping up her sandwich and tossing it in the nearby trashcan. "Hey, Cuz," she continued, "you want to head back to the Hall for our tour? T.J., are you hearing me?"

The boy was staring out at the water and the mountains.

"Yo, Big Mon," prodded Bortnicker. "You there, my brother?"

"This lake's part of it," he stated flatly.

"Part of what?" asked LouAnne.

"The Clemente thing."

"But how?" asked Bortnicker. "What's a lake have to do with baseball?"

"Listen. You two go back to the Museum and get the tour from Jody. Take a couple camcorders with you. Film each other doing sound bites in front of the various exhibits and such. It's one-thirty. Meet me on the Village Green at three and bring a camcorder. We'll do local color around town for an hour."

"And what're *you* doing right now?" asked Bortnicker. "Going for a swim?"

"No," said T.J., rising from the grass and dusting off his jeans. "I'm gonna go find the Chief."

* * * *

As they walked up Pioneer toward Main, Bortnicker found himself in the same uncomfortable position with LouAnne as the previous night, but she quickly put an end to his anxiety.

"Let me get this out there," she said, looking straight ahead. "I've been dealing with some stuff at home and I'm kinda on edge. I shouldn't have fired out on you last night. You were only trying to be a friend - I get it. I've just got things I've got to work out, okay?"

"Sure," he replied. "I just didn't want you to be - I mean, of course I accept - that is -"

"Bortnicker, just shut up, okay?" she said sweetly.

"I can do that."

"All right, then," she continued, "now that we're past that, what was up with my cousin zoning out at the lake?"

"Don't know. It was like he just went somewhere else for a while." He frowned.

"What?"

"Okay, I'm gonna share something. A few weeks ago, T.J. was talking to Mike Weinstein, and Mike said he suspects T.J. has, you know, paranormal abilities."

"You think?" she asked seriously.

"Well, he does always seem to be where the action is, ever notice that? But, I think he's a little frightened by it, to tell the truth. 'Cause in the background there's always -"

"The thing with his mom?"

"That's my guess. He wants to know, but then again, I feel he's terrified of it."

LouAnne was clearly concerned. "Let me think on this, okay?"

"Sounds like a plan," concluded Bortnicker, relieved.

They reentered the Hall and flashed their passes, then proceeded to the Halper Gallery and picked up a camcorder as per T.J.'s instructions. The ever-efficient Jody was waiting for them in the lobby.

"Hi, folks. Where's T.J.?" he inquired.

"Walking around town and communing with nature," said

Bortnicker. "But we're all ready for the tour. We'll give him the highlights later."

"Sounds good. Follow me."

First up was the majestic Plaque Gallery, where Jody explained the rules of induction and the arrangement by year of the plaques on the blonde oak walls. Overhead skylights in the vaulted ceiling cast an ethereal glow on the gallery, giving it a cathedral-like effect. Which was perfect, because these were indeed the gods of the sport, though many could not necessarily be classified as saints.

"Let's look at Clemente's," said Bortnicker. "I want some footage of the plaque and we'll do a sound bite."

"Easy enough," said Jody. "Let's go over to the class of 1973. As you know, a special dispensation was awarded to Clemente in light of the extraordinary circumstances surrounding his death."

The teens waited until the immediate area was vacant and removed their jackets. Then Bortnicker filmed LouAnne as she delivered her sound bite: "I'm standing in front of the induction plaque of Roberto Clemente here at the Hall of Fame. One of the all-time greats, he is the subject of our investigation."

Bortnicker zoomed in on the plaque which read:

ROBERTO CLEMENTE WALKER
PITTSBURGH N.L 1955-1972
Member of the exclusive 3,000-Hit Club. Led
National League in batting four times. Had four
seasons with 200 or more hits while posting
lifetime .317 average and 240 home runs.
Won Most Valuable Player Award 1966.
Rifle-armed defensive star. Set N.L. mark
by pacing outfielders in assists five years.
Batted .362 in two World Series, hitting
in all 14 games.

"Okay, Jody, we're done here," said Bortnicker, turning off the camera. "Lead on."

They ascended the ramp past the concealed lighting panel to the

Baseball at the Movies exhibit, which Bortnicker especially enjoyed, having seen most of them, and the Scribes and Mikemen room, dedicated to the great baseball writers and announcers of the past. LouAnne made sure to look up the late Harry Kalas, whose voice she indicated she would always associate with her beloved Phillies.

From there Jody escorted them to the Grandstand Theater, where they joined other Museum patrons in the re-created stadium for a fast-paced multimedia presentation of "The Baseball Experience" which culminated with the audience singing "Take Me out to the Ballgame." Bortnicker and LouAnne belted it out with gusto, swaying back and forth in their seats. "Too bad T.J.'s missing this," said Bortnicker. "I wonder what he's up to right now."

* * * *

After his friends had left, T.J. spent a while more at the lake, taking footage and narrating. Then he ventured up Pioneer and hung a right on Main. He entered the parking lot to Doubleday Field, filmed the outside façade, and went right to the field entrance up the first base line. The gate again was open, but the ballpark seemed deserted. Disappointed, T.J. nevertheless let himself in and took some footage of the stands and field for future use. He was heading for the gate when a familiar voice called, "Looking for me?"

He turned to find John Goodleaf ten feet or so behind him. *How does he do that*? he wondered. *I know Native American hunters could be super stealthy, but this is weird.*

"Uh, hi, Chief," he stammered. "Yeah, I was looking for you, actually." He reached for the camcorder, hoping to get some footage of their conversation. But Goodleaf seemed to cringe.

"What's that?" he said, pointing to the camcorder.

"A video camera, Chief. Is it okay if I film you?"

"I really don't think that's necessary. Makes me nervous, you understand."

T.J. quickly returned the device to his jacket pocket, not wanting to offend the man.

"Where's your friend?"

"At the Hall of Fame with my cousin, doing a tour. But I wanted to talk to you, instead."

"About what?"

"Well, I guess about death. I mean, you said this whole area was originally all Indian Territory, right?"

"Yes; the Mohawk, which I am, Mahicans, Algonquins and Iroquois. It's pretty complicated, because their territories overlapped. But that's not what you're really interested in, is it?"

"Ah, not exactly. What I want to know is, when you see those old Western movies on TV the Indians are always referring to the 'happy hunting ground' or something corny like that to represent Heaven or the afterlife or whatever. I want to know what the real deal is on that."

"Walk with me, son," he said. They began inside the first base foul line, heading toward the outfield. Goodleaf's hands were stuck in the front pockets of his jeans, and he moved smoothly and deliberately. "This 'happy hunting ground' thing you're mentioning means nothing to me. Never heard it used by my people.

"That being said, different tribes looked at the afterlife in their own way. In general, my people believe that every person, and animal, has two souls. The body soul, or shadow, is associated with the heart and provides the person with his memory and intelligence in life. It remains with the body after death forever, usually resting quietly. But the 'real' or free soul is associated with the brain and gives the person his sensations. We believe this free soul, after death, makes its journey to the afterlife."

"Where is it supposed to be?" asked T.J., totally engrossed, as they began crossing the outfield to the other foul line. "Up above? Down below?"

"The land of the dead is vague as far as location, but we believe it to be a generally pleasant place. However, we also believe that the souls there have no memories of their previous existence. Some tribes believed the souls ate food there. Maybe those 'happy hunting grounds' people based their belief on that, while others discounted that part completely."

"Do your people believe that the dead, or their spirits, can interact with the living?"

"Yes, to a degree. Why do you ask?"

"Because I've *seen* it, Chief. Twice." T.J. went on to describe his experiences in Gettysburg and Bermuda. Goodleaf listened intently, never interrupting. By the time the boy finished they were into their second lap around the ball field.

"Interesting," he said finally. "So I must ask you, T.J., what is it, actually, that brought you to this place?"

"Well, Chief, there was this famous ballplayer, Roberto Clemente, who died a tragic death back in 1972. It's believed his body was broken apart and …well…it's pretty grim. But he's been spotted, or at least his ghost has, in the Hall of Fame, a couple of times in the past few months. My friends and I, based on our past experiences that I've told you about, were called in to investigate."

"And if you were to make contact with this man's spirit?"

"We'd try to return him to the afterlife."

"Really? And how would you do that?"

"I don't know," the boy replied honestly. "That's why I'm talking to you."

"Me? How would I be of help?"

"You *know* things, Chief," said T.J. "I can sense it. And you seem to be in touch with the land here." He took a breath and plowed ahead. "Do your people believe that the spirit world includes things besides humans and animals, things like trees and…lakes, for example?"

"I'd say yes to that."

"Even the very field we're walking on?"

"Perhaps."

"Because I've been getting vibes from two places since I got here: Lake Otsego and Doubleday Field. Not the building that sits here, but the land itself."

"Hmmm."

"Chief, do you know what a portal is? It's a place that acts like a kind of passageway to the afterlife. And I'm starting to think that Cooperstown, or at least this area within the town, is a portal. And that's why Clemente has come back here. His baseball connection made it the logical place, even though he died thousands of miles away. What do you think of all that?"

The pair had now traversed the playing field twice and found themselves at the gate. "I think you have told me a great deal, T.J.," he answered. "Things I have to consider for a bit. Give me a little time to think this over, maybe check with some tribal elders. You come and see me later."

"Later? *When* later?"

"Doesn't matter. Like I told you boys the other day, I am always around. This field needs constant attention."

"It's a beautiful place."

"That it is."

* * * *

Meanwhile, back at the Hall, Bortnicker and LouAnne received a visit from the president as they were exiting the Grandstand Theater.

"Enjoy the show, folks?" asked Bob Simmons as the exuberant crowd filed out on a baseball high.

"It was great, Mr. Simmons," said LouAnne. "I really liked how the baseball cards came down out of the ceiling at the end."

"And you, Bortnicker?"

"The stadium seats are cool and the wraparound crowd mural, too. You feel like you're actually at a Major League park, only it's cozier."

"Well, that's the desired effect, all right. Has my man Jody been a help so far?"

"Big time," said Bortnicker. "He helped set up all the computer stuff for tonight and is giving us a first-class tour."

"Attaboy," said Simmons, clapping the young intern on the shoulder. Then he lowered his voice. "Listen, I want to, uh, both commend and thank you for the way you've handled Fiona so far. She can be a handful."

"No problems, Mr. Simmons," said Bortnicker. "She actually saved me some extra work with the equipment today, and we told her she could help out with our videotape review tomorrow morning."

"Well, fine. You know, she's kind of a lonely girl at home, and you guys have been quite accommodating. I think you've got a fan for life, Bortnicker."

"Like he says, Mr. Simmons, he's just irresistible," kidded LouAnne.

"Now, before I let you continue your tour, are you all set for tonight?"

"The equipment's all ready to go," said Bortnicker, "except the remote DVR cameras we'll have to position when we get here. What time can we start, and how will we get in?"

"We're going to shoo everyone out by 9:00 PM," said Simmons. "At this time of year, it's not a big problem because the entire town rolls up the sidewalks early, as you've probably noticed. Dan Vines volunteered to let you in. That is, of course, unless you need Jody."

"No offense, Jody," answered Bortnicker, "but we'll be handling this ourselves. We're just more comfortable that way."

"No offense taken," he replied. "And I've got a date, anyway."

"All right, then," concluded Simmons. "We'll see you back here at nine." He moved off through the throngs of Museum patrons.

"On to the second floor?" asked Rieman.

"Ready when you are," answered LouAnne.

The intern escorted the teens up another ramp where the chronologically laid out exhibits told the history of baseball through hundreds of artfully displayed artifacts. LouAnne was taken with the 1850s-1890s exhibits, which naturally brought her back to her work as a Civil War civilian reenactor back in Gettysburg. Bortnicker was more enthralled with the evolution of equipment, from the early primitive lemon peel balls to the huge wagon tongue-like bats. Especially curious were the gloves, which began as fingerless leather sheaths resembling modern bike racing models and were only as big as yard work gloves by 1900.

And while the Ty Cobb/Babe Ruth era was intriguing, it wasn't until they hit the 1970s Clemente display that they stopped dead in their tracks.

"Gotta film this," said Bortnicker. They took video and stills from every angle, zooming in and out. "Definitely setting a DVR camera in this area later," he added.

"No doubt," agreed LouAnne. "Gee, that mannequin's lifelike. It's spooky."

"That's what that poor guy Florio thought before he keeled over," Bortnicker whispered in her ear.

The other area of note on the second floor was the Viva Baseball!

114

exhibit, which now displayed the Silver Slugger Award bat of Ozzie Mantilla. As expected, Clemente figured prominently in the collection, and a lot of footage was taken.

"Camera two in this area," said Bortnicker.

"Check."

Finally they climbed the stairs to the third floor, where Rieman took them through rooms dedicated to classic and modern ballparks, the World Series, and baseball cards. At every turn the young intern was a font of knowledge, answering their numerous questions easily without showing off.

"He's going places here," LouAnne whispered to Bortnicker when she had a chance.

The conclusion of the tour took them down a back staircase to the spacious gift shop on the ground floor opposite the Plaque Gallery.

"I'll leave you guys here to poke around," said Rieman. "Hope you enjoyed it."

"It was great, Jody," said Bortnicker, and they both shook his hand. "I'm sure we'll run into each other again before we leave."

As the intern moved off, Bortnicker looked at his watch. "Perfect. Twenty minutes to three. We can window shop a little and then go find T.J."

* * * *

T.J. was waiting for them on a park bench in the center of the Village Green, reviewing footage he'd shot on his travels without them.

"How was the Hall?" he asked.

"I think we walked every inch of it," said Bortnicker, "though I'm positive we missed a lot. And we got tons of footage and more than enough sound bites. I've scoped out at least four places to put the DVRs. You've gotta do the tour before we leave, Big Mon."

"Don't worry, I will. Now you two experts can show me the ropes."

"Did you find that Chief guy?" asked LouAnne.

"Oh, yeah. Let's get an ice cream up the street and I'll fill you in."

They strolled the crowded sidewalks with their cones, stopping occasionally for "local color" sound bites and the like, as T.J. related the highlights of his conversation with John Goodleaf.

"So he's gonna, like, get advice from some tribal elders or something to try to help us out?" asked Bortnicker, licking some dripping pistachio off the side of his cone.

"He was a little vague on that, but yeah," answered T.J., popping the bottom of his cracker cone into his mouth. "Another thing, I wanted to film him for the show, but he wasn't into that. Most people can't wait to get on TV."

"Maybe it's a tribal thing," said LouAnne. "Kind of like the Amish, you know?"

"Yeah," agreed Bortnicker. "I think I read once where some tribes felt that if you were captured on film your soul was stolen or something."

"Anyway, he sounds interesting," said LouAnne. "I'm looking forward to meeting him."

"Well, he's definitely different," said T.J. "I get a weird vibe from him I can't quite put my finger on."

Bortnicker caught LouAnne's eye and gave her a knowing nod, which she furtively returned. When T.J. walked over to a nearby trashcan to dump his napkin, Bortnicker mouthed *I told you*.

Chapter Eighteen

"Now this is my kind of place," said Coach Pisseri as he tore into his dinner of roast turkey and mashed potatoes. "How cool is it to have a restaurant like this right under your hotel?" Apparently, he wasn't the only one with that opinion. The Dugout was fairly busy for a Tuesday night.

The boys, who hadn't eaten much at lunch, now fortified themselves for the long night ahead with thick steaks, while LouAnne opted for the healthier lake trout and sautéed vegetables.

"How did the campers do today, Coach?" asked Bortnicker as he smothered his beef with A-1 sauce.

"Better. We've more or less got them in positions now, so they were able to get a lot of technique work in. We even put together a Home Run Derby contest for the afternoon, and it was a blast. The Hall of Famers held a secret draft beforehand, so the two squads were fairly even. Then, Ozzie Smith and George Brett played for one team, and Carlton Fisk and Jim Rice with the other. I helped Niekro and Eckersley throw to the hitters, which got pretty frightening with those former pro sluggers out there. They're not spring chickens, but they can still get around on a BP fastball. Thank goodness we had a pitching screen to hide behind, or I wouldn't have any teeth left. Only thing is, my shoulder is killing me now, like after I throw BP to you guys."

"Hey, Coach, you'd better watch it," said T.J. "We still have our whole season ahead, and we're gonna need your arm."

"Point taken. But enough about me. Let's hear about your exploits today."

All three of the teens reported on their travels in and around the Hall of Fame, and also related the details of Clemente's life - and death - which came to light in the library.

"Wow," said Pisseri. "It's weird to think that what you see in the actual Museum is just a portion of what they have overall. That underground vault must be something. Speaking of the Museum, the whole camp is scheduled to do a VIP tour of the building tomorrow morning from nine to eleven. The entire coaching staff and the Hall of Famers will be with us. They're not opening the Museum tomorrow morning till we're all done. It would be a madhouse otherwise, people trying to get autographs and whatnot. Then we'll bus over to the Clark Center. Is our tour going to interfere with your work?"

"It shouldn't," said T.J. "We have this exhibit room called the Halper Gallery all to ourselves, so we should be able to slip in and out with no problem. We'll be reviewing tonight's video and audio, I guess."

"And now that you're underway, how long you see the investigation taking?"

"That's a tough call. Typically, the max you'll see on the TV show is two nights. But the real reason we are here is to help Mr. Simmons, so it might take longer. Either way, I think what happens tonight will give us a good idea of whether we can accomplish anything."

"I say we'll be done by Friday," declared Bortnicker confidently. "How about you, my dear?"

LouAnne chewed her fish slowly. "I'm pretty much with T.J.," she said. "This thing could be over tonight, but I see at least one more day."

"That reminds me," said Pisseri, "Friday afternoon is our big intra-squad game at Doubleday Field. I'm hoping you guys have this all wrapped up by then so you can attend."

"You playing, Coach?" asked T.J.

"Technically, no, and neither are any of the staff or the Hall of Famers. This is a game for the campers, who are paying a lot of money to be here. Many of their families are coming in for the game, and there should be quite a crowd. But, as far as I can see we only have four pitchers to work with, which means two for each squad. If one gets tired or injured, I've been informed that I'm the next one in. But I'm hoping that doesn't happen 'cause like I told you, I'm pretty sore."

"Speaking of sore," said LouAnne mischievously, "how were the campers this morning after their evening of fun with the Hall of Famers?"

"Let's just say there were a lot of bleary eyes and gallons of coffee being brewed."

Everyone decided to skip dessert, and the waitress brought the check. "So, Coach," said T.J. as he handed over the credit card, "what movie are you guys taking in tonight?"

Pisseri, blushing, said, "Debbie suggested we see *The Hunger Games*, which is fine with me. She's actually a very nice person. If it's okay with you guys, I'm thinking I might ask her to dinner tomorrow night."

"With us?" asked Bortnicker.

"Uh, that would be a 'no', Bortnicker," said Pisseri. "I'm thinking of revisiting that cute Italian place from last night."

"Go for it, Coach," said LouAnne. "We don't mind. Besides, if she had to watch Bortnicker eat, it might put a damper on the evening."

T.J. signed the credit card slip and they climbed the stairs to Pioneer Street. It was early evening and the sky was darkening. A Nissan Altima pulled up to the curb. Debbie McCray lowered the power window and greeted the group. "We've got to hustle to make the eight o'clock show in Oneonta, Todd," she said. "Hop in!"

"See you tomorrow, guys," said Pisseri. "Good luck tonight. Say hi to Roberto for me. You doing breakfast again tomorrow, Bortnicker?"

"You know it, Coach," he replied. "Now get going. Don't keep the lady waiting!"

Pisseri climbed into the passenger seat and they sped off up Main Street. "Okay," said T.J. "We've got some time to kill. Let's go to our rooms and change into our show shirts. I'd also like to give my dad a call and tell him we're all safe and sound. We'll meet in the lobby in an hour and stroll over to the Hall. By then it should be emptying out."

"Yeah, I think I'll check in with my parents, too," said LouAnne. "Bortnicker, you might want to call your mom as well."

"Capital idea," he joked. "She must miss me terribly."

* * * *

"So, has Clemente showed up yet?" said Tom Sr. in Arizona.

"Hopefully tonight, Dad," answered T.J. "How's your trip?"

"Same-old, same-old. We sit around the table, go over the building plans, and talk about contractors. You know the drill. How are Bortnicker and LouAnne?"

"They're okay. Bortnicker weaseled his way into the kitchen and is helping with breakfast. It's a cool place. Very 1800s."

"How about your cousin? She didn't seem quite herself the other day."

"I don't know, Dad," he said truthfully. "She's kinda up and down. You know how girls are."

"Don't remind me. Well, you two guys take care of her, or Uncle Mike'll be after you."

"Got it."

"Let me know if there's a break in the investigation, okay?"

"Sure thing, Dad."

"All right. Be safe, son."

"You too. Talk to you soon."

Bortnicker, who'd already spoken to his flighty mother, had been listening from his position on the bed, where he was munching on Saltines, his favorite snack, and pouring over Clemente information on his laptop from the Hall of Fame website.

"Hey, Big Mon," he said casually, "you really think your cousin's behavior is just a typical girl thing?"

"How the heck should I know?" he snapped. "It's not like she says much."

"Okay, okay," Bortnicker replied, backing off. He decided again not to relate his experience of the previous night. It would only upset his friend, and T.J.'s mind had to be clear for tonight. They all had a job to do.

* * * *

"Well, here you are," said the eternally grumpy Dan Vines as he met the teens at the front entrance. "We've cleared the building out, and I personally walked the entire facility and checked every nook and cranny to make sure no stragglers were missed."

"Thanks, Mr. Vines," said LouAnne brightly. "That was very kind of you."

"Yes. Well. Now come with me and I'll show you how to turn out all the lights. I've already disarmed the alarm system." He led them through the lobby to the Plaque Gallery. In a small hidden alcove near the ramp to the Bullpen Theater was a hinged wall panel that swung out to reveal a bank of switches. "Just flick all of these to the OFF position and you're ready to go," he said. "When do you see this wrapping up?"

"For tonight, I'd think around 1:30 AM, Mr. Vines," said T.J. "Sound about right, Bortnicker?"

"Yup, that should do," replied his friend, eyeing the toggle switches.

"All right," said Vines. "I've set the front door on automatic lock, so when you leave tomorrow morning pull it closed - hard - until you hear a distinctive click. Please don't forget to do this. It's making me nervous just telling you about it."

"Try not to worry, Mr. Vines," said T.J., flashing his winning smile. "We're pretty reliable about things like that."

"Well, I still think this is crazy, kids, but good luck." He turned and waddled toward the lobby.

"Not exactly a ringing endorsement from old Dan-O," observed Bortnicker.

"Whatever," said T.J. "Let's go set up."

The Halper Gallery, whose walls were adorned with panoramic ballpark photos from the current bimonthly exhibit, provided a pleasant backdrop with the two tables of equipment that Jody Rieman, Bortnicker and Fiona had laid out for the evening. Cables and wires snaked from the computer terminals to nearby wall outlets. One by one Bortnicker flicked them on. He took his role as tech specialist seriously.

"Okay," he said. "First thing, everybody grab a walkie-talkie and the flashlight. We need to be in constant contact, because we'll all be on our own most of the time."

"Yes, Sir!" said T.J., snapping a smart salute.

"Not funny, Big Mon. Now, the way I figure it, we'll have to man this computer table in shifts. I'll take the first ninety minutes, then T.J., then LouAnne. The terminal here on the left will be divided into four pictures giving a live feed from four sites. We're going to set up the

121

infrared DVR cameras on tripods at these places: Clemente's slab in the Plaque Gallery, the Sacred Ground Room on the third floor where there's some artifacts from Forbes Field and Three Rivers Stadium, where Clemente played, the Viva Baseball! exhibit, and of course the Clemente mannequin case. I need you guys to go set these up right now. I'll guide you on the positioning by walkie-talkie."

"Bortnicker, I'm impressed," said LouAnne as she gathered up a tripod and camera. "I'll do the Plaque Gallery."

"Let me get the ballparks room," said T.J., "and then LouAnne and I do the other two."

"Good idea," said Bortnicker, "'cause they're on opposite ends of the second floor."

A half-hour later it was done, and the cameras switched on. Bortnicker had his friends maneuver the tripods into the most advantageous angles so that all four targets were covered. "Perfect," he concluded. "Now, each of you take a camcorder, K-2 meter and EVP recorder with you. Do a running narration whenever you can for TV purposes. Use whichever device you want at whatever time. If I see something come on the screen at any of these sites, I'll radio you. There's actually enough ambient light from the roof skylights to get by in the Plaque Gallery, but for everywhere else you'll need flashlights. Ready to go 'lights-out'?"

"Let's do it," said T.J.

"Aren't we forgetting something, you guys?" said LouAnne.

"I left something out?" asked Bortnicker, perplexed.

"Only the most important thing. The official *Junior Gonzo Ghost Chasers* cheer."

"Oh yeah," said T.J., remembering their ritual in Bermuda. "Everyone put their hands in." They formed a tight circle and placed their hands in the center.

"One, two, three—*Gonzos Rule!*"

* * * *

As in any paranormal investigation, the first fifteen minutes under "lights out" conditions were exciting and anxious. But then as the teens' eyes became acclimated to the darkness and no ghosts magically appeared, it became a rather tedious grind. T.J. recalled something Mike Weinstein had told him the previous summer in Bermuda: "Remember, Dude, after you take away the commercials, a typical episode of *Gonzo Ghost Chasers* is like forty-two minutes. Hours and hours of footage get left on the cutting room floor, most of it useless and boring."

After going over a rudimentary map of the Museum, he decided to start on the third floor and work his way down while his cousin did the opposite. The only sound was the barely discernible hum of the central air system that kept the humidity level low in the display cases while supplying heat to the building to offset the chilly mountain temperatures of April. He decided to start scanning his environs with the thermal imaging device. But no matter where he pointed, no hotspots emerged. He then switched to the EVP recorder and started asking questions, leaving pauses for possible responses.

"Is there anyone here with me? I'm searching for Roberto Clemente. Are you here, Mr. Clemente? Would you like to speak with me? My name is T.J. Jackson, and I am an outfielder, just like you. People are claiming they've seen you. Why have you come back?"

There was no audible response to his many questions. Of course, they might show up later when he replayed the tape. But it was odd…the entire time he crept through the roomy aisles, T.J. felt he was being watched.

* * * *

Meanwhile, LouAnne was experiencing some disquieting phenomena of her own. She didn't know exactly if her eyes were playing tricks on her or if clouds were passing in the heavens above the skylights over the main staircase, but there seemed to be shadows darting here and there, especially in the 1800s area. She gamely tried to capture some of them, but like her cousin, she wouldn't know for sure until she reviewed the tape.

* * * *

In the Halper Gallery, Bortnicker removed his thick glasses for a quick polishing. Staring at the screen was making him cross-eyed. A few times he'd seen what appeared to be shadows, and had directed either T.J. or LouAnne to those areas for a closer look. Whether they'd caught anything was anyone's guess. He couldn't wait to turn over his uncomfortable folding chair to T.J. and take a turn walking the Museum himself.

* * * *

Finally, near the end of T.J.'s shift, things began happening. He was in the vicinity of the Viva Baseball! exhibit when he decided to try the K-2 meter. Taking a seat on a stadium chair from old Shibe Park in Philadelphia, he laid the meter on the carpet before him.

"I'm placing this device on the floor here," he announced. "It cannot harm you. But if you come close to it, the little lights at the top will go on and I'll know you're here. If you'd like me to know you're here, come closer."

He waited a few seconds with no response, and was about to speak again when the outermost bulb blinked on and off.

"Okay," he said evenly, "that was good. Now, just to make sure this gadget is working properly, would you please make it light up again?"

This time *two* bulbs flashed, and it seemed like a cold spot was growing around him. Keeping his excitement in check, T.J. said, "Is this you, Roberto Clemente?"

All five bulbs flashed.

"Yessss!" he hissed to himself, pulling out the EVP recorder again. "Mr. Clemente," he said, "please tell me if you are in my presence." Pause. "Do you want to be here, at the Hall of Fame?" Pause. "Is there a reason you've come back?" Pause. "Do you want me to help you?"

When Bortnicker broke in over the walkie-talkie with "Need you down here for computer time, Big Mon," he almost had a heart attack.

"Be right down," he said, composing himself. "I think I've made contact."

* * * *

By this time LouAnne was sure the spirits were playing with her. The Plaque Gallery seemed alive with activity, and it kept moving around. Like T.J., she'd set up the K-2, and it started blinking almost immediately, before she even got to her Clemente questions. So she kept her inquiries on the EVP general, calling for any and all spirits to check in. She was also hearing strange sounds, almost like people murmuring, in various sections of the huge room. Were they murmuring about her? An especially hot spot was in the area of the induction class of 1946; why? She had no clue. But this was getting better by the minute.

* * * *

"He's here," said T.J. triumphantly as he entered the Halper Gallery.

"How do you know, Big Mon?" said his friend, gathering equipment from the table for his walking shift.

"He lit up the K-2, and I think I might have an EVP on him."

"Really? Let's give a listen."

They both sat down and in a flash Bortnicker had connected T.J.'s player to the computer. He plugged in a set of earphones, rewound the tape, and closed his eyes, listening carefully. After a minute his eyes snapped open and he flashed his crooked smile. "You done good, Big Mon," he said, handing over the earphones. "Your turn."

T.J. put them on and sat back in the folding chair. What he heard excited him:

"Mr. Clemente, please tell me if you are in my presence."

Estoy contigo.

"Do you want to be here at the Hall of Fame?"

No de esta manera.

"Do you know why you've come back?"

No. Estoy confundido.

"Do you want me to help you?"

Por favor.

"Wow," he said, removing the earphones. "That was fairly clear. Well, you're the Spanish major here. What did he say?"

"He's saying he's with us, he's confused, and he wants to leave. He's saying he needs us, T.J."

* * * *

As Bortnicker went on his way, T.J. slid into the computer chair and contacted his cousin. "How's it going with you?" he asked.

"Crazy good," she answered. "I'm in the Plaque Gallery, and it seems like stuff is flying all over the place, but it's all jumbled. And I'm hearing faint voices, I think. Could it be that they're *all* in here?"

"Well, maybe the deceased ones are."

125

"How'd you do?"

"Great. Tell you about it later. Bortnicker's out walking now."

"Cool. Over and out."

* * * *

Feeling like he was missing out on the fun stuff, Bortnicker made a beeline for the second floor and the Clemente mannequin. When he got there he tried the thermal imager, but it came up cold. If there was anything in that case with the mannequin, it wasn't registering. Then he tried replicating T.J.'s success with both the K-2 and EVP recorder, but it just didn't feel like he was on to anything. Easily frustrated, he started toward the Viva Baseball! exhibit.

* * * *

It was now past midnight, and T.J., entering the last thirty minutes of his computer shift, was experiencing the same computer terminal screen hypnosis as Bortnicker before him. He kept shifting his eyes from one box to another, and once or twice he was sure an infrared DVR had caught a shadow, but he feared that his wishing was clouding his perception.

And then, he saw something near the Clemente case.

Something with the human shape.

Something solid.

Riveted to the screen, he started fumbling for his walkie-talkie. But before he could depress the TALK button, a huge burst of light erupted in the picture and a shrill voice screamed *"BORTNICKER!"*

Chapter Nineteen

"Bortnicker!" T.J. barked into his walkie-talkie. "Where are you?"

"Coming down the staircase from the third floor," he replied. "I heard a scream."

"Go to the Clemente display on the second floor! I saw something on the monitor!"

"Be there in a second."

"I'm on my way up from the Plaque Gallery," said LouAnne, who also sounded like she was sprinting.

"T.J., get up here," Bortnicker wheezed seconds later. "Somebody's laid out on the floor."

He took off for the stairs, bounding upwards two at a time, and pounded into the 1970s wing to find his friend and cousin kneeling over someone. Bortnicker looked up. "It's Fiona."

"*Fiona?*" gasped T.J. "What's she -"

"She sneaked in, obviously," was LouAnne's curt reply as she gently shook the girl's shoulders. "I think she fell and cracked her head on this stadium turnstile."

Foggily, the young girl moaned and then opened her eyes. "Uh, hi," she whispered with embarrassment.

"Are you okay?" asked Bortnicker, straightening her glasses and taking hold of her limp hand.

"My head hurts...whacked it on something."

Bortnicker turned to T.J., who was punching numbers on his cell phone. "You calling 911?"

"No. I'm calling Uncle Bob."

* * * *

The president of the Hall of Fame, whose home on the lake was almost a mile away, made it to his workplace in record time. The teens had not moved Fiona, though she protested that she was feeling better. It was only when Simmons came on the scene that they allowed her to sit up.

"Young lady," he began, "I can't tell you how upset I am with you. How dare you sneak out of our house in the dead of night? Your parents have entrusted us with your safety. Your Aunt Mildred is mortified!"

"Sorry, Uncle Bob," she murmured. "I just wanted to help out with the investigation, but they told me I couldn't. I'm sorry I screwed the whole thing up."

"Listen, Fiona," said T.J., "when we were in Gettysburg two years ago the three of us did the same thing - snuck out at night to go to the battlefield in search of a ghost."

"And we found him," said Bortnicker, who had never let go of her hand. "But, see, it was all three of us. The difference is, you went out alone and put yourself at risk."

"What happened, Fiona?" asked LouAnne.

"Well," she said, "before I left today I cracked open Uncle Bob's office window, 'cause it's on the ground floor. Tonight I sneaked out the back door of the house after they thought I was asleep and walked the whole way here. Took me around a half-hour. I let myself in and went through the connecting hallway to the library; then I started wandering around the Museum—"

"Which is why I saw a shadow cross the screen in this hallway," said T.J. "But there was this crazy flash of light before we heard you scream. What was that?"

"It came from that case over there," she said, pointing a quivering finger at the Clemente display. They all looked over to the case, where the Clemente mannequin stared out impassively. "I was going by and I felt like something moved in there, so I took out this flashlight I brought and...and..."

"And what?" said Bortnicker.

"It looked like there were *two* guys in there," she said, beginning to tear up. "I kinda staggered back, and there was this burst of light; then my feet got tangled and I went down. Must've hit my head on the end of this thingamabob."

Indeed, the girl had a golf ball-sized lump that was turning purple coming in above one eye.

Simmons had calmed down by now, somewhat relieved that his niece was in no great danger.

"Well, we're all glad you're okay, Fiona," he said. "Nevertheless, I'm going to run you over to the medical center to get that bump checked out and make sure there's no concussion."

Fiona was about to launch a protest when Bortnicker said, "I'll come along, if you want me to."

"You'd do that?" she whispered.

"Sure. It's past midnight, anyway, and I doubt if we're ready to resume the search tonight after all this. Right, guys?"

"Yeah," said T.J. "Enough for the first night."

"Thanks, Bortnicker," said Simmons, as they helped Fiona to her feet. "She's still a bit woozy. My car's right outside the front entrance. We'll walk her out and get her over to the med center. I'm sure she's okay, but it's a precaution. Then I'll drop you back at the inn."

"Sounds good. Let's go, nice and easy, Fiona." He helped the still-shaky girl down the hallway.

"We'll lock things up and get out of here," volunteered T.J. "Don't worry about us. See you tomorrow at breakfast."

"Okay, Big Mon," he called over his shoulder. "Night, LouAnne."

As they left, LouAnne turned to T.J. "Man, what was that kid thinking?" she asked. "We're lucky she wasn't hurt badly."

"No question. But still, I can't wait to review the DVR stuff tomorrow. It could be really cool. Something was definitely going on here, and I think we caught it. Besides, I got Clemente on the EVP recorder."

"That's fantastic!" she gushed, the most animated he'd seen her since they'd arrived.

They made their way back to the Halper Gallery, shut down the computers and turned off the lights. As they clicked the main entrance door closed T.J. said, "Jeez Louise, that got me going so much my heart's still pounding."

"Me, too," LouAnne replied. "Want to walk it off?"

"Sure."

They headed up Main and stopped at the entrance to the empty Doubleday Field parking lot. The ballpark loomed darkly in the pale moonlight. "Want to see if it's open?" said T.J.

"Yeah. Let's check it out."

They entered under the archway and walked up one of the ramps to the box seats. There was barely a breeze but the old edifice creaked and groaned. A few pigeons who had nested in the eaves of the roof cooed softly. Other than that, it was deathly silent in the deserted grandstand. Small overhead lights built into the underside of the roof provided muted light. As for natural illumination, there was little; clouds had partially obscured the full moon.

T.J. and LouAnne sat directly behind home plate about halfway up, the dim panorama of the playing field before them. Though it was quite cool they were barely touching. T.J. couldn't remember when he'd ever felt so apprehensive around a girl - any girl. He decided to make an attempt at light conversation.

"It seems like Coach P. is really getting along with Debbie McCray. I wouldn't be surprised -"

"His name is Tommy DeMarco," she broke in woodenly, staring into centerfield. "He's a junior like me, the quarterback of the football team." She took a deep breath and blew it out.

"Around town they call him 'Touchdown Tommy' or just 'T.D.' This past season he threw twenty-five touchdown passes and led our team to the state semifinals. He's being recruited by Penn State, Pitt, Michigan, and a bunch of schools I can't remember."

So this is it, thought T.J., *my worst case scenario.* With each statistic his heart sank a little more. But he bit his tongue and kept his gaze fixed on the second base bag. *Let her get it over with and give me the boot.*

"He's six-one with black, wavy hair and blue eyes, and he drives a red Mustang convertible. The girls in school melt when he walks by. Even a nod from him makes their knees buckle. All the phonies on the cheerleading squad claim to have gone out with him. His teammates idolize him. They sit around him at their own table in the cafeteria like some kind of fraternity. The JV players bring him his lunch and run errands for him, trying to gain acceptance into the varsity scene."

"I get it," said T.J. quietly.

"No, T.J., you don't get it," she replied in kind. "You don't get *anything*." From the corner of his eye he could see a tear rolling down her cheek.

"Tommy and I had very few classes together, mostly because I was on an academic college track and his coaches and advisors got him into the easiest courses to keep him eligible for sports. Of course, in the classes where he actually had to do papers and stuff, some girl would usually volunteer to write them for him. But anyway, we found ourselves in home ec together last semester, and from day one he was hitting on me. I mean, he could be kinda charming in a way, but behind it was always this sense of entitlement, like I was supposed to be so thrilled the great Touchdown Tommy DeMarco was paying attention to me.

"But I was focused on my schoolwork and track, and I didn't have time for any of his 'Big Man on Campus' nonsense. Not that I wouldn't go to a movie or something with a nice guy; I even have a few boys I consider friends at school, guys I'd rather hang out with than a lot of girls I know. It's less drama, you know? But there's no steady boyfriend, if that's what you're wondering.

"So there I was, being chased by the star quarterback, other girls either envying me or hating me or thinking I was a complete moron because I wasn't going out with him. But you know how some people are. They want the one thing they can't have, and they don't rest until they get it."

The story had started to turn, and T.J.'s mind began transitioning from blinding jealousy to something darker. He fought to keep his hands, which were resting on his knees, from shaking. As for his cousin, her fists were clenched so hard he feared her fingernails would draw blood. After an excruciating pause, she continued her tale:

"Tommy never officially asked me out. He never figured he had to. Instead he would mention that there would be a kegger at one of the guys' houses after the game, or some such gathering. But I never went to those. I heard stories. People getting really drunk and making fools of themselves, especially the girls. I just focused super hard on cross country, which is probably why I made All-County. I had a really good season, Cuz." She managed the briefest of smiles, then pursed her lips, took another breath, and forged ahead:

"One day I went to work out in our field house, where we have a small indoor track. My season was over, but I just wanted to do some stretches and get loose. If you remember, in Bermuda I got a really bad charley horse in my calf during the 5K race, so since then I try to do a lot of stretching, even on my off days. But I'd had to go to the school library first to finish up a paper, so I didn't get down to the track 'til like 4:00 PM.

"It was the first week of December. Our football team had been eliminated from the state playoffs the previous week, but because of Tommy, everybody figured we'd be a lock to win it next year. Well, a bunch of guys on the team started working out immediately for next season. We have a huge weight room that was built back when my dad was coaching, and our booster club keeps it stocked with state-of-the-art equipment. Remember, football is king in Pennsylvania. So while I was out on the track loosening up, a few of the varsity guys were clanking weights. I could tell because they have a stereo in there that they blast the whole time they're working out. Gets 'em psyched up or something. But by the time I was almost done, the room was silent. They filed out and went to the boys' locker room to change. I noticed them out the corner of my eye and didn't pay them much attention. But...I *knew* they were watching me, and whispering. And Tommy was right in the middle of it. So I stayed even a little longer than I normally would have to let them all clear out of the building.

"When I figured I'd waited long enough, I went to the girls' locker room to change and call my mom for a pickup. I was sitting on the bench in front of my locker, unlacing my sneakers, when I heard the door creak open. I looked up and there he was, still in his workout shorts and cutoff T-shirt.

"He said, 'Stayin' kind of late, aren't you?'

"'This is the girls' locker room,' I said, trying to sound brave. 'You don't belong here.'

"'And who's going to tell me to leave?' he said. 'Besides, this is a good opportunity for us to talk.'

"'I have nothing to say to you in here,' I said. 'Now get out.' He leaned up against the locker next to mine and crossed his arms over his chest like I was amusing him. Then he gave me this creepy smile. 'Why don't you like me, LouAnne?' he said. 'I'm always nice to you in class. A lot of girls would kill to have me pay this much attention to them. Or do you think you're too special to be with me?'

"'This is stupid,' I said. 'I don't think that about myself.'

"'Yeah, right,' he said. 'Everyone knows LouAnne Darcy is one of the hottest girls in the school.' Then he said, 'Hey, wait a minute. Is it the Hollywood thing? You get on a TV show and now you're too good for us common people in little old Gettysburg?'

"'It's nothing like that,' I said. But he knew he'd hit a nerve and he kept going.

"'You know what?' he said. 'I bet you're in love with that pretty boy cousin of yours from the show. What's his name? J.R.?'

"'It's T.J.' I said.

"And he said, 'Well, why would you want a T.J. when you could have T.D.?'"

She was sobbing now, and T.J. wanted so badly to hold her that he had to fight himself to stay under control and let her finish.

"What happened next is a blur, it was so fast. He picked me up off the bench and started tearing at my track shirt, and I tried to scream, but he clamped one of his big, sweaty hands over my mouth and jacked me up against the lockers..." She bowed her head and was wracked with sobs. T.J. now half-turned and looked at her, frightened to death, but hanging on every word.

After a minute, LouAnne wiped her nose with her sleeve, and T.J. had his opening.

"Cuz," he said gently, "did he -"

"No, T.J., he didn't," she said, setting her jaw. "Tommy made a big mistake, standing me up like he did."

"How come?"

"Well, you've been around my dad, and you know he was a bigtime college linebacker back in the day. I guess a small part of him always wished he had a son, but my mom couldn't have kids, which is why they adopted me. Anyway, even though Dad was awkward around girls, especially young ones like me, he never forgot would guys could be like.

So he taught me, at a very early age, *exactly* what to do if someone ever got out of line with me. He told me it was the same technique he used to coach his punters on the football team." She managed a thin smile at the memory of her father's instruction.

"And you used the technique on Touchdown Tommy?"

"Uh-huh," she sniffled. "If it was a punt it would've gone forty yards...with a lot of hang time."

It was at this moment that T.J. felt confident enough to put his arm around her and pull her close to him. But LouAnne wasn't done.

"Tommy went down like a sack of potatoes," she said, her head on his shoulder, "screaming in pain and cursing. I bolted out of that locker room, crying my head off, calling for help. I practically crawled up the stairs to the hallway and ran right into the arms of my guidance counselor, Miss Kaplan. I tried to tell her what happened, but I was so hysterical at that point that it took a while. But when she figured it out she tore down to the locker room, where Tommy was still rolling around on the floor. I'm surprised she didn't kill him, she was so mad."

"So, what happened after that?"

By this time his cousin had stopped sniffling and her voice took on a sarcastic edge. "After that? Well now, let's see. Miss Kaplan called my parents and his parents and the principal, though she stopped short of calling the police.

"As you can imagine, my dad went absolutely ballistic. This kid was laying his hands on his little girl! Mom was just plain horrified. They took me home, and a meeting was set up for early the next morning in the principal's office. Then the principal, Mr. Purcell, was going to determine what school actions should be taken, and my parents would have to decide whether to press charges and have Tommy arrested.

"So the next day, Mom and Dad drove me to school at like 6:00 AM. We went into Mr. Purcell's office. Miss Kaplan was already there, and she was still pretty upset. Mr. Purcell asked me what happened and I told him. Now, I don't think I mentioned that Mr. Purcell, before he became an administrator, and my dad were both on the faculty together at Gettysburg High until Dad retired a few years back, so he knew how crazed Dad was at the moment, and that something major had to be done to satisfy him.

"After I told my side we were asked to sit in Miss Kaplan's office while Tommy and his folks got interviewed by Mr. Purcell. Miss Kaplan sat in on that one, too."

"Did Tommy confess?"

"He didn't have much choice. But, still, he did try to say that I had an attitude around school, even hinted that I had kinda 'asked for it', but nobody was buying it. At one point, his own father even yelled at him to stop. Good thing, because Miss K. might've slapped him."

"So then the principal called the police, right?"

She sighed. "My poor, innocent T.J. Life isn't that simple, Cuz. Here's what happened. Mr. Purcell called Dad back to his office, along with Mr. DeMarco. But here's one detail I left out. Tommy's dad had played for my dad at Gettysburg High on the first team he'd ever coached. So he knew Dad pretty well. Mr. DeMarco is a sanitation worker in town, and their family kind of scrapes by. They were counting on Tommy getting a scholarship to be able to go to college. DeMarco literally begged my father not to press charges on his son, promised him the moon, started crying, the whole bit. Dad said it was embarrassing.

"What they came up with was this: Tommy would immediately transfer to a school on the other side of the state, where he had family; the incident would be more or less swept under the rug; Touchdown Tommy could play his senior season of ball; and Gettysburg High - including LouAnne Darcy - would be rid of him."

"And your father went for this?"

"He was pretty conflicted. He wanted Tommy to pay, but he didn't want this incident splashed across the local papers or dragged into court. And, being the man he is, he didn't want to ruin his former player's family. So, yeah, he went for it, but to this day he's still fighting himself over it.

"And so, all of a sudden, poof! Touchdown Tommy was gone. His parents actually ended up moving away a month or so later. I haven't seen his face since, and good riddance.

"But the tale he told his buddies on the way out about why he had to leave was nothing like the truth. And you know what happens at school when a story is told and retold. I'm now known as the self-centered temptress who single-handedly ruined the prospects for next year's football championship. Yeah, my closest friends know the real deal, but Tommy was king of the school, and I am still around to take the abuse. The TV jealousy only makes it worse. And it just doesn't stop. Stuff whispered in the halls when I walk by...hateful crap written on my locker...mean-spirited emails and texts that I get all the time -"

"Like on Monday?"

"What do you mean?"

"You were crying in your room the other day, but I wasn't brave enough to knock on your door and ask you if you were okay."

She shook her head. "No, T.J., You were *smart*. Yeah, I'd just read a nasty one, but if you'd tried to help I would have bitten your head off. Didn't Bortnicker tell you how I went off on him the first night here?"

"Actually, he didn't."

"Well, he should've. I've been a real witch."

"Are you gonna tell him, Cuz?"

"I'd rather not," she said. "It's too embarrassing to relive again. Would you do it, please? I'm sure you could put it in such a way that he'd understand without wanting to hunt Tommy down and destroy him. You're good at that."

"No problem, I'll do it. I just wish I'd been there for you."

"And what would you have done, T.J.?" she asked. "Challenge him to a fight and get your butt kicked, like that time you told me about when you stuck up for Bortnicker back in middle school? What good would that do?"

He shook his head. "Well, that explains a lot. I *knew* there was something going on at Christmas."

"You mean my lame 'flu' excuse? You saw through that?" She finally managed a smile. "I feel like I've just run a marathon, but I'm so glad I told you. The thought of telling you was really weighing on me."

"How come?"

"Because I *care* what you think about me, T.J. This disaster made me question a lot about myself...how other people perceive me...how I act. I would never want the person I care most about to think less of me."

He held her tighter. "LouAnne, that will never, *ever* happen."

They sat in silence a while longer. T.J. felt like he'd just gotten off a roller coaster. As he was trying to equalize his breathing, he scanned the park that had served as the backdrop for his cousin's story. It could have been shadows or his mind playing tricks, but he could have sworn that he saw the silhouette of John Goodleaf in the last row of the third base grandstand, still as a statue.

They left the ballpark and walked the deserted streets, his arm protectively around her shoulders. "We running tomorrow morning?" he said by her door at the Glimmerglass Inn.

"You know it," she answered. "It's time for me to get off my butt and get serious about spring track."

"Tomorrow's gonna be a big day," he said. "I can feel it."

"Well, tonight is a big night," she replied, taking his face in her hands. "My sweet, sweet T.J." She kissed him lightly on the mouth, her eyes brimming once again. "Thank you for giving me a reason to be strong." She unlocked her door and slipped inside, closing it gently behind her.

He crept into the dark room, past where his best friend snored aloud, closed himself in the bathroom, put a towel to his face and cried.

Chapter Twenty

It rained hard in Cooperstown toward dawn, but by the time T.J. awakened on Wednesday morning the sun was streaming through the windows of his room and its warmth was a welcome indication that spring was finally here. No sooner had he sat up and stretched when there came the tap-tap-tap of his cousin on the hotel room door. "Let's go, sleepyhead," she whispered.

"Coming!" he called back, while Bortnicker still snored away in the other bed. As he dressed, T.J. harkened back to the previous night at Doubleday Field when LouAnne had bared her soul to him. He hoped that this moment would offer a new beginning for her, and perhaps a deepening of their relationship.

As they descended the stairs to the lobby together, it was clear that his cousin had more spring in her step. It was as if she couldn't wait to hit the pavement. During their pre-stretch on the sidewalk she said, "Hey, how about going in the other direction today, towards the Farmer's Museum. Is it too far?"

"I don't think so; what we have to do is go up Lake Street past the Otesaga Hotel, then follow Route 80 along the lake. Should be scenic."

"Scenic schmeenik," she said, slipping into a hamstring stretch, "I need a workout."

He smiled. The old LouAnne was back.

Once they took off, it was like the previous summer in Bermuda during their ill-fated 5K race. LouAnne was obviously the superior runner, and with her renewed sense of purpose T.J. had to labor to keep up. But he was never so happy to have his butt kicked by a girl. They blew past the Otesaga and turned right on 80, past the hotel's meticulously manicured golf course and then the wooded banks of Lake Otsego. Not long afterwards, the museum came into view - a collection of farm houses which stored exhibits, a church, and a schoolhouse all moved to the site from other places. Split rail fences similar to those in Gettysburg served as barriers for assorted livestock. Towards the rear of the compound, the squawking of chickens and roosters could be heard. It was at once pastoral and calming, a window into the Cooperstown of the early 1800s. But, as LouAnne had made clear, she wasn't in it for the scenery. Once they reached the site, she effected an abrupt U-turn and took off back to town with T.J. struggling valiantly to keep pace. By the time they got to Pioneer Street, he was dragging. Their post stretch on the sidewalk provided blessed relief. Nothing about the previous night had been mentioned during their run. There was no need.

T.J. let the hot shower pound on him a little longer as he anticipated another breakfast adventure from his best friend. He was also excited to review the previous night's tapes from the Museum, feeling they would point the way for a momentous second investigation. Now that his cousin's drama had crested, the three ghost hunters could buckle down and solve what was becoming an intriguing case.

* * * *

Bortnicker, who was whistling away as he poured batter into Clara's aged waffle iron, almost jumped when LouAnne sneaked up behind him and gripped him in a bear hug. "Which Beatles song involves people eating bacon?" she whispered in his ear.

"Why, 'Piggies' of course," he replied in his nasally best John Lennon voice. "Although it was actually me mate George's song. Am I to understand from this that you're somewhat hungry, dear girl?"

"Starving," she said.

"Give me a couple minutes," he asked, returning to his normal Bortnicker voice. "As you can see, our blueberry waffles - with fresh blueberries Clara got from the local farmers market, I might add - will be done shortly. Pour yourself some OJ in the meantime."

T.J. entered the kitchen and came upon this harmonious scene, which made him glad. He'd tell Bortnicker later about his talk with

LouAnne. "How did things go at the hospital last night?" he asked.

"Not great," said Bortnicker, stirring another batch of batter. "Fiona was embarrassed over what had happened. She kept telling her uncle she was fine and asking to go home. A lady doctor came in and checked her eyes and a bunch of other concussion stuff, but it all came up negative. In the end, the kid was lucky to come away with just a bump on her noggin."

"Well, you were sweet to stay there with her," said LouAnne.

"Yeah, I think her uncle appreciated it. She was pretty nice to me, anyway. She'll probably show up sometime this morning to give us a hand."

Shortly thereafter, Coach Pisseri bounded into the room, smiling broadly. The movie date with Debbie had obviously gone well, and as the group settled into their seats around the dining room table, positive vibes abounded.

"We've got traditional maple syrup and blueberry syrup for your waffles," sang Clara Frank. "I must say, I'm thinking about hiring our Mr. Bortnicker as a full-time chef."

"It was no big effort," the blushing boy said, waving her off.

"Nonsense, young man. You have a talent!"

"Hear, hear," said Pisseri, raising his coffee cup.

As Clara left to join her husband for some in-town shopping, the coach related some much anticipated details about his date.

"The movie wasn't bad," he said. "A little dark, but okay. Afterwards we went out for ice cream in Oneonta. Bortnicker, you would've loved this place. It was kind of an 1800s old-fashioned ice cream parlor deal, with fountain service and everything."

"What did you have, Coach?" said Bortnicker, drizzling his waffles with blueberry syrup.

"Classic banana split," he replied. "I went with vanilla, chocolate and mint chocolate chip as my three scoops, with crushed nuts, hot fudge and whipped cream on top - and a cherry, of course!"

"Sounds like you'll have some working off to do today," quipped T.J.

"You got that right. I think I'll run a few laps before our pre-practice stretch. But what about you guys? Any breakthroughs?"

"Bigtime, Coach. We still have to review the tapes, but it looks like Roberto Clemente was with us, in some shape or form." He related the events surrounding Fiona's extraordinary experience near the Clemente display case. LouAnne followed with the weird goings-on in the Plaque Gallery.

"Wow," Pisseri said, pouring himself another cup of coffee. "Imagine the spirits of all those baseball immortals swirling around in there. Think you caught any on video or audio?"

"We'll find out," said Bortnicker through a mouthful of waffles.

"Uh-huh. And are you guys okay with me taking Debbie out to dinner tonight?"

"Sure, Coach," said T.J. "Don't feel that you have to keep an eye on us. It's kinda hard to get into trouble in this town."

"I know what you mean," he replied. "Not much going on here after 9 PM."

T.J. looked at his watch. "Right. Well, we've got about a half-hour till we're supposed to be at the Hall. Bortnicker, I'll help you clean up here." He gave his cousin a secret nod, implying that he wanted to be alone with his buddy.

LouAnne winked in response. "I'll be freshening up in my room," she said. "Just give me a yell when you're ready. Breakfast was fabulous, Bortnicker."

"Thank you, my dear," he replied, sopping up the last of his syrup with a forkful of waffle.

Once they'd cleaned up and brought the dishes to the sink, Bortnicker said, "Boy, your cousin's in a good mood today. Hugs, compliments, the whole deal. You notice that?"

"Yeah," said T.J. "That's what I have to talk to you about." Slowly, carefully, he recounted LouAnne's harrowing tale, rounding off the hard edges a bit; nevertheless, he could see his friend's mouth opening slowly in shock and a film grow over his eyes behind the Coke bottle glasses.

"The poor kid," he said finally. "That Tommy guy sounds like a real creep." He shook his head sadly. "Think she's really over it, Big Mon?"

"Well, last night was a start," T.J. replied, "but you gotta figure something like this is going to take time. I don't see how what happened to her doesn't change her in some way."

"Good thing she has you."

"No, good thing she has *us*."

* * * *

When they arrived at the Hall of Fame, Dan Vines was there to let them in. "The fantasy campers are due shortly," he said, "but the Halper Gallery is open and ready for you. Bob phoned me about some strange goings-on last night?"

"Yeah, Mr. Vines, it did get interesting," said Bortnicker nonchalantly. "Hopefully, we're on to something."

The trio of teens settled in to their folding chairs at the computer table. "Are we filming ourselves while we do the review?" asked T.J. "For the TV show, you know."

"Good point," said Bortnicker. "Give me a minute to set up a couple camcorders on tripods." In a short time they were mounted, focused in and ready to run. "Remember what Mike told us in Bermuda," he said. "It's okay to overplay it a bit when we catch something."

"Something tells me we won't have to exaggerate," said LouAnne.

"You're probably right, Cuz," agreed T.J. "Okay then, let's get after it."

"Why don't we start by giving a listen to all our EVP recordings?" asked Bortnicker. "I have headphones here that we can plug into the computer; we'll run each person's EVP tape through it. Sound good?"

They were just about to put on the 'phones when there was a gentle knocking at the door. They looked up as it cracked open and Fiona's head appeared, a white gauze bandage hiding the lump over her right eye. It seemed to have receded a bit from the night before. "Can I come in?" she asked tentatively, quite a change from her bravado of the previous morning. "The Museum's closed except for a bunch of old guys walking around in a big group. Uncle Bob had to let me in himself."

"You're just in time," said Bortnicker, waving her over. "And we've got something for you," he added, shooting his friends a wink. From under the table he pulled out a spare *Junior Gonzo Ghost Chasers* T-shirt and tossed it to her. "That should fit," he said.

"Really? For me to keep?" she asked.

"Yeah. We figured since you gave up your body for the cause, you deserve one. Put it on!"

She pulled the black shirt over her Abercrombie thermal and looked to the teens for approval.

"Looks great," said LouAnne. "Now let's get to work."

"Uh, before we do," said Fiona haltingly, "I'd just like to say I'm, uh, sorry about last night. Hope I didn't mess up the investigation too bad."

"Nah, we're okay," assured T.J. "We're just about to start listening to the EVP tapes."

As he spoke, Bortnicker was plugging in a fourth set of headphones. "All right," he began. "Let's start with my stuff, because I was on the floor for the shortest time." They all concentrated hard as they listened to the replay of Bortnicker's questions to Clemente at the display case and Viva Baseball! area. After a half-hour the tape ran out.

"Nothing," said T.J., removing his headphones.

"Agreed," responded Bortnicker. "Now let's play LouAnne's stuff from the Plaque Gallery."

It wasn't long before all their eyes started to widen. "I hear jumbled voices," said Fiona. "Like they're whispering to each other. And not necessarily all in English. Might've been some Spanish in there, too."

"That's what I thought I was hearing," confirmed LouAnne. "The question is, who was it?"

"You said something about the year 1946 being a little noisy," offered Bortnicker. "Well, last night when I got back to my room I did a little research. LouAnne, I think you might've made contact with a long-lost neighbor."

"Really? Who?"

"Eddie Plank. Also known as 'Gettysburg Eddie'. He was a lefty pitcher in the early 1900s who went straight to the pros, namely the Philadelphia A's, from Gettysburg College. Won over three-hundred games. Old Eddie was born and died in Gettysburg."

"You think he was trying to talk to me?"

"Could've been. Or maybe talking *about* you to his friends."

"Creepy," said Fiona.

"Unfortunately," said T.J., "we can't make out any specific conversation. The only word I think I heard a few times was 'moment'."

"Me, too," said LouAnne.

"Wait a minute," said Bortnicker. "Could it be *momen* you were hearing?"

"What makes you say that?" asked T.J.

"Only the fact that 'Momen' was Clemente's nickname when he was coming up. As the story goes, when Clemente was a kid he couldn't be rushed into a response without thinking through his answer. So, he would say '*momentito*' while he collected his thoughts. After a while, his friends and family shortened it to 'Momen' and used it as his nickname. He even had it inscribed on some of his early Louisville Slugger bats."

"So, maybe the others were talking *to* him?" asked Fiona.

"Who knows? Could be that Clemente's just a popular guy."

Of course, it was T.J.'s EVP that was the star of the audio show. Clemente's responses, in his faint high-pitched voice, were fairly clear, albeit in Spanish.

"Hey," said Fiona, catching on, "isn't this the guy whose body double is in the case that blew up on me last night?"

The teens looked at each other, uncertain of how much to disclose.

But Fiona was no dummy. "You're here about *him*, aren't you?" she said finally. "This is about Roberto Clemente. Why didn't you tell me?" She seemed genuinely hurt.

"It's not that we didn't want to," said T.J. reassuringly.

"Actually," continued Bortnicker, "your uncle requested that this be kept under wraps. We figured if he didn't let you in on it, we shouldn't, either."

She chewed on her lower lip for a second. "I guess I understand," she relented. "But I still want to know why his ghost or whatever showed up in that case, and what caused that flash of light."

"Tell you what," said T.J. "We've been at this a while, and this folding chair is killing me. Why don't we break for lunch, then come back and focus on the videotape?"

"Sounds good," said LouAnne. "Why don't we try the Main Street Diner up the street? I'm almost starving, even after all those waffles this morning."

"The diner it is," decided Bortnicker. He turned to Fiona. "Want to come along?"

"I can't," she said dejectedly. "Uncle Bob and Aunt Mildred are taking me on a picnic down at the lake, like I'm five years old or something. But I'll be back with the afternoon, for sure. I'd like to see the video of exactly what happened to me last night."

"So would we," said Bortnicker.

* * * *

As usual, the charmingly tiny Main Street Diner was practically full, with only a few stools at the counter available. Luckily, three of them were together, so T.J., Bortnicker and LouAnne seated themselves. As the matronly counter waitress slid menus to the teens, she paused and regarded them somewhat warily. "I've seen you three before," she said in a not-unfriendly tone. "You been on TV or something?"

Remembering Bortnicker's spouting off in a local Bermudian café in their last expedition - which led to a myriad of problems - T.J. smoothly replied, "Yes ma'am. Actually, we're here at the Hall of Fame to do a little investigating for a paranormal show."

"I thought I recognized you all, especially this one over here," she said, pointing to Bortnicker, who blushed.

"Well, he has a memorable face," joked LouAnne.

"Wasn't it some kind of pirate thing you were into?"

"You're right again," said T.J. "In Bermuda."

"Now I remember," she said. "You're the *Junior Gonzo Ghost Chasers*, right? You work with that cute Mike Weinstein. I wouldn't mind him investigating *me*."

T.J. chuckled. "Yes, that's us."

The woman, who seemed old enough to be their grandmother, leaned across the counter until she was almost nose-to-nose with T.J. and whispered, "Have you found anything? Because you know we've had other teams up here in the past year or so. Seems like hunting ghosts is quite the fashion nowadays. In fact, one of those groups came in one morning for breakfast. Acted like big shots, like they owned the place. I don't think they found anything," she said with a sniff.

"Well, ma'am," said LouAnne charmingly, "we're not like that at all. In fact we *love* your town. Hopefully, we'll have more success than they did."

"What's recommended on the menu?" asked Bortnicker, deftly changing the subject.

"Today's special is the open turkey sandwich with a side of mashed potatoes and peas. It's really good."

T.J. looked at his friends, who gave approving nods. "Make it three," he said pleasantly.

* * * *

After settling the bill the teens crossed the street, where again they detected the faint aroma of cinnamon buns from the corner bakery. "That tears it," declared Bortnicker. "Let's drop in for dessert. It's on me."

They entered the old-fashioned establishment and were assaulted by heavenly smells. Had they not just finished a substantial lunch, there would have been a major assault on the various pastries, cupcakes and buns neatly arranged behind glass counter cases. But normal rules did not apply to Bortnicker. "I smelled your cinnamon buns from down the street," he rhapsodized to the stout woman with huge forearms behind the counter. "Please tell me you have some left."

"Why, yes, young man," she replied, pointing to the case below her chin. "Would you like yours with or without nuts?"

"I'll take two of each and share them with my friends," he said, rubbing his hands together in anticipation. Carefully the woman removed the generously-sized buns with plastic tongs and placed them in a small white box. "No need to tie it shut," said Bortnicker, handing over some greenbacks. "We're going to enjoy them right now!"

They strolled down Main, wolfing their cinnamon buns while repeatedly licking their fingers of white icing. "A return trip is in order before we leave this town," said Bortnicker, popping a large chunk of "with nut" into his mouth.

"Totally unhealthy, but sooo good," agreed LouAnne, who had finally seen her appetite restored.

They were just finishing their dessert when they came upon the entrance to Doubleday Field. "Let's stop in," suggested T.J. "See if Chief is here."

Sure enough, as they approached the field entrance a lone figure could be spied atop the pitcher's mound, his arms outstretched, face turned toward the sky.

"That's him?" asked LouAnne.

"Yup," said T.J. "First time he hasn't sneaked up on me."

"What's he doing?" asked Bortnicker. "Meditating or something?"

"Let's find out."

They approached cautiously. Indeed, John Goodleaf seemed to be in some kind of trance. His eyes were closed and his lips were moving silently. Bortnicker and LouAnne, who was laying eyes on Goodleaf for the first time, looked to their leader to make contact.

After an audible clearing of his throat didn't work, T.J. said, in his most respectful tone, "Excuse me? Chief? Is it okay for us to talk to you? I hope we're not interrupting something important, and if you want us to come back later -"

The man slowly lowered his arms, then bowed his head for a moment. When he raised it again his eyes bore into the boy. In a faraway voice he said, "He comes tonight, as in a dream."

Bortnicker began to say, "Who -" but T.J. placed his hand on his friend's chest to stop him.

"I understand, Chief," he said earnestly. "C'mon, guys." He led his friends from the pitcher's mound toward the field entrance.

"What was *that* about?" asked Bortnicker, looking back over his shoulder.

"Yeah, Cuz," said LouAnne. "Was he talking about Clemente? Your friend Chief seems a little out there, don't you think?"

"He may be out there," replied T.J., "but I think he's right. Tonight we're going to meet Roberto Clemente, guys. Let's get back to the Hall."

* * * *

They entered the Museum and wound their way through the crowd to the Halper Gallery. When they slipped inside they found Fiona, seated at the computer, ready to go. "How was your picnic at the lake?" asked T.J., pulling up a chair.

"Not bad," she replied with a shrug. "We had chicken salad sandwiches, and Aunt Mildred baked special chocolate chip cookies. I fed my sandwich crusts to the ducks. To tell the truth, I couldn't wait to get back to work."

"That's what I want to hear," said Bortnicker, fiddling with some wires. "What I'm trying to do here is patch the DVR video from last night into one terminal, and our handheld camcorder tapes into the other one. Fiona, you and I will watch the DVR footage. But I warn you, it gets a little boring at times and you'll find yourself spacing out if you don't take care. T.J., you and LouAnne check out the camcorder stuff. Stop the tape if you see something and we'll all take a look."

He set the tripod camcorders on RECORD and returned to his seat alongside Fiona at the DVR station.

At first, all four of the examiners squinted hard at their respective terminals, intermittently asking their partners to stop the tape and rewind it for a slow-motion viewing. As their eyes became acclimated to the dark screens, they became more adept at discerning possible shadow figures from random shadows cast by themselves, or floating dust motes and the like.

Their first hit came, predictably, on LouAnne's camcorder tape. Granted, she was filming in a room with ambient light from a glass ceiling, but under close inspection it seemed like shadows were zipping all over the place, as well as anomalies too defined to be classified as motes. And the activity seemed to pick up more when she spoke out and tried to make contact. LouAnne and T.J. called Bortnicker over to check them out, then marked every such occurrence on the video for future reference. Conversely, T.J.'s video was not the bonanza of his earlier audiotapes. Even when he made intelligent contact with Clemente, the area surrounding him remained blandly indistinct.

The star of the show, of course, was the DVR of Fiona's accident. After she and Bortnicker viewed it the first time - emitting gasps of wonder - they called T.J. and LouAnne over. "You've gotta see this, Big Mon," Bortnicker said, rewinding. They crowded around the terminal. This section of tape, no more than twenty seconds in length, began with Fiona entering from the rear and walking toward the camera, which was angled toward the Clemente case. She was not quite past the camera when she stopped and looked back over her right shoulder. And though the angle was not straight on to the case so as to avoid reflection, it was clear to see that some kind of activity was going on behind the mannequin, a liquid-like black mass that started to take shape and then burst forth like a thousand flashbulbs. Fiona could be seen tumbling backwards out of the picture, her right arm flailing behind her.

"Wow!" cried LouAnne. "Play it again!"

They must have watched it ten more times, and each time their reaction was the same.

"See, guys?" said Fiona. "I didn't make it up...I really saw something!"

"I'll say," agreed Bortnicker. "Looks like you're a part of the granddaddy of all ghost videos, my dear." He offered her a high-five, which she enthusiastically returned.

"Well, team," said T.J., "we could stop right here and we'd probably have enough to carry a show, between this and my audio. But this just makes me want more."

"No question," said Bortnicker. "I'm totally psyched for investigation number two, tonight."

"But, Fiona," said T.J. gently, "you've really gotta do the smart thing tonight and stay home. We can't take any more chances."

"I get you," she said. "Anyway, my aunt and uncle are probably going to have me under video surveillance, on total lockdown. I wouldn't be able to sneak out again if I tried. The other thing is...and I hate to admit it, but...I was really scared last night. And now that I've seen the tape, I think I'll pass on investigating live and leave it to you guys. But can I come back tomorrow morning for the tape review, like today?"

"Of course," said LouAnne. You're one of us now."

"We might even sneak you into the credits," said Bortnicker.

"Cool!" She literally skipped out of the room, but not without a gentle shoulder rub for her hero.

Choosing to avoid the opportunity to rag on his friend, T.J. said, "Okay, then. We'll label these tapes and pack them up, then take a break before dinner. Remember, Coach P. won't be with us tonight. What's everyone feeling like eating?"

"There's a pizzeria on Main Street we haven't hit yet," suggested LouAnne.

"Sounds good. But no anchovies this time, Bortnicker," he cautioned, remembering his buddy's favorite topping that he sometimes ordered just to be annoying.

* * * *

T.J. was just coming out of the bathroom when Bortnicker sang out, "I've got Ronnie coming in on Skype! Go get your cousin!" He sprinted across the hall and knocked on her door.

"Can't a girl take a nap around here?" she called in mock anger.

"Cuz, Bortnicker's got Ronnie on Skype from Bermuda," he answered. "Want to say hi?"

"Be there in a sec."

Soon the three teens were huddled around Bortnicker's laptop as the image of their Afro-Bermudian friend who had been so instrumental in their previous case came onto the screen. As always, Ronnie Goodwin's corkscrew curls shot out in all directions, framing her smooth mocha skin and blue eyes.

"Wow," she said in her Bermudian lilt, "it's the Three Musketeers, all together. What's the occasion, guys?"

"We're on an investigation in upstate New York," said T.J. "How are things in sunny Bermuda?"

"Still a bit of chill in the air," she said. "The water's starting to warm up, though."

"Are you at home?" asked LouAnne.

"No, I'm here at the dive shop. It's not even the high season yet, guys, but business is booming. Once Dad made the announcement last July after you'd left that we'd discovered the *Steadfast*, our dive business was in all the papers, as we had expected. It even made CNN. Then the TV special became a 'must watch' on the island. It opened the floodgates, so to speak, for wreck diving on the island. We were booked solid for the rest of the summer and the fall, and now it's picking up all over again. My dad can't thank you enough."

"Hey, Ronnie, remember that it was your father who found the ship first. We just stumbled on its bell by luck," said Bortnicker.

"Nonsense. All of you put in a lot of work to make the investigation a success. By the way, have you ever heard from that crusty old Mrs. Tilbury?" she inquired, referring to the head of the Bermuda National Heritage Trust, who was against the idea of their island investigation from the start and had been a thorn in their side for virtually their entire stay, despite the astounding findings they'd made regarding their subject, Sir William Tarver.

"Yeah," said T.J. "We received a letter of 'thanks' from her through The Adventure Channel which was read at the premiere party in New York City last fall. Of course, she didn't mention that she'd confiscated the only clear audiotape of any ghost ever recorded."

"Or that we were basically kicked off the island," added LouAnne.

"That's our Mrs. Tilbury for you," said Ronnie with more than a trace of sarcasm. "Pleasant to a fault. But anyway, when are you all going to come visit us again? My parents and Dora, the restaurant lady, are always asking about you. And Bortnicker, Mr. Chapford wants to know if John Lennon's been whispering in your ear anymore since you left."

Indeed, Bortnicker had been convinced, along with their middle-aged Bermudian driver, Nigel "Chappy" Chapford, that the deceased Beatle - a personal acquaintance of Chapford - had been speaking to him directly during their visit.

"Sorry, Ronnie, old John hasn't had any messages for me since we left. I guess I have to be on your magical island for everything to click into place."

"Too bad. So what's your current investigation about?" asked the Bermudian beauty.

All three Americans volunteered information on their current expedition with great excitement, while explaining the significance of Roberto Clemente and Cooperstown in American sporting history.

"And you think things are going to pop tonight?" she said finally.

"We hope so," replied T.J.

"I'll fill you in if something happens," promised Bortnicker.

"You'd better. And tell me, LouAnne, is our culinary expert having to fight off the ladies now with his newfound fame?"

"You have no idea, Ronnie," she replied with a smile. "Why, there's even one up here in the mountains who's taken quite a shine to him."

"Aw, c'mon," the boy said, reddening.

"My word. And does this girl have a name?"

"It's...*Fiona*," said T.J. dramatically.

151

"*Really?* Well, I shouldn't wonder, with his good looks and cooking skill. Keep an eye on him for me, will you?"

"No problem," answered LouAnne. "We're on it."

"Well, all right then. Listen, guys, a bunch of tourists just came in. I have to be off. It was great talking to you. Ta-ta."

As they switched off Bortnicker said, "Didja have to mention Fiona? Really?"

"I think it was a great move," retorted LouAnne primly. "Letting the girl think she's got a little competition can't be a bad thing."

Bortnicker brightened, flashing his crooked smile. "You know, you might be right," he said. "How can I ever repay you guys?"

"Simple," said T.J. "No anchovies on the pizza tonight."

"Done."

Chapter Twenty-One

After a couple hours to rest up, the trio found themselves at a back table in Luigi's Pizzeria, a small eatery that catered mostly to the takeout trade. Predictably, the boys found it wanting in comparison to their beloved Pizza Palace in Fairfield. But that didn't stop them - with LouAnne's assistance - from polishing off an entire large cheese pie (no anchovies) and a pitcher of Coke. It seemed like the town's tourist population was growing more each day of this Spring Break week, probably because of the forecast of fair weather for its duration. They had to wait a bit for the table, but once there they took their time and chatted about Ronnie's Skype and the upcoming investigation, which they were confident would be epic.

This time when Dan Vines let them in he was grudgingly respectful, actually wishing them luck and reminding them to be careful. Of course, he also reminded them to make sure they locked the door correctly on the way out.

"Okay," said T.J. once they were inside the command center. "Should we change our plan of attack at all from last night?"

"I'd say no," volunteered Bortnicker. "We should set up the four DVRs exactly where they were last time. We had success with it, didn't we?"

"I agree," said LouAnne. "Only tonight, let me lead off at the computer. I haven't had my turn yet."

"All right, then. Everyone grab a DVR and a tripod and let's go set them up."

When all four stations were operable and focused in, the teens came together in the command center and put their hands in. "Remember, guys," said T.J., "'He comes tonight, as in a dream.' I hope Chief is right. One, two, three -"

"Gonzos Rule!"

As Bortnicker headed upstairs to the Clemente case, T.J. went towards the Plaque Gallery, stopping to switch off all the lights in the museum. He hoped to experience the crazy phenomena his cousin had seen and heard the previous night. Pointing his infrared camcorder, he slowly scanned the entire room for darting shadows. He tried a few EVPs as well, but wasn't encouraged with the results. After a half hour or so he moved upstairs to the Viva Baseball! exhibit.

At the Clemente case, Bortnicker was getting just as frustrated. He got up close and examined every inch of it with his camcorder, and then for hot or cold spots with a digital thermometer, but no luck. The two boys actually ended up running into each other in the Sacred Ground exhibit.

"Anything?" asked T.J.

"Nada, Big Mon. I think Chief was off the mark on this one."

"Don't give up on it just yet. I still think something's gonna happen."

Shortly thereafter their walkie-talkies crackled. "Hey, guys," said LouAnne. "Maybe I'm just going cross-eyed looking at this screen, but there seems to be something going on in the Plaque Gallery. A shadow, I think."

"I just came from there, Cuz," said T.J., "but what the heck. Give me a minute to go back down."

"I'll come with you," said Bortnicker.

The boys descended the main staircase to the ground floor, cut through the lobby, and entered the Plaque Gallery. And although it was very dark, they could discern a faint silhouette at the other end.

"Uh-oh," said Bortnicker quietly, "that's right near the class of '73." They approached stealthily, holding their breath. "It's getting colder, Big Mon," whispered Bortnicker. "Can't you feel it?"

T.J. nodded. He deftly pulled out his digital thermometer to gauge the temperature drop in the room. It was stone dead. He gently shook Bortnicker's arm. "See if your EVP recorder works," he whispered.

"It's out."

T.J. then tried his camcorder. "No juice. If this is him, he's killed every device we have on us by manifesting. Wonder if LouAnne's still getting the video feed from here?"

"No way to know. Walkie-talkie's fried, too."

"Want to keep going?"

"No question."

They continued to creep along, covering some thirty yards of tiled floor, until they were only ten or so feet from the figure. It was a man, perhaps six feet tall, with his back to them, facing the wall of plaques under the sign that read '1973'. If he was wearing clothes, it was no more than a polo shirt, trousers and shoes - no baseball uniform or hat. The boys looked at each other and Bortnicker nodded to his friend.

"Mr. Clemente?" asked T.J., his voice wavering slightly.

The man turned slowly, a faint shaft of ambient light illuminating one side of his face, which was itself as dark as the night. He was a handsome man, with high cheekbones, close cropped hair and piercing eyes, which he now trained on the boys, his head cocked slightly to one side. Then he said, "*Sí, yo soy Clemente. ¿Son ustedes que me buscan?*"

"What's he saying?" whispered T.J. sideways.

"Yes, I am Clemente. Are you the ones who seek me?" translated Bortnicker.

"Ask him if we can speak in English."

"*Señor* Clemente," said the boy in halting Spanish, "*sería posible conversar en inglés?*"

Clemente gave a wry smile, then chuckled softly. "Ah, yes, my English. Forgive me, but it was a sore spot for much of my life."

Just then LouAnne appeared at the far end of the gallery. "Hey, guys," she panted, "I tried to get you on the walkie-talkie, but it's like everything cut out at once-the computers, too. I was starting to freak out—"

"Cuz," said T.J. softly, "come this way. I'd like you to meet someone."

She approached cautiously, then gasped at the apparition, which seemed to be about 90% solid, the remainder going in and out.

"Good evening, *señorita*," he said with a slight courtly nod. "I am

Roberto Clemente. And what is your name, please?"

"L-LouAnne Darcy," she replied.

"And you boys?"

"Mr. Clemente, I'm T.J. Jackson, and this is my best friend, Bortnicker."

Clemente looked at Bortnicker, it seemed, for a few extra seconds before saying, "Your Spanish is not great, *amigo*, but I appreciate the attempt. As I was saying before the *señorita* arrived, my English was always a problem while I was in the States."

"How so?" asked T.J., his heart rate finally stabilizing.

"Well, before I answer that, I must ask you how you know who I am, and why you have found me in this place."

"You are Roberto Clemente," said T.J. "Hall of Fame right fielder for the Pittsburgh Pirates. And we know this because we've taken the time to learn your life story."

"I'm honored," he said with another slight nod. "Now, with the language. Let me tell you something, *amigos*. I am from a poor area of Puerto Rico where no one spoke English. So when I came here in 1954 to play baseball in the minor leagues, I could barely understand people or have people understand me. I learned to say a few words, like 'ham and eggs', which I would eat three times a day. I also went to the movies a lot and watched American TV shows, mostly cowboy stories, to learn the language. But my whole career, no matter how much I tried, some sportswriters made fun of me, making me sound stupid in their newspapers."

Bortnicker, seeing that the ballplayer was becoming agitated at the memory of these insults, tried to change the subject. "Mr. Clemente," he said, "we'd like to learn more about you than what's here on the plaque. Would you tell us more about your life?"

"To what end?" he replied cautiously.

"So we can…help you return to where you came from," said T.J. "I mean, you don't want to be stuck in Cooperstown forever, do you?"

"No," he agreed. "This is a wonderful place, but my plaque - and that *thing* upstairs - is enough of me to have here."

"You mean the mannequin?" asked LouAnne.

"Yes," he said with a frown.

Roberto's Return

"I've got an idea," said T.J. "If it's okay with you, would you like to walk around the Museum with us to other places where we can see objects from your career? Are you able to do that?"

"I believe so," he replied. "Lead the way, *amigo*."

* * * *

As the group made its way to the Viva Baseball! exhibit, the teens could not help but watch Clemente as he moved among them. Once a graceful athlete in real life, he now seemed to almost glide over the floor, his casual shoes making no sound at all on the tiles. Also, he never became totally solid, which could be a bit distracting at times. But outside of the obvious fascination with their connection to an ethereal being, there was no fear in the young people, as there had been with both Major Hilliard in Gettysburg and Captain Tarver in Bermuda. Clemente seemed to have a quiet dignity which both put them at ease and held them in awe.

When they reached the exhibit, he stared for a few moments at the large map which identified the origins of major Latino players, including himself. He seemed to take a deep breath, perhaps replaying his early memories.

"My father's name was Melchor," he said. "My mother, Luisa, had been married once before but had lost her husband. Are you aware that in my homeland, slavery was not abolished until the late 1800s, only a few years before my father was born? He worked hard, my father, earning a dollar a week cutting sugarcane in the blazing sun. To make ends meet for their seven children, my mother sold groceries out of our crowded house. She was a strong woman, *amigos*. Do you know she could butcher an entire cow by herself?"

"Maybe that's where you got your throwing arm from," offered LouAnne.

He smiled. "Of that there is no doubt, *señorita*. Nobody ran on the arm of Clemente."

"When did you first become interested in baseball?" asked T.J.

"As young boys with little money, my friends and I used whatever we could as equipment. A rubber ball or tennis ball wrapped with tape, even a tin can, would do. If we could find a broomstick we would be

157

ready to have a game, or at least batting practice. My older brother, Matinoa, who was a good ballplayer, gave me tips, but I learned a lot on my own. You see, I was a shy child, but in baseball I could express myself." Clemente reached out and seemed to gently touch the island of Puerto Rico on the map.

"Did you have any ballplayers you looked up to as a child?" asked Bortnicker.

"Well, there were two ballplayers I tried to emulate. Have you ever heard of Hiram Bithorn?"

The teens shook their heads.

"A shame. Hiram Bithorn was the first Puerto Rican to play in the Major Leagues. He was signed by the Chicago Cubs, which was only possible because he had white skin. This was in the 1940s, before Jackie Robinson broke in. Unfortunately, Bithorn was called to serve in the military during the Second War, and when he came out he wasn't the same player. But he was still a hero to Puerto Ricans, and I tried to emulate his basket catch. People think I copied it from Willie Mays, but it was my countryman, Hiram Bithorn."

"I play outfield, Mr. Clemente," volunteered T.J.

"Do you? Are you good at getting rid of the ball quickly after a catch?"

"I could be better," the boy confessed. "I don't have the strongest arm, so I need to do the transfer faster."

"Hmmm," said Clemente. "Maybe I shall teach you the basket catch."

The teens gave each other a look, wondering if the ghost had a true grasp on his situation here.

"Of course," Clemente continued, "there was another player whom I idolized, who you've probably heard about. Monte Irvin."

"New York Giants outfielder, Hall of Famer," said Bortnicker.

"Yes, *amigo*. The great Monte Irvin, a man of color, played winter ball in my country for the San Juan Senadores, near where I lived. The Senadores played at Sixto Escobar Stadium in Old San Juan. I would show up early at the game and wait for him to arrive. Once he got to recognize me, he would hand me his suit bag so I could walk into the park with him for free. I felt so important! He was another player I patterned myself after."

"I think his jersey is on display here, Mr. Clemente," said LouAnne. "Should we go see it?"

"Why not? I will follow you, *señorita*."

As they proceeded to the 1950s section T.J. asked, "So, how did you get discovered, Mr. Clemente?"

"I was signed to my first contract at fifteen years of age," he said. "The Brooklyn Dodgers held an open tryout at Escobar. Word had spread about my play in the youth leagues, and people had been telling me to try out, so I did. A scout for Brooklyn liked what he saw, so the next thing I knew they were putting a contract in front of my father. It was only $15,000, but to us it was a fortune. Of course, it meant that I would have to leave my homeland with little more than clothes on my back, and no idea of the English language. But I was determined to make my family proud.

"When I was signed the Dodgers were loaded with talent, and they had more black players than any team, so that should not have been a problem. But it was hard to make the team, they were so good. So I was sent to their top farm club, the Royals of Montréal, in Canada."

"That must've been some change for you," said T.J.

"In every way. I did not understand English *or* French, and I was not used to the cold of the early season. And I missed the food of Puerto Rico. Even something as simple as rice and beans, I could not find it. As I said, I learned how to say 'ham and eggs' and I ate that until I was sick of it. But at least in Montréal there was some acceptance of blacks. In the U.S. there was little."

They had reached a display case which housed Irvin's Giants home white jersey, with its black and orange letters and piping. "A great player," Clemente said, "but even the great Monte Irvin had to waste years of his career in the Negro Leagues because of others' ignorance."

They started walking again, and T.J. noticed that Clemente carried himself with a quiet grace that seemed to permeate everything he did. He found himself trying to emulate his gait.

"How did you end up in Pittsburgh?" asked Bortnicker.

"A funny thing. Mr. Rickey, who signed Jackie Robinson and all the black players for the Dodgers, he tried to hide me in Montréal until

Brooklyn had a need for me. But word got out that the Dodgers had a good young prospect up in Canada. Then, the Dodgers let Rickey go, and he went to run the Pirates. Of course, he remembered me, so he drafted me off the Royals. This was good and bad. I was happy to get a chance to play in the Majors, but I would be going from a top organization in Brooklyn to one of the worst in Pittsburgh.

"There were problems from the start. First, I had gotten in a car accident in Puerto Rico during the off-season in 1954 and wrenched my neck. It affected how I batted, how I threw, everything. I was always trying to get it loose, like when I came up to bat. Some sportswriters made fun of my mannerisms. And Rickey himself was not pleased with certain parts of my game, like how I ran. Thought it wasn't smooth enough. He was a hard man to please.

"Then there was Fort Myers in Florida, where the Pirates had Spring Training. It was totally segregated. I could not stay in camp with the team; instead, I had to room with a Negro family in the black section of town. But you see, I was not even a true Negro, in some people's eyes, because I did not speak the language. So I had the worst of both ends." He frowned at the memory. "In camp, on the field, I was okay. But on road trips to play other teams in Florida, I had to sit on the bus while my teammates ate at roadside restaurants. Someone would have to bring me my food. In my own ballpark in Fort Myers, blacks had to sit in a section away from whites. I hated Florida.

"But I made the team, and went north with the club. I hit only .255 the first year, but I kept improving. Even so, because I played the game with passion and great effort some sportswriters called me a 'hot dog' and said I had a bad temper. When they interviewed me they printed my words in a way that made me sound ignorant. In the papers it would read, 'I heet ball good.' And even though Pittsburgh was in the North, and had a black community where I lived, there was still the problem of having few Latinos I could socialize with."

"What happened after the season was over?" asked LouAnne.

"I came home a famous person, a hero, but there was no time to rest. I found there was always pressure to play winter ball, and I played almost every season. I also spent time with a doctor back in Puerto Rico learning all about muscles and bones so I could lessen my pain and even help others. In fact, in later years many people with back problems came to my house for care. I was hoping that after I retired I could open a clinic to help many more people, but..." His voice trailed off.

"Let's go somewhere else," said T.J.

They passed through the 1960s, where Clemente briefly paused before a photo of the National League All-Star outfield of the mid-'60s: Mays, Henry Aaron and himself. He nodded and smiled. "You know why we beat the American League so many times in the All-Star game? Because the National League was quicker to integrate than the American League. We had many more black and Latino players, and that was the difference."

But that brought them to the display case housing his effigy. Clemente put his hands on his hips and again slightly cocked his head, appraising his likeness. "You see how I am here?" he said, with a trace of bitterness. "Alone. In this entire Museum there is not another display like this. And even though I don't like it, this does represent the truth. I was too serious, I think, early on. I was not one to go out drinking with the boys or tell jokes. Maybe it was my fear of the language, or being left out of things because of my color. People took it as me being unfriendly.

"Do you know that when we finally had a good team in 1960 and beat the Yankees in the World Series, I finished eighth - *eighth* - in the MVP vote? Two of my white teammates who had lesser seasons actually came in ahead of me. They were my friends, and good players, but my statistics that year were clearly superior. So why was I not voted? Was it my color? Was it because I had started to make my feelings known about racial injustice? Was it because my manager sometimes felt like I was faking injuries to take days off, when the disc in my back stuck out so much I had to push it back in myself?" He threw a hand in the air in disgust. "Please excuse my anger, *amigos*," he said.

"Mr. Clemente," said Bortnicker, "believe me, people today are aware of how good you were and how hard you played. Many consider you the best right fielder of all time."

"Thank you, my friend," he said with sincerity.

"Mr. Clemente," said T.J. gently, "we've come here to help you. Tell us what it is we can do."

The ballplayer thought hard. "You know what? I would like to play on a ballfield one more time. To break at the crack of the bat, track the flight of the ball, make the catch…fire the ball to third base."

"Like in the 1971 Series?" asked Bortnicker.

"You've seen the play? Against the Orioles?"

"It's considered a classic."

"Good. Yes, that is what I'd like to do most."

T.J. said, "We can do that for you. How about tomorrow night?"

"Bueno. You have a place we can go?"

"Sure. Doubleday Field, right up the street."

"Ah, yes. I remember. My Pirates played there twice in exhibition games. A jewel of a park, with short fences." He paused. "But will we be able to leave *here?*" He swept his arm across the room.

"I don't know," said T.J., "But we can try."

"And can you three children help me go *home?*" His voice was heart-wrenchingly hopeful.

"We'll do our best," promised LouAnne, her eyes brimming with tears.

"Then I will see you again, *mañana,*" he said. "Until then, *adios.*" He turned and glided down the hallway until he was swallowed by the darkness.

"Too cool!" said Bortnicker.

"Yeah, maybe," said T.J. "But jeez Louise, guys, how are we gonna do everything we promised?"

"You'll figure it out, Big Mon," said Bortnicker. "You always do."

* * * *

They returned to the Halper Gallery to switch off the electronics that had come back to life with Clemente's departure (the battery operated devices would need replacements), then let themselves out of the Museum, their amazement and sense of accomplishment over that night's happenings tempered by the apprehension that their promises to help the ghost of Clemente might be for naught.

They made small talk on the short walk back to the Glimmerglass Inn, mostly about their conversation with Clemente, but the entire time T.J.'s mind was racing. After agreeing with his cousin to take the next morning off from running, he bid his friends goodnight at the hotel front door and told Bortnicker not to wait up for him.

"It's like 1 AM, Big Mon," said his friend with a yawn. "What more can you do tonight?"

"I'm gonna check in with Mike Weinstein down in Jamaica," he replied. "Run some ideas by him."

"Are you serious? You're calling him at this time of the morning?"

"Bortnicker, down there it's only like midnight. Mike's evening is just getting started, whether he's on an investigation or out clubbing."

"Good point. See you at breakfast. How do you feel about French toast and ham steaks?"

"Sounds good, man. I'll be up in a bit."

* * * *

T.J. was right on the money. "Heyyy, Mon," said Mike in his best Rasta dialect. "How goes it up in the Catskills? You've gotta talk loud because this connection is weak and the bar I'm in is out of control!"

"Okay, I'll keep it short," he said loudly, his voice echoing on Pioneer Street. "Mike, we made contact -"

"*Again*? Clemente showed up?"

"Yeah."

"And you got it on *tape*?"

"Not tonight. He zapped the electronics when he manifested."

"But you talked to him? You saw him, like the others?"

"Well, yeah. That's what I'm trying to tell you."

There was a long pause on the other end. Weinstein heaved a sigh that suggested a mixture of envy and frustration. "I must be living wrong, dude. So, okay, what do you need from me?"

T.J. told his somewhat inebriated mentor about the team's conversation with Clemente, and how he'd asked for help to "go home".

"And you're all bent out of shape because you just don't know what to tell him, right?"

"Yeah, I guess."

"Dude, you've got to think hard. Have you seen or heard anything, *anything* in that town that might be a clue as to how to connect him with the other side?"

And then it dawned on T.J., so clearly that his heart started pounding. "Gotta go, Mike," he yelled into the phone. "Just got an idea. Talk to you soon!" He clicked off and started running toward Doubleday Field.

* * * *

There had been an American Legion game played at the ballpark in the late afternoon, but one would never know it. The infield dirt was smoothed out, a small tarp covered the pitcher's mound, and the bases gleamed white in the pale moonlight. T.J. entered the grandstand behind home plate, seated himself and waited. Sure enough, he detected the faint footsteps padding up the ramp only a few minutes later.

"Thought I heard someone up here," said John Goodleaf, settling on the plank bench next to him. "Why are you out so late?"

I could be asking the same thing of you thought T.J. "Well, Chief," he said, "remember the other day when we were talking about portals?"

"Yes."

"So today you told me 'He comes tonight as in a dream,' remember?"

"Yes. I had a vision about it."

"That's what I thought. Well, you were right. We met Roberto Clemente - or his ghost, I guess - at the Museum tonight. He told us two things. First, he wants us to bring him here to the ballpark tomorrow night. And also, he asked us to help him 'go home', as he put it. But how can we do that? I mean, in Gettysburg we sent Major Hilliard back when LouAnne's dad blasted him with a bullet from the Civil War, and in Bermuda we dug up Captain Tarver's bones and they reburied them in a proper grave. But this one is tough. Since we're in a place of Indian spirits and customs, I would like to know how your people would handle it."

"I think you give me too much credit, son," Goodleaf replied. "Making the dead move between worlds is a little out of my reach."

"Okay, but in the old days, if your people were to, let's say, send a great warrior on his way to the next world or whatever, what would they have to do to prepare him?"

"I suppose we would follow the custom of burying him with his prized possessions, or objects he would want or need with him in the next world. In the old days it was sacred talismans or weapons. I don't know what would be appropriate in this man's case. But maybe you do. Think of what object from his past you could provide that would help conduct him to the hereafter."

"Okay, Chief. Thanks. Let me sleep on this one." As T.J. finally made his way back to the inn, his footfalls echoing on the sidewalk, an idea took shape in his head. He only hoped he'd be able to manage a few hours of sleep before he put it into motion.

Chapter Twenty-Two

As T.J. was habitually an early riser, he found himself awakening as the first shafts of sunlight penetrated the drapes of his bedroom at the Glimmerglass Inn. He turned toward Bortnicker's bed to find his friend gone, a pile of tangled sheets in his place. The faint smell of coffee wafting its way upstairs signified that his buddy's French toast breakfast was well underway.

Lying awake, he revisited the previous night's events, from the *Junior Gonzos'* extraordinary encounter with Roberto Clemente, to his discussions Mike Weinstein and John Goodleaf. There would be much to do today, and job one was to call Bob Simmons to arrange an emergency Board meeting. And after a leisurely hot shower, he did just that.

"My, this is early," said the Hall of Fame's president from his lakeside home. "Did something happen last night to prompt this, T.J.?"

"You could say that, sir," he answered enigmatically. "It's really important that we meet because I have some ideas I have to run by you and the Board."

"And are we close to a resolution here, then?"

"Well, Mr. Simmons, my gut tells me this is all going to end tonight."

"Wonderful, T.J. I'll start making calls. Let's plan on nine-thirty this morning in the board room."

"Sounds great. See you then."

He went downstairs and joined the communal breakfast that was in full swing. A stack of French toast, lightly sprinkled with powdered sugar, was being attacked by his friends and coach.

"'Bout time," needled LouAnne. "We were going to eat your portion. Why so late?"

"Tell you in a minute. First let me get some coffee."

Bortnicker's mouth fell open. "*Coffee*? You? What's the deal here?"

"Not exactly a healthy choice," agreed Pisseri, forking a golden brown ham steak onto his plate. "Are you drowsy or something?"

"Nah, Coach," he confessed, "I just didn't get much sleep. There was a lot going on last night."

"I'm listening."

T.J. and his friends then explained about their meeting with Clemente, from beginning to end. Not too far in, Pisseri stopped chewing, hanging on every word. At the conclusion he blinked a few times, then took a gulp of coffee.

"You're telling me that you guys were actually walking and talking with the ghost of Roberto Clemente," he said in a reverential tone.

"That's about the size of it, Coach," said Bortnicker nonchalantly, spearing another slice of French toast. "Think I overdid this one," he added for effect.

"And you weren't scared?" asked the dumbfounded baseball coach.

"He's not really a scary guy," replied LouAnne with a shrug of her shoulders. "He's kind of sad, actually."

"And you think you can actually help him?"

"Well, that's what we promised," said T.J.

"Hey," said Bortnicker, changing the subject, "how was your dinner at the Italian place?"

"It went fine," said Pisseri. "We actually have a lot in common. Unfortunately, Debbie's determined to make a career here at the Hall of Fame, so it will have to be more of a long-distance friendship, at least for now. Tonight she'll be working on all the arrangements for the Fantasy Camp game at Doubleday tomorrow. We're having a draft today and practicing as two separate squads at the Clark Center for the game. You guys are coming to the game, aren't you?"

"Wouldn't miss it," said T.J. "So what are you doing then tonight, Coach?"

"I'll probably just hang out at The Dugout with the locals, take in a ballgame on the tube."

"You can always join us," offered Bortnicker with a devilish grin. "I think we might have an extra shirt floating around."

"That's quite all right," he replied. "As I told you guys, I'm not into the whole ghost thing."

"Bortnicker told me you were going to talk to Mike Weinstein last night, Cuz," said LouAnne. "How did that go?"

T.J. chuckled. "Well, just as I thought, Mike was out partying it up in Jamaica. But he gave me a good idea, and I actually ended up talking to Chief about it."

"Who's he?" asked Pisseri.

"He's the groundskeeper over at Doubleday Field, Coach. Anyway, I went over there on a hunch, and he just showed up."

"At 1 AM in the morning, Cuz? What's up with *that*? This guy is strange."

"Maybe, but now I know what we have to do."

Bortnicker asked, "And that is?"

"We've got to go meet the Board in a half-hour and talk them out of a baseball bat."

* * * *

At precisely nine-thirty Bob Simmons ushered the *Junior Gonzo Ghost Chasers* into the boardroom of the National Baseball Hall of Fame and Museum. Fiona, who had accompanied her uncle to work that day with the intention of helping out with the previous night's film and audio review, was made to promise to stay in his office until the conclusion of the meeting.

Upon entering, T.J. was surprised to find only Sarah Martin and Jody Rieman, along with the ever-suspicious Dan Vines. Simmons quickly explained that Bryan Davis was in Oakland to collect some artifacts from an early-season no-hitter that had been tossed the previous night, and Pete Alfano was away on family business. T.J. secretly wished it had been Vines who was out of town for the day.

"All right, then," began Simmons, getting comfortable at the head of the table. "Thanks for coming together on such short notice, everybody. T.J. and his team have some news to tell us, I believe." He gestured to the boy that he had the floor.

"Thanks, Mr. Simmons. Well, as you all know we were asked to come to Cooperstown because of supposed sightings of Roberto Clemente's ghost. And last night -" he paused for effect - "we confirmed that the ghost of Roberto Clemente really is haunting the Hall."

Vines, predictably, rolled his eyes. "And how do you know that, son?" he asked condescendingly.

"Because we talked to him, that's how," snapped Bortnicker.

Vines was not shaken, though Sarah Martin seemed to go white. "Do you have proof of this encounter?" he asked coolly.

"Actually, no," replied T.J. diplomatically. "When he manifested he sucked all the energy out of our equipment, even the computers."

"How convenient."

"Now, wait a minute, Dan," said Simmons, trying to intervene before the escalation of another war between his second in command and the bespectacled boy across the table who was staring him down.

"No, *you* wait a minute, Bob," he retorted. "With all due respect, I've gone along with this wild goose chase from the beginning, but it seems like all we have to go on is hearsay. I would appreciate some tangible evidence that a ghost is skulking around this Museum, and these kids have been poking around long enough to have something to show us."

This isn't going well thought T.J. "I suppose then, Mr. Vines," he began delicately, "that this would be a bad time to make a request?"

"T.J., before you do, could you please take us through exactly what happened last night?" asked the president.

"Oh, sure, Mr. Simmons," replied the boy. "Sorry. I was getting ahead of myself. Okay, here's what happened. Two nights ago on our first investigation we started encountering a lot of crazy phenomena, especially in the Plaque Gallery. Lots of darting shadows and garbled language" - he looked directly at Vines - "which we did capture on tape. And then, as you know, there was the incident with your niece at the Clemente case which was, we believe, his first attempt to manifest."

"Want to hear my theory?" said Vines. "I think it was an electrical short in the air conditioning wiring of the case."

"Are you *serious*?" cried Bortnicker, springing to his feet and leaning forward aggressively across the table. "There was a ball of light, man! That wasn't any electrical short!"

As he had done in other situations, T.J. reached up from his seat, grabbed the back of his friend's shirt, and pulled him back down. "Mr. Vines," he said, "all you have to do to disprove our claim is call in an electrician to confirm that a wire shorted out in the case. But as far as I can tell, the AC is working just fine in there."

Vines harrumphed and sat back, and the moment passed.

"Please continue, T.J.," said Simmons. "And Dan, just cool it, will you?"

"Okay. So anyway, last night we started out again, and all our electronics blew out. This takes an awful lot of energy, and the only answer was that Clemente's ghost was manifesting. Sure enough, we encountered him in the Plaque Gallery."

From there, LouAnne took up the report. "We confirmed that he was Clemente through simple questioning. He was actually pretty friendly."

"What did he look like?" asked Sarah Martin.

"He was pretty solid," she replied. "I mean, no doubt it was him. He looked just like his photos."

"What was he wearing?" probed Vines.

"If I had to guess, it was the clothes he had on the night he died," said T.J.

"And his clothes - or himself - wasn't mangled or anything?" asked Jody Rieman.

"Nope. He looked pretty regular to us."

"So, what did he say?" asked Simmons.

"Well, we walked around the Museum with him, and he told us about how he started in baseball, then got signed by the Dodgers and later went over to the Pirates."

"We got as far as the 1960s," said Bortnicker, who had calmed down. "He was telling us about the discrimination he faced because of his skin color and language, which confirms everything we learned through all our research that we did on him. But, I'll tell you what, he's a pretty proud guy. Personally, I wouldn't have wanted to mess with him back in the day."

Simmons nodded. "So how did you leave off with him?"

"Well," said T.J. tentatively, "here's where we need your help. Mr.

Clemente told us that he, uh, wants to go home, is how he put it. And I have it on pretty good information that the way to do this is to return to him something he prized in life."

"Such as?"

T.J. turned to Sarah Martin and trained his doe eyes on her. "Such as the game-used bat you showed me and LouAnne the other day, ma'am. It's the only way." His words hung in the air for an agonizingly long time.

Surprisingly, it was Simmons who said, "Out of the question."

If T.J. was stunned, he didn't show it. Instead, with only the slightest waiver to his voice, he asked, "Why is that, Mr. Simmons?"

"Bob, may I?" intervened Sarah Martin.

"Sure, go ahead," he said.

"T.J.," she began gently, "as I told you and LouAnne the other day, all the items in our collection here at the Hall are donated. We don't pay one penny for any item, no matter how exclusive or historic. When we accept an artifact, it is with the expressed understanding that we will never part with it, for any reason. That bat was given to us in good faith many years ago, and we must honor our commitment to the donor, who is now deceased, by keeping it in our possession always."

"Even if it means you'll never rid yourself of the ghost?" asked the incredulous Bortnicker.

"I'm afraid so, son," said Simmons with resignation. "But I think that if there's another way to solve this problem, you kids will come up with it."

T.J., who was frankly crushed over this turn of events, briefly pinched the bridge of his nose as he always did when composing himself. "All right, Mr. Simmons," he said evenly. "If that's the way it's got to be." He paused and looked at the ceiling, as if pondering something. "But is it okay if we borrow Jody one more time? We need help with something that needs to be done today."

"Of course," said Simmons. "I'm sure Jody would be happy to assist you."

"For sure," chirped the intern.

"Okay, then," said T.J., masking his disappointment. "We're going to go to the Halper Gallery to check out last night's stuff for a while, but if you could hang out here a minute, Jody, I'd like to fill you in."

"Very well," said Simmons. "Thanks for coming, everybody." The board members filed out, but not before Dan Vines shot a triumphant wink at the simmering Bortnicker.

* * * *

After outlining the task for the eager intern, the somewhat dispirited teens collected Fiona from her uncle's office and picked their way through the thick crowd of Museum patrons to the blessedly quiet sanctuary of the Halper Gallery. Once there, T.J. suggested that LouAnne and Fiona do the video review of the previous night's relatively brief footage. "Bortnicker and I have to run a little errand for tonight," he explained.

"What's that?" asked Fiona, her disappointment over Bortnicker's departure obvious.

"We've gotta do some shopping."

"So where are we going, Big Mon?" said Bortnicker as the two boys exited the Hall's main entrance.

"We're going to need a bat for tonight," replied T.J. "The Doubleday Bat Company shop is right up Main Street. We'll stop in and have one made."

"You're gonna try to fool Clemente with a fake bat? I wouldn't recommend that, Big Mon."

"Nah, I wouldn't dare try that. But, we are gonna need a bat to hit flyballs with, aren't we?"

"Good point."

They entered the brightly lit shop whose walls were lined with custom made wooden bats of all shapes and sizes, many emblazoned with team logos, stadium reproductions or Hall of Fame players' career statistics. It was actually a bit overwhelming, and T.J. had a curious desire to forever chuck his aluminum bat for one of these hand-turned beauties.

"Can I help you?" asked the young man behind the counter.

"Actually, yes. I need a bat made, but I need it pretty fast."

The employee nodded. "Not a problem. You came at a good time." He pointed to a vertical side rack which featured blank blonde wood bats in graduating size from left to right. "Go through those until you find a length and weight that suits you," he said. "If you want it engraved, we can put anything you desire on the barrel for an extra charge. Takes about a half-hour."

"Could you put something similar to the Pittsburgh Pirates logo and the name CLEMENTE in block letters?"

"No problem."

T.J. began hefting one bat after the other. Finally, he handed one he liked to Bortnicker. "Can you swing this?" he asked.

Bortnicker took a medium-sized cut. "Yeah, this isn't bad," he said. "But why do you care if I like it?"

"'Cause you're gonna be hitting fungoes later to Roberto Clemente," his friend whispered.

"Me? And just where are *you* going to be at that time?"

T.J. smiled. "Learning how to do the basket catch."

* * * *

Back in the command center, LouAnne was gazing intently into the computer monitor at the previous night's footage when she felt the eyes of Fiona Bright boring into the side of her head. She removed her earphones and asked, "What?"

"You're just so...pretty," the girl confessed. "It's like you don't even try to be. I guess that's why T.J. looks at you the way he does."

Blushing profusely, the teen shook her head. "Fiona," she began, "if you only knew. Listen, when I was younger, and not so long ago, I was kinda skinny and mousy. I'm nearsighted, so I was wearing these big old glasses -"

"Like mine?"

LouAnne grinned. "Yes, kinda like yours. And I didn't really spend any time brushing my hair or trying to dress nice. I more or less fell out of bed every day and went to school."

"Did the other kids make fun of you?"

"Oh yeah, especially the girls. Today you would classify it as bullying. But you know, I didn't help it any. I had kind of an attitude, and overall I guess you could say I was annoying. Even T.J. tried to avoid me at family gatherings, though he was just my cousin by adoption. Can't say I blame him.

"But then, I think it was when I was around your age, I just decided one day that I was going to start taking care of myself, beginning with the inside. I tried being nicer to people, and it made me have a more positive outlook. And then, with a little more concentration on my appearance, not to mention that I started exercising and watching what I ate, I started changing. And I liked what I saw."

She paused, and then closed her eyes for a moment. "But you know," she said, "even with all that, some things - really, really bad things - have happened to me this year. What you're going to find is that whether you are pretty or not, or popular or not, there will always be people trying to drag you down. You just have to rise above it. And I've also learned that you have to be willing to confide in the people who really love you. I did, and it took a lot of weight off my shoulders."

Fiona pushed her bushy curls away from her glasses. "LouAnne," she whispered, "before you leave Cooperstown, will you show me how to be pretty?"

LouAnne Darcy bit her lip and thought. "Yeah, I can do that," she said finally. "But you're going to have to handle the inside part on your own."

"It's a deal," said Fiona, hugging the stunned teen tightly.

* * * *

By the time the boys returned from the Doubleday Bat Company, their customized club encased in a plastic slipcover, the girls were finishing up with the footage from the previous night.

"Anything?" asked T.J., looking over his cousin's shoulder.

"Not really," she replied. "I guess the action in this place comes and goes. I hit it big in the Plaque Gallery two nights ago, but yesterday was a dud."

"Yeah, said Bortnicker, "but we hit the jackpot with Clemente."

"I can't believe you actually talked to a ghost," marveled Fiona. "All I got was a flash of light."

"I have to admit, it was pretty cool last night," said LouAnne. "But remember, Fiona, you were the one who he first tried to make contact with."

"What's doing with lunch today?" asked Bortnicker, who was always preoccupied with food.

"There's an outdoor place in Pioneer Alley, behind the shops on Main Street," said T.J. "I passed it when I cut through on my way to Doubleday Field. Why don't we try that?"

"I've eaten there with my uncle," volunteered Fiona, fishing for an invitation. "It's actually pretty good. They have some tasty sandwiches."

"Sounds like a winner," said Bortnicker. "Let's check it out. Fiona, you coming?"

"Why not?" she replied, grinning broadly.

As they dined on the patio, the group chitchatted about music, school, and other things. Fiona was intrigued by Bortnicker and LouAnne's running Beatles trivia contest and blown away over the 'John Lennon whispered message' story from Bermuda. She was clearly taking LouAnne's advice to heart, and made a conscious effort to be positive and upbeat while making an effort not to step on anyone's dialogue when they were speaking. It made LouAnne feel good.

"Hey, guys," said T.J. after they dismantled their order of BLTs, turkey clubs and fries, "I need to loosen up my arm for tonight, I hope. I haven't really thrown all week. Who wants to have a catch?"

"I brought my glove, Cuz, remember?" said LouAnne. "Let's go down to that little park by the lake and toss the ball around."

"What about you, Bortnicker?" asked T.J. as he motioned to the waitress for the check.

"I think I'll walk around town," said the boy, "do a little shopping for souvenirs for my mother."

"Can I come along?" asked Fiona, trying not to sound too anxious.

"Yeah, I wouldn't mind some company. You can help me pick out a T-shirt for her."

"Cool!"

"And what about dinner tonight?" asked T.J. "I've gotta text Coach P."

"You're thinking about food already?" chided LouAnne. "We just ate!"

"I say, back to The Dugout," suggested Bortnicker. "I think tonight's special is prime rib."

"All right, then. Cuz, let's go get our gloves. Bortnicker, I'll see you back in the room around four o'clock."

"You got it, Big Mon."

* * * *

After stopping by the inn to pick up their gloves and a baseball that T.J. always kept in the pocket of his, the cousins strolled in the spring sunshine down to the lakeside park. Everything seemed to be in full bloom, and a row of ducks paddled happily along the still water, only a few feet from the shoreline near picnic tables where people ate sandwiches. They backed up to about fifteen feet apart and started soft-tossing, the ball making a crisp popping sound in the pastoral quiet.

"Hey, Cuz," asked T.J., "in Bermuda, didn't you say you almost drowned in a lake once?"

"Thought you'd forgotten about that," she replied, never missing a beat with their game of catch. "It's something I try not to think about."

"Oh, forget it, then."

"No, I'll tell you. There was this summer rec camp I went to at my elementary school. Well, every so often we'd have an outing or field trip. One day we went to this lake near York, about a half-hour from Gettysburg. I was around seven years old and all excited. Remember, we don't have any beaches in Pennsylvania, so going to the lake was a big deal.

"Anyway, there were counselors with us, mostly high school and college kids, and they were supposed to be watching us, but they were mostly watching each other, if you know what I mean. Meanwhile, a bunch of us kids decided to swim out to this wooden floating raft thing about fifty feet from shore. I wasn't the best swimmer, but when my friends dove in I followed them 'cause I didn't want to wimp out. Also, at the time I was kind of an outcast, and I didn't want to give them a reason to rag on me anymore than they already did.

"So, of course, about halfway out I started sucking air. I tried to turn back but then I got a bad stitch in my side. I opened my mouth to call for help, but a wave from the other swimmers hit me in the face and I swallowed the water. Next thing you know, I went under.

"On the lake bottom it was dark and all reeds, and even though it was only like six feet deep, I managed to get my legs tangled in them. It was like they were reaching up and grabbing at my ankles. At first I thrashed around like a crazy person, but then...I don't know, I figured, *Hey, maybe drowning isn't so bad. You breathe in a few gulps of water and just kinda float away.*"

T.J. held the ball and stared at her.

"See, at that time my life was going so bad, being bullied by other kids and whatnot, that I was ready to just pack it in. Pretty stupid, huh?

"But then, suddenly, somebody grabbed my hair and yanked me up and out of the water. It was an adult who was there with his kids and saw me go under. He actually did CPR on me and then turned me on my side so I could sick-up the lake water. My so-called counselors really caught it from the camp director for that one.

"So that's my near-death drowning story. Now can you see why I didn't want to go scuba diving in Bermuda?"

"*Scuba diving?*" said T.J. "After that, I can't believe you even went *snorkeling* with me. I mean, at one point we were in like twelve feet of water."

"Yeah," she replied, "but you were holding my hand the whole time, remember? As long as you were holding onto me, I figured I was okay."

He smiled. "Hey, what ever happened to that bottle I found for you? The handmade one from the 1800s with the stopper still in it that I picked off the bottom? You told me you'd use it to hold all your wishes."

"Uh-huh."

"Do you still have it?"

"T.J., what do you think I've been wishing into the past four months?"

"And what did you wish for?"

She paused before throwing. "A week just like this one," she said before snapping a return toss.

His heart soaring, T.J. nodded and said, "Can we back up a bit? My arm's getting loose."

She stopped again, hands on hips. "What, you don't think I can reach? You think I throw like a girl or something?" She retreated a few steps and then zipped a throw that stung his hand right through the glove. Gradually they backed up more and more, the ball *whocking* into their gloves as seagulls careened overhead.

* * * *

As advertised, The Dugout's Prime Rib Night was spectacular. Coach Pisseri and all the teens except for Bortnicker ordered their meat medium rare; he wanted an end cut, well done. Steaming baked potatoes and butternut squash rounded out their heaping portions.

"How did the draft go at camp today, Coach?" asked T.J. between forkfuls of potato slathered in sour cream.

"Not bad. I believe the squads are pretty equal, and I think there should be a fairly decent crowd at Doubleday tomorrow to watch the game."

"That reminds me," said Bortnicker, "Fiona said she'll be seeing us at the game."

"How was it shopping with her in town this afternoon?" asked T.J. with a raised eyebrow.

"Surprisingly, not bad at all," he replied. "She actually helped me pick out a couple things for my mom. And...I don't know but, it was like she was trying so hard to be *civil*, you know? Like, she really made an effort. Wonder what's got into her?"

"I have no idea," said T.J. "Cuz?"

"Don't ask me," LouAnne said, smiling inwardly.

Chapter Twenty-Three

They marched purposefully toward the Hall of Fame, three abreast, the Doubleday Bat slung over T.J.'s shoulder, Bortnicker toting the baseball gloves in a small zippered duffel bag he'd brought on the trip. They didn't talk much; there wasn't much to say.

The full moon shone brightly overhead as Dan Vines let them into the Museum with nary a word. It was just as well, for the group was pretty fed up with him, and an argument on this night could be disastrous. However, someone on the staff had come through big-time. As they entered the Halper Gallery, a good-sized canvas ball bag awaited them on one of the tables. T.J. peeked inside. "Way to go, Jody," he said to himself. The intern had done them a huge favor driving to a sporting goods store in Oneonta, where he purchased two dozen regulation baseballs before taking them back to town and spray painting them Day-Glo yellow. T.J. plucked one out - it was perfectly dry. "Yeah, that'll do," he said, satisfied.

"Are we setting up the equipment?" asked LouAnne, removing her windbreaker jacket. All the teens had brought an outer layer of clothes just in case their Doubleday excursion would come off. The boys had even included their Bridgefield JV hats; LouAnne opted for her tattered Phillies cap.

"Might as well," said Bortnicker, flipping on the computers, "though from what we've seen, he causes a major blackout every time he shows up."

They split up, setting the DVRs in pretty much the same locations as last time. As T.J. was adjusting the tripod for his camcorder he was almost shaking with excitement. *This is the night* he thought as he pointed the camera at the Clemente case and turned it on. "How's the feed, Bortnicker?" he asked into his walkie-talkie.

"Pull it back a little, Big Mon," his friend answered as he peered into the computer. "That's it. Perfect."

"How does the Plaque Gallery look?" asked LouAnne.

"Just a little more to the right and you've got it," he replied.

On the way back to the command center T.J. extinguished the lights for what he hoped was the last time. He reentered the command center a few seconds later than his cousin, who was arming herself with handheld gadgets. "I guess I'm starting out on the computer tonight," he said. "If I see anything even remotely weird I'll call you guys on the walkie-talkie. You geared up, Bortnicker?"

"Yup," he replied. "All systems go."

"Okay, then," said T.J. quietly. "Let's do this." He held out his hand, which was quickly covered by the others'. "One, two, three -"

"Gonzos Rule!"

* * * *

Bortnicker swept the Plaque Gallery with his thermal imager, looking for hotspots and trying to catch some EVPs. Sure enough, there was what looked like a palm print near the plaque of Clemente's deceased Pirates teammate, Willie Stargell. He zoomed in on it. "Wonder if Clemente left this?" he said to himself. Then he tried to raise Clemente for an EVP response, but just got what sounded like mild static. "You've gotta try harder than that, old boy," he advised. Seconds afterward, laser-like shafts of light started bouncing off the walls. "T.J., are you seeing this?" he barked into his walkie-talkie.

"Yeah. It looks kinda like a pinball machine," answered the boy from the command center. "Any temperature change?"

"Nada. But wait. Everything just went dark again. Back to square one."

"I think he's trying, though."

"It would appear."

"How's it going upstairs, Cuz?" T.J. called to LouAnne, who was approaching the Clemente case.

"All quiet here," she whispered. "No, wait. T.J., can you pick up detail on the case's glass? It seems like some kind of condensation is forming." She strode to the case and felt the glass. "It's got a chill to it. I think something's about to happen!"

"Bortnicker, meet us at the Clemente case," said T.J., sliding his seat back from the table. "It's game on!"

The boys converged at the bottom of the staircase just as a cracking noise emanated from above. They looked at each other for second. Bortnicker managed a "Wha-" before a crash of shattering glass made them bolt up the stairs toward LouAnne.

* * * *

They encountered a frightening scene upon their breathless arrival; shards of glass from the Clemente case were everywhere, the camera and tripod had been dashed to the floor, and LouAnne lay next to the far wall, Roberto Clemente on one knee leaning over her. They ran over as Clemente rose and took a step back.

"You okay, Cuz?" asked T.J. softly, a comforting hand moving a strand of hair from her eyes.

"Woo, boy," she said, sitting up slowly.

"What happened?" asked Bortnicker, briefly glancing over his shoulder at Clemente, who looked as distraught as anybody.

"Well," she said, shaking her blonde mane from which a few stray glass splinters flew, "the glass started getting, like, misty. I put my hand on it and the drop in temperature was obvious. And the colder it got, the more opaque. Then I heard the surface start to spider-web, and I backpedaled as fast as I could before it just blew out."

"Was there a flash of light, like last time?" asked her cousin.

"Not really. The whole glass frosted over, and *whammo*. I got back just far enough, I guess."

At that point Clemente, who had been hanging back, his hands clasped at his waist as if in prayer, stepped forward and said earnestly, "*Señorita*, please accept my sincere apologies if it was I who caused this. You are not injured, I hope?"

In response, the girl rose to her feet and assumed an almost defiant stance. "I'm good to go, Mr. Clemente," she said, her chin tilted upwards. "I'll say one thing, though. You sure know how to make an entrance."

Even Clemente had to smile at the girl's spirit.

Bortnicker looked back at the case, of which only the outer fringes appeared intact. The mannequin remained upright and perfectly rigid; only its Pirates cap was ever so slightly askew. "Well, *he's* come through it okay," he observed sarcastically.

"Could we move somewhere else, please?" requested Clemente, who appeared uncomfortable with the situation he'd initiated.

"Sure," said T.J. "Why don't we go sit for a minute in the Plaque Gallery?"

"That would be fine."

They turned toward the room's exit, careful not to step on any broken glass. Clemente paused for a second to look upon the upended camcorder and tripod - glanced at T.J. with a suspicious expression - then followed down the stairs, gliding along as usual. Of course, all of their ghost hunting appliances had winked out with his manifestation, though LouAnne had left her EVP recorder on just in case, as when she'd captured Captain Tarver's voice in Bermuda.

The group came to a halt in the center of the long hall; Clemente sat upon one of the centrally located cushioned benches as the teens settled at his feet on the cool tile. Moonlight from the vaulted ceiling provided him a warm glow, accentuating the fact that he wasn't quite solid to begin with.

"Mr. Clemente," said LouAnne, "the other night when I was in here by myself I thought I heard voices. Do the deceased Hall of Famers come here to...uh...visit each other?"

"From time to time," he replied, scanning the enormous room. "You never know who shows up. Ruth was here the other night, and Josh Gibson, the Negro League catcher. They were both saying they had hit the longest home run ever. I just laughed. Who cares? Whether you hit a line drive or a bloop that falls in, it counts for the same in the box score, no? And of course, Ted Williams thinks he knows more about hitting than anyone. So scientific. Me, I see the ball and I hit it. Simple."

"Are there any guys you don't get along with?" asked Bortnicker.

"A few. I'm not too sure I like Ty Cobb; and that Judge Landis, who kept the blacks out of the Majors, I have no time for him. But I *respect* everyone in here, and I expect the same."

"LouAnne thought she heard some Spanish being spoken," said T.J. "Is that true?"

"Oh, yes," replied Clemente with a chuckle. "Some of us, like Martin Dihigo, who was from Cuba, we speak in our native tongue. Most of the Hall of Famers who played winter ball in the Caribbean understand us, anyway. And if they don't, too bad." He smiled, his teeth a gleaming white.

"Can I ask you what you think of the baseball of today?"

A cloud came over Clemente's face, and his smile vanished. "Sometimes I wonder if it is the same game," he said with a trace of derision. "When I played, I would face great pitchers who finished what they started. Sandy Koufax, Juan Marichal, Tom Seaver! Today there is a pitcher for every inning. And the hitters who come to bat covered in padding. Ridiculous! In my day, if you even dug in your spikes at the plate, Don Drysdale or Bob Gibson would knock you down as easily as look at you. And I would get back up and sneer at them and hit a line drive. *That's* baseball.

"But what is worse, from what I have seen, I think many players today do not have the passion, the joy. Yes, many are as rich as kings, but are they happy? And why do some disgrace themselves by cheating the game? When I played for the Pittsburgh Pirates, I gave my all. I played hurt, even though I was criticized for admitting it. Even on the Pirates today, there are those who miss a few weeks, or months, with ailments I would endure. And why? Because I was always scared someone would take my place, and because I was too proud to sit. Maybe that is why my Pirates have been so bad for so long. But I tell you, *amigos*, things will turn around for them. I can feel it."

"Well, Sir," offered Bortnicker, "what you *can* be happy about is how many great Latino players there are in the game today. And you were the first."

"*One* of the first," he replied, "but there was none more proud."

T.J. took a deep breath. "Mr. Clemente, you made a request last night. Do you still want to play some ball?"

"I am ready to try."

"I'll go get the equipment from the command center," said Bortnicker, who was off in a flash.

Inwardly, T.J. was worried to death. He couldn't help recalling the plight of Captain Tarver in Bermuda. The old sea dog had returned to his palatial plantation home all right, but wasn't able to venture past its walls. Would Roberto Clemente suffer the same fate at the Hall of Fame?

* * * *

Slowly, T.J. eased open the front entrance door of the National Baseball Hall of Fame and Museum. He looked out both ways at the deserted sidewalk, then brought his head back in. "The coast is clear, as far as I can tell," he said. "You guys ready to do this?"

"You know it, Cuz," said LouAnne, hefting the brand-new bat.

"I've got the ball bag. Bortnicker, do you have the gloves?"

"Yup."

He turned to Clemente, who seemed anxious, and winked. "Follow me, then."

Anyone who came upon this troupe on Cooperstown's Main Street that night would not have sensed anything out of the ordinary: three teens in ball caps, jackets, jeans and sneakers; and a fortyish black man, a bit underdressed in the pleasant April chill. Clemente continuously looked around - at the buildings, at the sky, at the cars parked overnight along the street. His eyes seemed bright with anticipation.

At Pioneer they turned left and then hung a quick right into Pioneer Alley, passing the café where they'd eaten lunch that day. It was Clemente who broke the silence, perhaps out of nervousness:

"I was never a good sleeper," he said. "Maybe a couple hours each night. In Pittsburgh, when my wife was with me she'd tape the window drapes shut to keep out the morning light. Then there were the nightmares. I had dreams I would die in a plane crash, you know." The kids left that one alone.

A few minutes later the outline of Doubleday Field's façade came into view. Clemente picked up his pace, the teens in tow. Finally they stood before the entrance and the ballplayer took his time, drinking in every detail of the classic building. "*Bueno*," he said to himself.

T.J. cleared his throat respectfully. "Uh, Mr. Clemente, there's a side entrance to the field if you'll follow us."

The gate, thankfully, was unlatched, and the foursome entered and stepped onto the manicured grass of Doubleday Field, which shone silver in the moonlight. Clemente took the bat from LouAnne, walked purposefully to the plate, settled into the batter's box, twisted his neck and upper body as he had done millions of times before, and gazed at the expanse of the outfield. "My 3000th hit was my last," he said wistfully. "A double, up the left-center gap at Three Rivers Stadium. I went into second base standing, and then returned the cheers of the crowd by removing my cap and saluting them." He sighed and shook his head, then looked T.J. in the eye. "But I did not come here to hit, *amigo*. It was fielding - and throwing - that gave me the most pleasure. And I believe I promised to show you a few things."

"Yes, Sir," said T.J., his heart hammering. And then, something he fully expected occurred. Over the ballplayer's shoulder, leaning against the visiting team dugout, was John Goodleaf, doing his magician trick again. He nodded to T.J. and smiled knowingly. *You called it, Chief,* thought the boy.

Then disaster struck, or so it seemed. Organizing the workout, T.J. instructed Bortnicker to take the bat and ball bag to home plate for fungo hitting, and for LouAnne to play third base and take throws from right field. "I'll be in the outfield with Mr. Clemente to shag flies," he said, but no sooner had the words escaped his lips than T.J. realized he was one glove short. In his haste to get the bat made and the balls bought and painted, he'd failed to do the math.

Reading his face, LouAnne remarked, "We've got a problem, huh?"

"No, we don't," announced Bortnicker, unzipping the small bag. "Here's your glove, Big Mon," he said, tossing T.J.'s Wilson A2000 over. "LouAnne, this is yours, I believe." He handed her the worn Derek Jeter model with the frayed laces. Then, as his friends gaped in wonderment, Bortnicker reached *again* into the bag and brought forth a mahogany-colored Rawlings XFG-1 fielder's glove which he held out to Clemente. "This should do the trick, Sir," he said, the slightest tremor in his voice.

The ballplayer hesitated, then took the glove and slipped it on. "My *glove*," he said lovingly. "But…how is this possible?"

"You gave it to my father the night you died," the boy replied.

T.J. and LouAnne looked at each other pie-eyed.

"Ah, yes, I remember," said Clemente. "The sad little one. I promised I'd return to play catch with him."

"Well, we're here now," said Bortnicker, his crooked smile evident in the moonlight. "Let's play."

"*Gracias, amigo.*" He tucked the glove under his arm, turned, and jogged out toward right field.

The cousins, still agog at this revelation, stared at their friend.

"So," Bortnicker said, "are you two just gonna stand there or are we gonna get after it?"

This broke them from their reverie, and they sprinted to their positions, but not before LouAnne, her eyes filmy, planted a kiss on Bortnicker's cheek.

* * * *

Todd Pisseri was bored. As planned, he'd gone back to The Dugout to catch the Yankees-Red Sox game on the bar's TV. The place was pretty lively, with a number of fans of each team in the crowd, but by the seventh inning he had started getting antsy. Now the game, a New York victory, was long over, and the interminable post game show was heading into its second hour. He'd already had a couple beers and four or five bags of bar snacks, and a cute girl across the bar who was from Texas had even come over and tried to make conversation, but he just couldn't get his mind off what was supposed to be happening up the street at Doubleday Field.

The time he'd spent in Cooperstown had been a dream. From helping middle-aged ballplayers live out their fantasy, to getting an exclusive tour of the Hall of Fame alongside of some of its members and hanging out with a very sweet lady whom he hoped to see again, the experience couldn't have been more rewarding. And tomorrow's game at Doubleday would tie everything together in a neat bow.

But still…what were those kids *doing* over there? Was there any chance at all that the ghost of Roberto Clemente was actually within the confines of Doubleday Field? He looked at his watch, then the TV screen, then his watch again.

"Check, please," he said to the bartender.

* * * *

Bortnicker, the open ball bag at his feet, held a Day-Glo yellow orb aloft with his left hand, the Doubleday Bat on his right shoulder. "Ready in the outfield?" he called.

"Let 'er rip," replied T.J.

He looked down the third base line to where LouAnne straddled the bag, pounding her glove. "Ready, my dear?"

"Bring it," she said.

"Okay, here goes." He flipped the ball in the air and took an uppercut swing, sending the sphere in a grand arc towards Clemente and his protégé in right field.

Despite the absence of overhead stadium lighting, the Pirates star immediately drew a bead on the ball. "*Yo lo tengo,*" he said quietly but assertively, then quickly translated, "I've got it." He backpedaled a couple paces, then formed the basket below his waist into which the ball plopped softly. In the blink of an eye he performed the transfer and fired it on one hop to the waiting LouAnne, who shoveled it sideways down the third base line towards Bortnicker.

"You see?" he said to T.J., who studied him intently. "It's all in the positioning. You have to track the ball and get behind it, then come in. Now, you try."

Bortnicker skied another one, and T.J. nervously settled under it. After a slight bobble on the basket catch, he whipped it in with a smile of relief.

"Way to go, Cuz!" called LouAnne.

After that they alternated, the baseball legend and the high schooler, until it became second nature. Clemente was clearly relishing every catch, every throw, and as T.J. calmed down he found himself marveling at the sheer incongruity of what he was doing on this moonlit night in the Catskill Mountains.

While Bortnicker was gathering the scattered balls around home plate into the bag for another round, Roberto Clemente turned to T.J.

"I have a question, *amigo,*" he said with gravity.

"Yes?"

"In the Museum. That camera on that, what do you call it?"

"A tripod?" answered the boy nervously.

"Yes, on the tripod. What was it for? What were you doing?"

"Um, well, Mr. Clemente, we were trying to shoot some video film for, uh, a TV show."

"About me?"

"Yes, Sir."

"And what is the name of the show?"

T.J. wished he could crawl in a hole. "Uh, it's called *Junior Gonzo Ghost Chasers*."

"Junior Gonzo Ghost Chasers," Clemente repeated slowly, and the words were like knives. "So it is a program about ghosts, not baseball?"

"Yes."

"*Why?*"

The boy was so mortified he didn't know what to say.

"Can you imagine the sadness - the *horror* - my poor wife, and my boys who are grown men now, would feel if this program was actually shown for the world to see?"

T.J., struggling for words, managed, "B-but, wouldn't you want them to know you're okay on the...other side?"

"T.J.," he said firmly, "you must understand. They know I am at peace, and that I am always with them in spirit. And that is enough."

Thankfully, Bortnicker launched another fly ball towards right field. "*Yo lo tengo,*" said Clemente, his lips tight.

* * * *

Pisseri crept into the first base stands near the side entrance and began stealthily sliding along the aluminum bleacher bench toward right field. Immediately he saw Bortnicker hitting fungoes and T.J.'s cousin doing an admirable job of manning third base. That girl was a natural athlete. And there was some other guy hanging around in the shadows near the third base dugout. But what the coach wanted to see - *had* to see - was happening out in right field. T.J. was there, Bridgefield cap and all, but could it be that the man with him was actually *Roberto Clemente*? He blinked a few times and refocused as he slid ever closer.

188

Roberto's Return

* * * *

They were almost done with the second round of baseballs when T.J. said, "May I ask you a question?"

"For the TV or for you?" Clemente replied, still miffed.

"For me."

"If you wish." The ballplayer effortlessly basket-caught a fly ball and fired it in.

"Do you remember your death?"

Clemente stopped, hands on hips, and faced the boy as Bortnicker sent another rainbow skyward.

"Yo lo tengo," said T.J., trying anything he could to get into Clemente's good graces, as he circled below the ball.

"Hold the glove a little lower," advised Clemente. "That's it," he said, his voice softer.

T.J. made the catch, crow-hopped and threw.

"Here is what I remember. I climbed aboard as the pilot - he was American - was doing his last check of the instruments. He was confident we would make the flight with no problem, and I wanted so much to believe him, because I was determined to help those people in Nicaragua. I strapped myself into a seat in the small cabin area behind the cockpit. The pilot received clearance from the control tower and he said 'Here goes,' and we started to roll down the runway.

"I never liked to fly, *amigo*. Which is funny, because I made thousands of trips during my career, all across the United States, Canada and the Caribbean for winter ball. I even went to Europe once with my family. But I was always uneasy in the air. With the Pirates I had flown through some pretty bad storms, especially before we used jet planes. How I would suffer as the plane bounced and dipped, although I would try to hide my fear from my teammates.

"But this time was different. From the start I felt something was off. The propeller motors on the old plane seemed to labor, and as we gained speed down the runway I could hear the body shaking and some of the cargo boxes shifting. From my seat I could see the pilot, and he was pulling back on the throttle, trying to get the nose of the plane into the air, but it seemed there was too much weight in the tail - the cargo. He was saying, over and over, 'Come on baby' and the stick was vibrating

189

in his hand."

T.J., riveted to the story, held up his throwing hand momentarily to stop Bortnicker.

Clemente looked skyward, moonlight bathing his handsome face, and drifted through time. "We finally began to rise, and then we were over water. I looked out the window and the waves below were black and evil. And then the pilot, or somebody, shouted something, and we started going down. I prayed to God to take care of me and look out for my family and then…then it all went dark. There was no sound, no pain. Only darkness."

They looked at each other, T.J. breathing hard through his mouth, struggling not to cry.

"One more round, *amigo*?" asked Clemente.

T.J. motioned to Bortnicker.

* * * *

Omigod thought Pisseri, who had closed to within fifty feet. *It is him. Roberto Clemente. Talking to T.J. Jackson…fielding fly balls with effortless grace. This has to be an illusion.* Then he barked his shin on a railing.

Clemente, his reflexes quick as a cat, glanced over his shoulder as T.J. gathered in a line drive. "Who is that man in the stands?" he asked the boy. "A person from the TV?"

"No, Mr. Clemente," he responded. "It's my baseball coach, Mr. Pisseri. He came along on the trip as a chaperone."

"I see. Was he a ballplayer? He looks like he might have played."

"Yeah, he pitched in college and then the low minors. But then he got this mysterious pain in his shoulder and they couldn't figure it out, so they released him."

"And he became a teacher?"

"Yeah. He's a really good coach, too."

"Bueno." He looked in at Bortnicker and said, "Tell your friend to hit some in the alleys. I am ready to *throw*."

"Some gappers, Bortnicker!" called out T.J.

"Coming right up!" answered his friend, and cracked one to deep right center. Clemente was off like a rocket, running the ball down and

190

snagging it with a shoulder high backhand before spinning and launching a laser that LouAnne caught - *on the fly* - a foot above the bag.

"Jeez Louise," marveled T.J.

"Wow," whispered Pisseri. "Roberto Clemente."

The rest of the balls were like a highlight reel. Right, left, straight back, it didn't matter. He'd outrace the ball (in casual shoes!), glove it, and pirouette with the grace of a ballet dancer before unleashing yet another frozen rope, which never seemed to rise more than six feet off the ground before smacking into LouAnne's glove. T.J. admired his cousin for not yelping in pain, but then again, LouAnne wouldn't.

After the last relay Clemente smiled, turned to T.J. and simply said, "Enough."

"That's it, Bortnicker!" called out T.J., and his friend proceeded to spin around and fall flat on his back, his arms outstretched, in exaggerated exhaustion.

"Your friend, he is funny," said Clemente as the two outfielders jogged towards home plate.

* * * *

Once LouAnne had helped the overly dramatic Bortnicker to his feet, the teens and Clemente met at home plate, followed shortly thereafter by John Goodleaf, who hung back a little. "Call your coach over," said Clemente, and T.J. gave a waving gesture to Pisseri to join them. After pointing to his chest in question, he popped up and hustled the length of the bleachers and down onto the field. Now the group was complete.

"Uh, Coach Pisseri, I'd like you to meet Chief, and Roberto Clemente," said T.J. with as normal a tone of voice as he could muster.

Both Goodleaf and Clemente nodded first to each other, and then the still-awestruck baseball coach. "My friend, T.J., says you were a pitcher who was forced to give up the game," said Clemente. Is that so?"

"Uh, yes, Sir," stammered Pisseri. "I developed some kind of strain or something where my back and throwing shoulder meet, and they weren't ever able to fix it. I never made it past Single-A."

Clemente nodded seriously. "I have some knowledge in this area," he said. "Would you like me to look at it?"

"I...uh...well...sure," said Pisseri. "That would be great, Mr. Clemente."

"*Bueno*," said the ballplayer. "Come with me." He walked toward the first base side dugout, and pulled the wide team bench away from the back wall. "Take off your jacket and lie face down for me, please," he said in a businesslike tone. After a furtive look of panic at the kids, Pisseri did as he was told. Then Clemente gestured to Bortnicker to hand him the bat. Upon receiving it he smiled appreciatively at the Pirates logo and his name embossed on the barrel. "I am going to gently run the bat head around on your back, *amigo*," he said to Pisseri. "Tell me when I've found the area that afflicts you." He put his right hand over the knob of the bat and with his left gripped the barrel just below the trademark as if it were a boat oar. Soon he'd found the spot.

"Right there," said Todd, extremely anxious.

"Hmm, yes." With the barrel head he started working the area with a mortar-and-pestle motion.

"It's like when I make guacamole," whispered Bortnicker to LouAnne, who shushed him.

This scene brought back a bizarre memory to T.J., of the night he first encountered the Confederate cavalier Crosby Hilliard on the Gettysburg battlefield. He had turned his ankle, and when the ghost, who carried with him an ungodly stench of death and decay, knelt at his side and touched his skin it was all he could do to keep from screaming. (Fortunately, Clemente only smelled faintly of the sea.) The strange thing was, the next morning T.J.'s ankle was markedly better. He wondered if Clemente's grinding and kneading on Pisseri's back would have a similar effect. He also realized that not once had any of the three teens made physical contact with Clemente - or Chief, for that matter.

Finally, after about ten minutes of manipulation with the bat, Clemente stood back from the bench where the baseball coach lay in a state of apparent exhaustion.

"How does it feel, *amigo*?" asked Clemente, who'd seemed to exert himself more administering to Pisseri than he had shagging balls in the outfield.

"It hurts," he groaned.

"Good. Tomorrow, with the grace of God, you will see a change."

Pisseri sat up and T.J. handed him his jacket.

It got very quiet. And then Clemente said, softly, "It is time for me to go, *amigos.*"

"Back to the Hall of Fame?" asked Bortnicker.

"No, my friend. It's time for me to *leave.*" He looked around the park, seeming to drink in the entire scene. "I…want to thank you for bringing me here. For a while I was alive again." Then he nodded to Goodleaf, who returned the gesture, turned on his heel and strode, baseball glove tucked into the crook of his elbow, toward the exit. After quick glances among themselves the others followed.

It was an odd procession that filed out of Doubleday Field and headed through the parking lot and across Main Street: Roberto Clemente, totally focused and cruising along; T.J., LouAnne and Bortnicker, keeping pace while lugging their gloves and the ball bag; Todd Pisseri, wind-milling his throwing shoulder in painful arcs; and John Goodleaf, the Doubleday Bat slung over his shoulder like a marching soldier.

He's going to the lake, I know it, thought T.J. Sure enough, the column continued down the far side of Main Street past Maria Amelia's and the Village Green, turned left on Pioneer past the Glimmerglass Inn, and ventured downward to Lake Street. Then they were crossing the patch of grass where earlier that day the two cousins had played a leisurely game of catch among the picnickers. Now, save for a few seagulls perched on pilings in the boat marina, the shore of Lake Otsego was as lifeless as a morgue.

When the ghost of Roberto Clemente reached the end of the grass, he stopped. Instinctively, T.J., the next in line, turned and motioned to LouAnne and Bortnicker to join him standing on each side. When they'd taken their places, he silently held out his hands and they clasped on. It was the first time they had all held hands since their first night on the Gettysburg battlefield; but the bond they had formed in their three adventures was now so strong that all derived incredible strength and comfort from their shared touch. Behind them stood Pisseri, his heart thudding, and further back, John Goodleaf, still toting the bat.

Finally, after an interminable wait, the ballplayer turned to face the three friends, who were trembling with anticipation.

To LouAnne he said, with the most gentle of voices, "*Señorita*, you are an admirable young woman who has had to endure the unspeakable cruelty of others. I have known the taunts of people who would demean me and all I stand for. And I was able to rise above it. You must be strong, and look to those who love you in times of weakness."

"I will," she replied, her bottom lip quivering.

Clemente focused his gaze on Bortnicker. "I once gave this glove to a timid, frightened boy," he said. "He is now a man, but in reality he is still that little frightened boy. He needs you to find him and give him your strength and love. Will you do it?"

"I'll try," he promised, his Coke bottle glasses reflecting the full moon.

The ghost started to turn away, then reversed himself and looked deeply into T.J.'s eyes. "Your mother loves you, and is proud of you. She wants you to know that she is watching over you always, and will see you again someday."

Tears rolling down his cheeks, T.J. nodded and managed to smile. "Thank you," he whispered.

And with that, Roberto Clemente wheeled and walked steadily toward the water, never altering his pace as it covered his ankles, then his knees, waist and shoulders. All around the water glowed an electric green, and even after he was totally submerged the translucence lingered for a few moments before finally fading to the deep purple-black of before.

A good thirty seconds passed before Bortnicker whispered, "Far out."

Pisseri then came from behind the kids and faced them. "Please tell me I didn't see what I just saw," he pleaded.

"'Fraid so, Coach," said T.J. with a shrug.

"'And I was going to stay at The Dugout and watch baseball instead," he chuckled with a shake of his head.

"Well, Chief, you were right," said T.J., looking over his shoulder. "When you told me - *Chief?*"

John Goodleaf had vanished.

Chapter Twenty-Four

Dawn was breaking over the village of Cooperstown, but T.J. had been awake for quite some time, staring at the cracks in his room's plaster ceiling as Bortnicker snored away, spent from what was probably the most physical exertion he'd had in years. So when LouAnne tapped on his door for their agreed-upon morning run, he was already dressed and raring to go.

They quietly descended the Glimmerglass Inn's staircase and eased out the front door. Once on the sidewalk, she put her hand on his shoulder and searched his face. "You okay?" she asked.

"Don't really know," he said honestly. "There was a lot to wrap my head around last night."

"Ya *think*? First, we have the exploding mannequin case, from which I'm *still* picking glass out of my hair; playing baseball with a dead person; listening to him as he looked inside our souls; and oh yes, how could I forget, him walking to the bottom of Lake Otsego! I tossed and turned all night."

"Yeah, it was kinda intense," he admitted. "Are you still up for running?"

"Are you kidding, Cuz? It could be just what the doctor ordered. Let's get a quick stretch and go. Why don't we do that big loop from our first run? I crapped out the last time."

"Sounds like a plan."

As they were rising from their final stretch she asked, "Hey, are you calling Mr. Simmons about that broken glass?"

"Already done. We're debriefing at nine o'clock."

195

"That should be interesting."

They took off down Pioneer toward Lake Street, a soft breeze in their faces. By the time they reached the Otesaga Hotel, a comfortable pace had been established. "Can I ask you something?" she said between measured breaths.

"Sure."

"What'd you think about what he said about your mom? You looked like you were about to faint on us."

"I don't know what to think. It kinda opens up a Pandora's Box, you know?"

"Yeah. Listen, Cuz, I don't expect you to be able to discuss any of this rationally because it's so fresh, but promise me we'll talk when you're ready? Don't do what I did and have it eat you alive for months."

"I promise."

"And what did you think about Bortnicker's dad and the glove thing?"

"Beyond weird. You know, he hardly ever talks about his father. It's like the guy doesn't exist. But, if Clemente is on the mark, he's out there somewhere wandering around."

"How was Bortnicker when you got back to the room? I mean, *nobody* really said anything on the walk back from the lake, unless you count his humming Beatles tunes all the way."

"Cuz, I'll tell ya, all he really said was, 'I'm really beat. Gotta get some rest. Good night,' and then he seemed to go right out. But he wasn't snoring like usual. So there we were, both wide-awake, but I wasn't going to bother him."

They passed the Episcopal Church where they'd paused at Hannah Cooper's grave a few days before, then hit it hard up Main Street to the Village Green where they did a quick post-stretch. The sun was shining now; Coach P. would have optimum conditions for his one o'clock ballgame.

"Wonder what Bortnicker's got planned for our last Cooperstown breakfast?" said LouAnne as she performed a graceful standing calf stretch.

"Whatever it is, we won't be disappointed," predicted T.J.

* * * *

"And so here we are," announced Clara Frank, the quiet Nat at her side. "I say we raise a glass of orange juice to our guest chef of the week, Bortnicker!"

They toasted the boy who bowed deeply, his mop of hair falling forward.

"So, what's the special today?" asked Pisseri.

"For our final breakfast banquet we've got apple cinnamon pancakes, Canadian bacon, and a fresh-cut fruit cup."

"Wow," said the coach. "You've spoiled me up here. Next week at school I'll be back to my morning granola bar and bad cafeteria coffee."

"What, we have school next week?" joked T.J.

"And ballgames, too," replied Pisseri." I can't wait to begin our regular season."

Oddly, the small talk at the breakfast table involved everything but the previous night's adventures. Bortnicker even threw a Beatles trivia question at LouAnne to fill a lull, which she fielded as cleanly as Clemente's throws the night before. T.J. felt everyone was just dealing with it in their own way, which was probably for the best. Regardless, all four of them, Coach P. included, would be forever touched by what they'd seen and heard.

Of course, one person couldn't totally restrain himself.

"So, Coach," said Bortnicker as he doused his second helping of flapjacks with maple syrup, "how's the old wing doing?"

Pisseri stopped chewing and wiped his mouth. "Well, guys," he said in a conspiratorial whisper, "let's put it this way. I don't think I could run out there and toss a no-hitter, but I've got to admit, this is the first time in a long time I woke up without my shoulder barking at me."

"Just in time to start throwing us BP back home!" joked T.J., keeping it light.

"Right-o. Well, I've gotta get over to the Clark Center. There's stuff to do this morning, and I promised Debbie I'd help her. The fantasy campers will be busing over to Doubleday around noon to warm up. See you there."

* * * *

Bob Simmons seemed a little worse for wear as he ushered the

Junior Gonzo Ghost Chasers into the boardroom. There had been a flurry of activity at the Hall in the early morning hours as the shattered glass was cleaned up and the Clemente case covered with a tarp and cordoned off while replacement glass was ordered. And the kids were tired as well. Attired in their matching black logoed golf shirts as a show of solidarity, they took their place across the table from Vines, Martin and Rieman.

Simmons opened the meeting with, "Good morning, everyone. T.J.'s team has concluded their investigation, and he'd like to share their findings with us. I would ask that we all allow him to finish before asking questions. He has much to tell us. T.J.?"

"Thanks, Mr. Simmons. First, I'd like to thank Jody for doing us a big favor yesterday. Last night couldn't have come off without him." Everyone, including Dan Vines, offered light applause.

"Okay, here's what happened, and you can choose to believe it or not, because I'll tell you right up front, we have virtually no video or audio to support this from roughly 10 PM onward."

Vines shifted uncomfortably in his seat but wisely kept his mouth shut.

"A little after ten, LouAnne was near the Clemente case. Suddenly, the outer glass kind of froze over, and then it shattered. Fortunately, she wasn't hurt. Clemente then appeared to us, zapping all our electronics like last time. We spent some time with him in the Plaque Gallery, and then we all actually left the building and walked with him to Doubleday Field, where…and you can believe this or not, we did some fielding practice. He showed me how to make the basket catch, actually."

Every one of the board members' mouths dropped open, except for Vines'. The man looked like a teapot about to boil over.

"But there's more. Before we left the park he actually tried to cure a shoulder problem in our coach, Mr. Pisseri, who's doing the fantasy camp at the Clark Center. If you're not aware, Clemente had been doing this in the off-season in Puerto Rico as kind of a hobby.

"Then…and again, I'm not making this up…we all went down to the lake, where he said goodbye before walking into the water and disappearing."

Finally, Vines blew his top. "Of all the cockamamie hogwash I've ever heard, this takes the cake. A ghost shagging fly balls? Doing chiropractic work on a patient? *Walking to the bottom of Lake Otsego?* You seem like pretty normal kids, but you aren't on any kind of hallucinogenic drugs, are you?"

"Dan, that's out of line," growled Simmons.

"Mr. Vines," said T.J., somehow keeping his cool as his mates glowered, "I can't help it if you don't believe us. It's beyond bizarre, I'll give you that. But, I mean, I hope you don't think we actually broke that glass ourselves, staging the whole thing. Then you're kinda questioning our integrity, and I for one am not going to sit here and take that." Under the table his cousin patted his knee in appreciation.

Then he suddenly caught himself. "Hey, wait a minute," he said, snapping his finger. "I know who can corroborate our story. Mr. Simmons, could you call over to Doubleday Field and ask John Goodleaf to come meet with us? It's only up the street."

Simmons looked pained. "Who, T.J.?"

"John Goodleaf, the groundskeeper. You might know him as 'Chief.' He's a Native American, you know. Chief helped us conduct Clemente back to, um, the other side."

"T.J.," said Simmons patiently, "the groundskeeper at Doubleday Field is named Kris Szabo. He's been with us for over a decade."

The boy was shocked, but not totally flustered. "Well, is there any chance this Mr. Szabo has hired an assistant?"

Simmons turned to Rieman. "Jody, I've got another job for you. Call Parks and Recreation from my office and see if they have a John Goodleaf on the books. T.J., before he goes, could you give me a description of this man?"

LouAnne spoke up. "He's tall, over six feet, and pretty husky. He's got jet black hair kind of long and thick, combed straight back into a ponytail. And the times I've seen him he's been wearing kind of a lumberjack shirt, jeans and work boots."

"Thanks, dear. Get on it, Jody."

"Yes, Sir!" The intern practically bolted from the room.

"Could I ask you a question, T.J.?" said Sarah Martin. "Yesterday you told us that the only way to help Roberto Clemente cross over was to give him back an item he'd cherished in life. Unfortunately, we weren't able to grant your request for the bat in our collection. So how—"

"I can answer that, Miss Martin," volunteered Bortnicker. "Again, you might just consider this *hogwash*" - he looked directly at Vines -"but this is the truth." He proceeded to tell the story of his father's chance meeting with the baseball great only minutes before his untimely death.

"And you had the glove all these years?" she marveled.

"Yes, ma'am. But I never told anyone, not even T.J. or LouAnne. My dad isn't something I like to talk about. It's kinda painful, you know? So when I found out we were coming up here because of Clemente, I packed the glove. I figured, if nothing else I'd end up donating it to the Hall. But then, when T.J. got stiffed - er, *denied* the bat, I figured it was time for me to part with the glove. It was rightfully his, anyway."

"That's...remarkable," she said. "I had no idea an authentic Clemente glove even existed. It would have been a centerpiece in our collection."

Bortnicker looked directly at Vines before flashing his crooked smile and saying, "Oh well, them's the breaks."

Suddenly, Jody Rieman appeared, out of breath and excited.

"Looks like you have news, son," said Simmons. "Have a seat and compose yourself."

"I'm fine," he replied, refusing to sit. "But listen to this, everybody. I phoned Parks and Rec, and they have no record of anybody named John Goodleaf working for the town in any capacity."

"You see?" began Vines.

Rieman held up his hand. "*Please*, Mr. Vines, let me finish. When T.J. and LouAnne were describing this guy it jogged something in my head, from when I was studying up on Cooperstown history before my job interview here at the Hall. So I went online and printed this out. Want to hear it?"

"Please," said Simmons.

"Okay. I'll paraphrase as I go. So, anyway, anyone walking around Cooperstown will notice a stone wall on the west side of River Street. This retaining wall near a property called Greencrest runs alongside Cooper Park. It's thick enough to sit on."

"I know that wall," said Vines, edging forward.

"Right. Well, for much of the 20th century, people noticed something about the wall. At times it seemed perfectly straight, but at others it seemed to bulge out toward the street, like it was on the verge of collapsing.

"In the early 1960s some concerned town residents broke through the wall to find out why this kept happening, and if it needed to be reset. That's when they found something incredible."

T.J. looked sideways at his friends. "What?"

"Well, apparently they uncovered a buried skeleton of an Indian - uh, Native American - a Mohawk chief, along with some weapons and other artifacts.

"The thing is, there had been rumors and myths going on about this wall since James Fenimore Cooper's time. The legend was that a spirit inside of it had been kicking down the old, thinner wall, and some had even reported witnessing a skeleton sitting atop the ruins. So, it was rebuilt in its much thicker version, but even so, it would start bulging out, like I said before.

"There were different theories as to why this occurred. Some said the chief had been buried in a hunched over position, and was pushing his legs out to become more comfortable. Others theorized his tears of pain had weakened the mortar that held the wall's stones together."

"So what happened after the 1960s excavation?" asked Bortnicker.

"It's never been confirmed exactly what became of the skeleton and the artifacts," said Rieman, scanning the printout. "This could be because the skeleton was properly reburied following Mohawk custom, or that the artifacts ended up in some museum outside of Cooperstown. Or, he's still in the wall, but laid out comfortably." Rieman put the printout down, still breathing heavily.

"I've got a hunch," said T.J. "Who's up for a walk?"

* * * *

Minutes later the entire group found themselves traversing River Street. When they came to the spot where the Greencrest property met Cooper Park, they stopped short.

"Well, looky here, Mr. Vines," said Bortnicker. Atop the lichen-covered stone wall lay a brand-new Doubleday Bat with a facsimile

Pittsburgh Pirates logo and the name CLEMENTE burned into the barrel.

* * * *

"Didya see the look on old Dan-O's face at the wall?" cackled Bortnicker as he and T.J. crated the equipment in the Halper Gallery.

"Yeah," said T.J., labeling the useful audio and video tapes for The Adventure Channel people to sift through in Los Angeles. "And then he had the stones to actually ask us if we wanted to donate the bat to the Hall!"

They both cracked up over that one.

"Think there's enough material for a show here?" asked Bortnicker.

"No doubt, even aside from any mention of Clemente."

Just then, Bob Simmons entered the room and silently shut the door behind him.

"Where's LouAnne?" he asked. "I wanted to speak to all of you."

"She said she had some things to get done," replied T.J. "Bortnicker and I will have this stuff packed for you to ship out in no time."

"Great. Ah, boys, I was trying to think of a way to thank you all for the job you did, and what I would like to do is invite you and your coach to my house on the lake tonight for a cookout."

"A home-cooked meal sounds great, Mr. Simmons," said T.J. with a broad smile. "Say, could Coach P. bring a date?"

Simmons chuckled. "Yes, I heard that he and our Debbie McCray have hit it off. Of course she can attend. I'll send a car for you around six o'clock, okay?"

"Uh, Mr. Simmons," said Bortnicker uncomfortably, "there isn't any chance of Mr. Vines being there, is there?"

"No, Bortnicker," he said shaking his head. "I think Dan has done enough, staying late to let you guys into the Hall every night. He really does mean well, and he's always got the Hall's best interests at heart. It's just that...well...did you ever have a friend you love like a brother, but he drives you crazy?"

The boys immediately pointed at each other.

* * * *

By eleven-thirty everything was packed and ready to go. The boys were talking about a light lunch or maybe a nap before the game when T.J.'s cell phone went off. "It's Coach P.," he said, checking the caller ID.

"Hi, T.J.," said Pisseri. "How did it go this morning?"

"Long story, Coach, but okay," he replied. "And we're invited to a barbecue at Mr. Simmons' house tonight. And you can bring Debbie."

"That's fine, T.J., but I've got a more pressing concern at the moment."

"What's up, Coach?"

"I'll just cut to the chase. What do you think about playing some ball today?"

Chapter Twenty-Five

"Are you sure you're up for a ballgame today?" asked LouAnne as the trio strolled up Main Street towards Doubleday Field. "You hardly got any sleep last night, plus you already ran a couple miles this morning."

T.J. waved her off. "Listen, Cuz, I know all that, but Coach P. is in a bind. His centerfielder, who's really a cardiologist, was called into emergency surgery in New York City this morning. They actually flew him out of Oneonta Airport a couple hours ago. Coach asked if I could fill in. They're gonna give me a uniform and everything, even cleats. Pretty sweet."

"Well, you already have the glove," said LouAnne.

"And a bat!" added Bortnicker, holding the Doubleday Bat Company Clemente model aloft in triumph.

On this early spring afternoon Doubleday Field was awash in color and activity. An impromptu concession stand outside the first base pavilion sold hot dogs, peanuts, Crackerjacks and soda to the thousand or so spectators, many of them tourists who'd just happened upon the game. T.J. met up with a nervous Todd Pisseri, who handed him a brand-new Hall of Fame Fantasy Camp uniform - number 21, of course - and told him to change in the restroom under the stands. This he did, and emerged looking quite official.

"Do I get to keep the spikes?" he asked Pisseri.

"No question. Now get out on the field and stretch with your teammates. I'll introduce you." He led the boy to the outfield, where a bunch of fortysomething guys were playing catch and loosening up.

"Fellas," he said, "this is T.J., who's graciously filling in for Dr. Balcom today. He's my regular centerfielder back home, and he can really go get 'em."

"Our corner outfielders thank you!" cried a portly, bearded teammate to raucous laughter.

"And our pitcher, too!" yelled another.

After T.J. did some mild stretching and played catch with Pisseri - who was throwing free and easy - to warm up, the coach had another surprise for the boy. "C'mon with me," he said with a wink. "I want you to meet some Hall of Famers." He paused. "Live ones, that is."

And so it was that T.J. Jackson, Bridgefield High centerfielder and part-time ghost hunter, shook hands with Ozzie Smith, Jim Rice and Phil Niekro, the honorary coaches for Pisseri's squad.

* * * *

But T.J. wasn't the only one who was in for a surprise that day. Bortnicker and LouAnne, armed with boxes of Crackerjacks, had just settled into their seats behind home plate, a scant few feet from where she'd unburdened herself to her cousin a few nights before, when a girl nudged Bortnicker and asked if the seat next to him was taken.

"No, it isn't," he replied through a mouthful of caramel corn. "Feel free to -" he froze and his eyes nearly popped out of their sockets. "*Fiona?*"

Indeed, it was Fiona Bright, but not the one Bortnicker had known until then. Her hair was washed, brushed, and pulled back in a ponytail. Instead of a billowing hoodie she wore a crewneck sweater over a collared shirt. A hint of eye shadow and some understated lip gloss completed LouAnne's midmorning makeover.

"Who'd you think it was, silly?" she replied sweetly, dipping her freshly polished fingernails into his Crackerjacks as LouAnne grinned.

* * * *

The temporary PA system crackled to life, and both Hall of Fame Fantasy Camp teams were introduced, the players jogging from their respective dugouts to one of the baselines, where they stood shoulder to shoulder, acknowledging the cheers of the crowd, many of them family members who were snapping photos and waving madly. When T.J.'s turn came up, his personal cheering section stood and applauded.

"Playing centerfield and batting ninth," intoned the overly dramatic announcer, "and hailing from Fairfield, Connecticut, T.J. Jackson, number twenty-one." After high or low-fiveing his brand-new teammates, T.J. took his position and tugged the brim of his cap in salute to LouAnne, Bortnicker and...*Fiona?*

Of course, the Hall of Famers, who had graciously accommodated hundreds of autograph seekers near the stands during the pregame warm-ups, got the biggest hand. After a rousing audio recording of the national anthem by the United States Marine Corps band, the home plate umpire shouted "Play ball!" and both teams returned to their dugouts. As T.J.'s team was first at bat, he took a seat on the bench between Coach Pisseri and Ozzie Smith, who looked like he could still go out there and pick it at shortstop. "Hey, Coach," he whispered mischievously into Pisseri's ear, "weren't you stretched out on this bench last night?"

"Sssh," whispered Pisseri right back, trying mightily not to smile.

After his team was set down in order, T.J. and his mates took the field. It was a weird feeling, in a week of weird feelings, that he experienced as he jogged to the outfield that day. The night before he had been here under a full moon, talking and playing ball with one of the game's immortals. Now, hopefully, the man was finally at rest, though there were some loose ends he had to speak to Bob Simmons about. But right here, right now, everything was perfect: the sky was blue, the grass was green, the crowd was alive, and his mother was smiling down on him.

The contest itself wasn't remarkable in any way, just a bunch of middle-aged men playing a boy's game in the "Birthplace of Baseball." But there were two highlights, for T.J., anyway.

Having walked twice previously (eventually scoring both times on sloppy plays by the defense) he came up in the top of the seventh with a man on second and two out. The pitcher, a gangly left-hander with a deceptive herky-jerky motion, fooled him badly on two curveballs in the dirt. But when he tried to paint the outside corner with a fastball, T.J. was on it, lining the ball up the left center gap for a standup double - just like Roberto Clemente on September 30, 1972. He gave an embarrassed wave to his fans in the stands, who cheered and stomped their feet. "Hey, he's cute!" screamed one teenaged girl a few seats over from LouAnne, who nodded knowingly.

T.J.'s crowning moment, however, came in the final inning. He'd had precious few fielding chances that day, most of them ground balls that had skipped under infielders' gloves for base hits. But now, with one out and an opposing base runner leading off third, he prayed someone would actually get a ball in the air so he could make a play. As if on cue, the other team's cleanup hitter skied one to center as the base runner went back to third to tag up. T.J. broke back, then measured it and gave his glove a tap. And then, as he'd been doing at 1 AM the previous morning, he dropped his glove down to slightly below waist level, executed a perfect basket catch, and fired to home plate to nip the charging runner by a step.

In the dugout, Jim Rice said, "Hey, Todd, that's your boy out there, right? Who taught him to basket catch?"

"Oh, Roberto Clemente," he replied with the slightest trace of a smile, as if it were the most natural thing on earth.

Chapter Twenty-Six

"Can I get you another steak kebab, Bortnicker?" asked Fiona as the guests milled about on the spacious deck of Bob Simmons' log cabin lakefront home. A cool breeze intermittently came off the water and gentle waves lapped beneath the pilings that supported the hillside structure.

"He's already eaten like eight of them," observed LouAnne. "We might have to float him back to the inn."

It had been a full day for the *Junior Gonzo Ghost Chasers*. After their tumultuous board meeting and baseball game, they had actually experienced a few hours of downtime in the late afternoon. Coach Pisseri had finally gotten to visit the myriad of memorabilia stores on and around Main Street, as well as the Hall's gift shop. Bortnicker and LouAnne had crashed immediately, later joined by T.J., but not before he'd placed a call to Mike Weinstein in Jamaica.

"Dude, you caught me just in time," he said. "We're leaving for our last night of investigating in about ten minutes. Got some great EVPs so far. How did it go for you?"

T.J. described, as best he could, the events of the previous night and early morning.

"Walked into the water, you say," the ghost hunter repeated reverently. "That's just, well, beyond anything I can imagine. Dude, this leaves no doubt whatsoever in my mind that you have a gift. Which could be good or bad, depending. What's important is, how do *you* feel about all this?"

"I'm still figuring it out," the boy confessed. "Listen, Mike, I'm sure

208

from what we send The Adventure Channel they'll be able to put together a great show. We did sound bites all over town, and there's some good video and EVPs for them to work off. But...and I think Mr. Simmons is going to feel this way, too...we should leave Clemente out of it. I could tell when I talked to him on that ball field that he'd feel betrayed if we made all this public. And I wouldn't want to drag his family through this, either."

Weinstein emitted a sigh of resignation. "I get you. You're a righteous dude, T.J., you know that? Well, when I get home in a couple days I'll sit down with the LA people and help them go through the tapes. Don't worry, I'll do you guys a solid. Hey, I bet they run the *Junior Gonzo* Special during the All-Star break in July, maybe even put it up against the game!"

"Whatever, Mike. Listen, I don't need the money, 'cause my family's got enough, or the fame, either, if you want to call it that. It was worth it just to know, once and for all, that there's *something* past this existence. It's kind of comforting, actually."

"So, you're telling me you guys aren't necessarily retiring?"

"You never know. Take care, dude." He clicked off, made his way to his bed somehow, and collapsed.

Now there was a distinct nip in the air, and the party began moving inside, where Bob Simmons had a crackling fire going. Everyone was relaxed and the conversation flowed. Mildred Simmons turned out to be a charming host, and with her husband hung on every word as the teens regaled them with stories of their first two investigations. And Fiona couldn't have been more accommodating, helping to clear the picnic table and keeping the food and drinks coming. When Bortnicker mentioned offhandedly that they all would be keeping in touch with her and that they would make sure she was in the credits at the end of the show, she positively glowed. T.J. was especially gratified to watch Todd and Debbie enjoying the last hours of each other's company...at least for now.

It was during a lull in the festivities that Simmons asked the three teens to step outside on the deck with him for a moment. "Kids," he said with sincerity, "I can't thank you enough for what you've done up here this week. You surpassed my wildest expectations, and you did it with class and maturity. Because of you, I'm confident we'll be able to conduct our full slate of Latin Baseball events without a hitch. As a token of my gratitude, I'd like to extend to you from the Hall of Fame lifetime passes for your families.

"But even more so, it's hard to find the words to describe the change you've brought about in my niece. She came to me this week an angry, antisocial child and is being returned to her parents an optimistic, self-confident young lady. None of this could have happened without the compassion you showed her, or the example you set. Again, I am in your debt."

"Thanks, Mr. Simmons," said T.J., stepping up as usual in his role of team leader. "It was an honor being chosen to help the Hall of Fame. And we really believe we've brought closure to the situation. Roberto Clemente was a great man; he might have been misunderstood at times, but he showed us nothing but passion and heart, which we'll all take with us.

"The thing is, we were also up here to film a TV show, and that's where it gets tricky. The Adventure Channel wants ratings, after all. Why else would they send us here, ship all the equipment, and pay us for our trouble?

"I just want you to know that this afternoon I spoke to Mike Weinstein, and I made it clear that the script of the show, outside of maybe the shattered glass thing, will not mention Mr. Clemente in any way, which he made very clear to me last night was his wish. If that's okay with you?"

Simmons was visibly relieved. "Okay? That's music to my ears, T.J. Again, if there's anything else I can do for you -"

"There is, actually, sir," broke in Bortnicker. "I know the limo's picking us up early tomorrow morning for the ride home - not before we stop off for a big old box of fresh cinnamon buns, I might add - but is it possible that we could make a stopover in Catskill Park for a ride on the steam engine train? It's only an hour or so."

"Consider it done," said the president. "To tell the truth, I've always wanted -"

"Chocolate chip cookies just came out of the oven!" called Fiona, poking her head out the door to the deck. You coming, Uncle Bob?

Guys?"

"We're on our way, honey," Simmons replied, putting his arm around Bortnicker for the walk back inside.

"Give us a minute," said LouAnne. "T.J. and I will be right in."

Once the door was shut, he turned to her. "So what's up, Cuz?" he asked.

She walked to the railing and looked out over the tranquil waters of Otsego. "You know," she said, "for the longest time I've been deathly afraid of water, especially lakes. So last night…I don't know, it was sort of ironic, wasn't it? Water took Clemente's life, and then he returned to it. But, you kind of sensed that it would happen that way, didn't you, T.J.?"

"Yeah, kind of," he said, joining her at the railing.

"You're something else, Cuz," she smiled. "For a lot of reasons. Most important, you pulled me out of a hole I thought was way over my head. I learned a lot about myself this week."

"We all did," he said, putting his arm around her.

"I'll tell you one thing, and you can write it down. I'm going back home and making All-County this spring. I've got some catching up to do, but it's doable."

"What about school?"

"Just got to stay focused. Those people trying to bring me down aren't worth my time. There'll be bumps in the road, but I can handle it."

"And what about…you and me?" he asked in a near whisper.

She thought for a few seconds. "I've done a lot of thinking up here," she began, measuring her words. "In some ways it was the toughest week of my life. But what I saw, and what I learned, was nothing short of amazing.

"One thing this trip made me do was ask myself what love is. And I'll tell you what: if love is caring about someone so much that their approval and respect means more to you than anything else in your existence, then I guess I love you, T.J. Jackson." She turned to him and kissed him tenderly, for what seemed to him an eternity, then looked into his eyes. "But I lied to you."

"*What?*" He stepped back and regarded her from arm's-length. "What are you talking about?"

211

She reached into her back pocket and brought forth her iPhone-sized EVP recorder. "Actually, *we* told the pretty big fib. Everybody thinks we never got Clemente on tape. Not true. Once we left the Hall last night, the batteries revived. The whole walk to Doubleday, like when he was talking about his premonition of dying, and then inside the park - it's all right here. I forgot about the recorder in all the commotion, until it fell out of my jacket back at the inn."

"And he's on there? You clearly know it's him?"

"Yup. So what do we do, Cuz?" she asked with an arched eyebrow.

"You look like you have an idea already."

"Yeah," she said. "I was wondering, after all that working out the past twenty-four hours, if you have one throw left in that arm of yours?"

"Well, let's see," he said with a wink, and after a Major League windup, T.J. Jackson let loose a throw that would have made Roberto Clemente proud. The recorder hit the water, skipped twice, then slipped beneath the waves of Lake Otsego.

Epilogue

Morty Barrett was in a foul mood. Things just didn't seem to be going his way lately at the Boca Vista Royale retirement community. To begin with, this year's shuffleboard tournament was turning into a joke because some of the participants, especially that Greg Burrell, were cheating on an almost daily basis.

Then, there were whispers that this past Valentine's Day bash at the main clubhouse would be his last as master of ceremonies, a position he'd held for virtually all the major soirées at the complex since he'd moved down to Florida in the 1980s after selling his shares in the Pocono Hideaway Resort, for what he'd thought was a sweetheart deal. But the joke was on him, because now that Pennsylvania had passed laws permitting gambling, the Hideaway's owners were raking it in as a casino business. Okay, so he might not have the energy of his younger self, when he knocked 'em dead in the resort's nightclub - he was pushing 90, after all - but he worked for free and still got laughs. People had no taste anymore.

But what put the cherry on top today was that Doris, for the *second* time this week, gave him egg salad for lunch instead of pastrami, and a watery egg salad at that. "Too much pastrami is unhealthy, Morty," she'd admonished while setting the plate before him. At least she'd given him some Pringles with the sandwich.

He was washing down his lunch with some iced tea while reading the *Boca Tribune* when the phone rang. "I'll get it," called out his wife, "because God forbid you'd get up while you're reading the paper." He chuckled to himself and crunched a Pringles.

A minute later she came to the table, with the phone receiver (whose cord was at least twenty-five feet long, because Morty didn't like to use a cell phone) in hand, and a puzzled look on her face. "It's your grandson," she said, her hand over the mouthpiece.

"What happened?" the old man asked. "He in trouble?"

"Do I look like a mind reader? Here, take the phone and ask him. I've got a hair appointment at one and I'm going to miss it if I don't get going."

"Okay, okay, give me the phone already," he said with a sigh. She handed it over, but not before she hissed, "Be nice! He's your grandson!"

"Sam-ela," he boomed, "to what do I owe the honor of your call?"

"Hi, Grampy," said Bortnicker, using the term of endearment from his childhood. "How are you doing?"

"How am I doing? Well, I guess okay. The sun is out, there's a nice breeze, and I didn't wake up dead, so I figure I'm ahead of the game. And by the way, how come you never visit? Your grandmother and I haven't seen you in over a year. What, you don't like Florida? Or is Bermuda your tropical paradise of choice now?"

The boy laughed. Same old Grampy. "No, no," he said, "I like Boca Raton. It's okay."

"No it isn't," said Morty. "Know why? Too many old people!"

At this the boy really cracked up. "You're too much, Grampy," he said.

"You see?" said the old man. "I've still got it. So, what can I do for you, Mr. Hotshot TV Ghost Hunter?"

"Well, I've got to ask you a question."

"So ask."

"Grampy, do you know where my dad is?"

"Your father? Why do you want to know? Is that crazy mother of yours sick? I only say she's crazy because she actually married my son. And also that feng shui stuff she's always pushing. She's actually a nice person -"

"Grampy, are you going to give me an answer?"

The old man sighed. "I wish I could, Sammy," he said. "Your father comes and goes. We'll get a call or a card from him, and they never come from the same place twice. What, he's not sending support payments to your mother?"

"No, he is, as far as I know. Mom doesn't say much about it."

"I don't blame her. Listen, your father was a difficult kid. Always whining and complaining about something, and of course your grandmother babied him and made it worse. But, as he got older it seemed to me that he just couldn't deal with being tied down, either to places or people. I still can't figure the kid out. Give you an example: he made a big deal about legally changing his name back to Bortnicker. See, I'd changed it to Barrett when I was in showbiz, so to speak. So, I figured this meant he was really going to become involved in family traditions and whatever. But then he became a gypsy. Yeah, he'd settle down for a bit, like when he married your mom and had a kid, who is you, but then he'd get happy feet and off he'd go. You see what I'm saying?"

"Yes, Grampy."

"So, is that it? That's why you called?"

"Well, there's something else."

"I'm listening."

"Do you remember the time you went to Puerto Rico?"

"Who could forget? We flew down there hoping for a great trip, and then *bam*, that tragedy with Clemente. To tell you the truth, I think it left a mark on your father."

"In what way?"

"Well, I think it showed him how fleeting life is, how sometimes you get crushed when you attach yourself to someone, like he was to that ballplayer. The man gives him his baseball glove, and an hour later he's dead. That's gotta have some kind of negative effect. After that your father kind of withdrew into himself. Put that glove away in a box and never took it out anymore. And, unfortunately, never followed baseball again. Wait, is this about that glove?"

"Yes, actually."

"Why? You want to sell it? If you do, I don't blame you. The dough they get for sports memorabilia today, you could make a mint. Maybe put a dent in your college tuition -"

"It's gone, Grampy."

"*Gone*? Somebody stole it?"

"No, Grampy, I...returned it."

"Returned it? How do you return something to a *dead man*?"

"Take my word for it, Grampy. The glove is where it belongs. I did the right thing."

The old man took a long pause. "Sammy, you've always had a good heart, so I guess I'll trust you on this one. I'll tell you what. The next time I get any communication whatsoever from your footloose father, I'll call you, pronto. But you've also got to promise you'll come visit me down here. I love your grandmother, but she drives me a little crazy, you know? Then you can tell me the story about the glove."

"It's a deal, Grampy. I'll come see you."

"Okay, but before I get back to this wonderful egg salad sandwich, I have to ask you one thing. You said you returned the glove. Fine. So what did *you* get out of it? What did you learn?"

Bortnicker thought hard, then looked at the photo on the wall of his room, the same photo of the three of them in Bermuda that LouAnne - and T.J., who had the third copy - saw every day. "Well," he said, breaking into his trademark crooked smile, "I guess I learned that you can replace just about anything, but the people who really love you can't ever be replaced, which is why you've got to grab hold of them and never let go."

Author's Note

Although the names of all the establishments in Cooperstown frequented by T.J. and his friends are fictitious, Doubleday Field, Lake Otsego, the Christ Episcopal Church and the National Baseball Hall of Fame and Museum most certainly are not.

One doesn't have to be a baseball fan to fall in love with Cooperstown. Having visited at least once per year since 1985 during various seasons, I can tell you that it certainly has an aura which must be experienced. The stories of Hannah Cooper and the Mohawk Chief are an important part of local lore - you can visit her gravesite and the "burial wall" on River Street. The morning mist over Lake Otsego is both spooky and majestic, and I defy you to find a more charming old-time ballpark than Doubleday Field. I've sat in the deserted grandstand at night as T.J. and LouAnne did, and I could *feel* the presence of its spirits.

Of course, the Hall of Fame never gets old for me. Every time I visit I discover something new, whether it be a recently acquired artifact or some nugget of information about its inhabitants like the great Roberto Clemente. In reality, Bob Simmons and his staff do not exist, but those who do work there are always knowledgeable, friendly and helpful. Simply put, it's the treasure vault of our National Pastime.

And don't forget to try the cinnamon buns.

About the Author

Paul Ferrante is originally from the Bronx and grew up in the town of Pelham, NY. He received his undergraduate and Masters degrees in English from Iona College, where he was also a halfback on the Gaels' undefeated 1977 football team. Paul has been an award-winning secondary school English teacher and coach for over 30 years, as well as a columnist for *Sports Collector's Digest* since 1993 on the subject of baseball ballpark history. Many of his works can be found in the archives of the National Baseball Hall of Fame in Cooperstown, NY. His writings have led to numerous radio and television appearances related to baseball history. Paul lives in Connecticut with his wife Maria and daughter Caroline, a film screenwriter/director. *Roberto's Return* is the third novel in the *T.J. Jackson Mysteries* series.

Visit him at **www.paulferranteauthor.com.**

Follow **T.J. Jackson Mysteries** on Facebook

Other works by the author at Melange

Last Ghost at Gettysburg, A T. J. Jackson Mystery
Spirits of the Pirate House, A T. J. Jackson Mystery

Made in the USA
Middletown, DE
28 September 2017